KINGS OF MOONLIGHT

EVA CHASE

BOUND TO THE FAE

BOOK
3

Kings of Moonlight

Book 3 in the Bound to the Fae series

First Digital Edition, 2021

Cover design: Yocla Book Cover Design

Ebook ISBN: 978-1-989096-95-6

Paperback ISBN: 978-1-989096-96-3

Talia

There are certain things magic can't do—or at least that faeries don't think it's worth wasting magical energy on when it's simpler to do it by hand. It turns out rearranging furniture is one of those things.

I give the wooden side table a little shove and step back to eye its position relative to the rest of the furnishings in the grand living room. When we moved into the castle two days ago, my fae companions banished the vines that had crept through the windows and whisked the dust from the floors with a few powerful words. Using the true name for the wood that makes up the entire building, which from the outside looks like several massive trees sculpted together into a towering fortress, they healed the cracks and the spots of rot that formed over decades of disuse.

The existing furniture has either been mended or replaced the same way. But now we're fitting in the bits and pieces we brought with us around them, which means I can finally actually help.

I'm the only human living with this pack of wolf-shifting fae, and while they've mostly welcomed me, it's pretty hard to forget that fact.

August comes up beside me, hefting a silver-framed mirror in his brawny arms. "That does look like a good spot for the table. And I think the table is the perfect spot for *this*." He sets the mirror on the tabletop so it leans against the wall and brushes his hands together with a satisfied air.

Interior design isn't August's typical line of work. As half-brother to Sylas, the lord of this domain, and part of Sylas's cadre, his main job is protecting the pack and leading the warriors into battle if need be. But thankfully he hasn't needed to do a lot of that in the two months since I joined them.

Of course, tomorrow that might change. And just like the few times he *has* needed to fight in the past couple of months, it'll be mostly because of me.

That knowledge hangs over all of us, but I'm trying to put on a brave face. I hate how vulnerable I feel compared to the nearly immortal, magically skilled beings around me. I hate how vulnerable caring about me makes *them*. The least I can do is act as if I believe they can get us through the conflict ahead okay, as impossible as that might seem.

"It looks great," I say to August with a smile, and turn to survey the rest of the room. Sofas and armchairs, their surfaces woven out of soft reeds and leaves, form two semi-circles facing the vast hearth that reflects the domain's name: Hearthshire. By the embedded stones that frame the hearth, a couple of pack members are just finishing arranging a set of fireplace tools—made out of bronze, since iron is toxic to the fae. At the far end of the room, a few others are arguing about the exact placement of a hanging tapestry. I'm not sure what else there is for me to do.

August is always quick to pick up on my moods. He wraps his arms around me from behind and presses a kiss to the top of my head. "You've pitched in plenty, Sweetness. You don't need to look for more work."

"Everyone else is still working," I point out, but I can't help leaning into his broad chest, letting his affectionate warmth reassure me.

Out of everyone here, August cares about me the most. Over the weeks I've spent with them, my feelings for Sylas and both members of his cadre have deepened from wary appreciation to tentative attraction to what I can only call love. I never expected any of them to offer that much devotion in return, considering they're not just fae but fae of high standing and I'm a mere human, but August has expressed his love in both words and actions so emphatically that just thinking about it makes me giddy.

"I'm sure you could find a few of our pack-kin slacking off if you looked." He nuzzles my hair with a chuckle and gives me a gentle nudge toward the doorway. "Why don't you take some time just to explore? The rest of us already know the domain pretty well. You should start settling in, get comfortable with the new surroundings."

He talks as if *he's* sure I'll be returning here after

tomorrow's meeting. I drag in a breath and nod. "All right. You make a convincing argument."

He laughs and waves me off, but I feel him watching me, making sure I'm okay, until I've limped into the hall.

On the way to the entrance room with its looming front door, a rhythmic tapping marks my uneven steps. The brace Sylas built for my warped foot helps me walk more steadily, but it is a bit noisy. And my foot still starts to ache if I'm on it for very long. None of my current companions has the magic to fix the warped ridge where my former captors broke the bones and let them heal wrong—it seems like that's one of those few things magic can't do at all. I'm a lot better off than before, when I couldn't do much more than hobble, though.

I heave the arched wooden door open just wide enough for me to slip outside into the vast clearing that stretches around Hearthshire's castle. The breeze tickles over the bright grass and my skin with an ever-present warmth. These fae are Seelie, belonging to the summer realm. Even if the Unseelie of winter weren't vicious villains, I'd be glad I ended up here and not in their freezing territory.

More pack-kin are bustling around the houses scattered throughout the clearing, which look like large tree trunks that've been twisted off into a spiraled point about ten feet up—a much smaller and less ornate version of the castle. A few are already urging plants to grow in small gardens. A couple are herding a bunch of bleating sheep that just arrived onto a forest path toward a pasture that's set at a distance from the village.

We've come a long way from Oakmeet, the domain

where I first joined the pack. The one they were banished to after Sylas's former mate took part in an attempt to overthrow one of the arch-lords who rule the Seelie.

It's that same arch-lord, Ambrose, who's demanded Sylas's presence tomorrow. Sylas's presence *and* mine, that is. Ambrose already campaigned to take me from Sylas once because of the unexpectedly vital role I've come to play in the lives of all the summer fae. Sylas was able to negotiate my freedom, but the arch-lord wasn't pleased about that. Most likely he's come up with some scheme to steal me after all.

The thought of having to leave Hearthshire gives me chills not only because I want to stay with the men I've come to love. The chances that *any* other fae will treat me as kindly as this pack does are small. The chances that Ambrose will, from what I've heard of him, are almost zero. He might throw me in a cage just like the fae who first tore me from the human world, the ones who broke my foot, starved me and taunted me—the ones Sylas and his cadre saved me from.

Watching the fae of the pack I can now call mine grin and chatter with each other eases my worries a little. They're happy just to be back in their former home, the one they've missed for ages longer than I've been alive. Even their magic is stronger here, closer to the Heart of the Mists that's the source of their power, which even I can sense from the quiver in the air.

Regardless of what August said, I'm not sure I'm up to exploring all that far from my new home yet. The massive trees that surround the clearing loom so high I lose my breath when I crane my neck to peer up at them. I don't think I've ever seen trees even half that tall before. Vines wind around their trunks, blooming with vibrant flowers that lace the air with a faint but heady perfume. Who knows what might lurk deeper within that forest that the fae wouldn't bat an eye at but that would mean certain death for a human?

I wander toward the pack village instead. I've only made it a few steps when a figure I'm pleased to see ducks out of one of the houses.

Harper, a young fae woman I've started to consider a friend, brightens at the sight of me. She tucks a few strands of her sleek pale hair behind her pointed ear and lowers her over-large eyes a little bashfully as she heads toward me. She has a bundle of what looks vaguely like birch bark clutched in her arms. When she reaches me, she thrusts it toward me.

"I made something for you. I hope you like them."

I hadn't expected to receive any gifts. And Harper already gave me a pretty big one recently: one of the gorgeous dresses she creates out of faerie-made fabric. I accept the bundle from her and unwrap the papery bark carefully in case whatever's inside is fragile.

I find myself gazing at a pair of boots. Not clunky snow boots like I might have put on as a kid in winters back in the human world or narrow leather ones like Mom sometimes wore with casual dresses. These are as intricate and graceful as Harper's dresses, different shades of brown wrapping around them and intertwining to look like rippled water, a ribbon of the same fabric woven up the sides to allow me to meld them perfectly to my feet.

When I turn them over to examine every side, a solid

frame within one settles against my fingers. They both have sturdy soles that feel as though they'll hold up to hikes in the forest—more hiking than my *foot* is likely to hold up to—but the righthand one includes additional support.

She's worked the material around a foot brace. A few days ago, she asked me to see if Sylas would make her one for some purpose she didn't totally explain. He must have given it to her soon afterward. I've gotten used to clomping around with the brace showing, not having the option of much in the way of footwear. Now I can keep my foot steady without having to show off my weakness quite so blatantly—and with a beautiful covering, too.

But we've spent all of the past few days preparing for and then carrying out the move. I glance up at Harper, both overwhelmed by her generosity and startled.

"They're gorgeous. Thank you so much. I never expected— When did you have time to make them with everything going on?"

She twists her hands where they're clasped in front of her. "Honestly, there hasn't been a whole lot anyone wants me to help with. I got my bedroom and my studio all set up in my parents' old house—I might take one of the abandoned homes just for myself later, but I don't know if it makes much sense to claim one if I might get the chance to start traveling around to the other domains—and it just seemed like… like something I could do that would be useful for someone. For you. Do you like them?"

"I *love* them." I hug the boots to me, curling my fingers around the shockingly soft fabric.

A shy smile curves her lips. "I also thought—everyone

else already knows this domain, but it's new to both of us. You told me that you wanted to see more of this world. Maybe these will make it easier for us to explore together."

I grin back at her. "That would be fantastic. I should try them on. I mean, I'm sure they fit. I'll wear them all the time."

Harper beams, but as I lower myself to sit on the grass, my attention is diverted. A carriage is drifting through the gateway formed by two massive trees bowed toward each other at the far end of the clearing.

Fae carriages have more in common with human boats than the things drawn by horses in past eras. This one looks ricketier than those Sylas has formed for us. It's definitely smaller, with only a rough canopy made of fluttering leaves. It hitches a little as it glides toward us, a couple of feet above the ground. Two figures peer at the castle and the village around it from beneath the dappled shadows of the canopy.

My muscles tense, and I shift into a crouch, tucking the boots to the side and letting my hand fall to the small dagger Sylas gave me that I keep in a sheath at my hip. So far, visitors arriving from any pack other than our own has always meant bad news. I may not be able to put up much of a fight against hostile fae, but I'll do my best with the defensive lessons August has given me if I have to.

I wish I had my pouch of salt, but it unnerves my pack-kin if it bumps against them when I pass them, and I hadn't thought I'd need that much defense right now. Silly me.

Harper stands stiffly beside me, equally uncertain. Someone must have run to tell Sylas, or else he's got magic that alerts him when anyone passes through the gate. As the carriage comes to a stop several feet from the castle and lowers onto the grass, he strides out to meet the unexpected guests.

Simply seeing his authoritative stride and the commanding confidence in his expression soothes my nerves a little. My shoulders come down, but I stay where I am, watching.

As Sylas passes out of the shadow of the castle, the sunlight picks up the purple tint in the coffee-brown hair that falls to his muscular shoulders. His one dark eye fixes on the figures emerging from the carriage. I'm not sure how much his other eye sees. Split through with a scar that runs through his brown skin from forehead to cheekbone, that one gleams ghostly white.

The fae who emerge from beneath the canopy make an odd pair. First comes a rosy-cheeked man with hair that's nearly mauve, who looks young enough to pass for a teenager in the human world. He offers his hand to a wiry old man whose skin is nearly as rippled as the sparse, translucent tufts sprouting from his head.

From the patience Sylas offers them, waiting for the old man to climb out, they're at least somewhat important. The sharp points on the elder's ears suggest he might be true-blooded: the most respected of the fae, the only ones allowed to become lords because their heritage has relatively little humanity in the mix.

"Lord Garmon," Sylas says, confirming my guess. His tone is respectful but not exactly friendly. He doesn't dip his head to either of the other men, but they don't to him either. "And I don't believe we've met…?"

The old man pats the young one on the shoulder. His voice is low and hoarse. "This is my great-grandson Orym."

"Lord Sylas," the young man says in acknowledgment with a quick bob.

Sylas's mismatched gaze slides over them. "Good of him to join you. We weren't aware of your intended visit, or I'd have been more prepared. We aren't quite set up for hosting yet."

Garmon lets out a couple of raspy coughs. "I hope I won't take up much of your time. I've only come to determine what's become of my grandson Kellan."

My pulse stutters. Sylas's expression doesn't shift, but then, he must have guessed this subject would come up. He knew who the man was.

Remembering Kellan makes the hairs on the back of my neck rise. The third member of Sylas's cadre—his former mate's half-brother—didn't think much of humans. After they took me in, he tormented me every way he could manage while avoiding Sylas's notice and then outright attacked me. Sylas leapt in to protect me and had to kill Kellan when he refused to back down.

The fae lord and the rest of his cadre have been keeping Kellan's death secret since then, making excuses and avoiding the subject, not wanting to disturb the pack further when they were facing so much other conflict. Will they have to own up to it now?

How is Sylas going to explain why he did what he did? When fae can live thousands of years if given the chance, killing one is a grave crime. Even though Sylas believes it was the right thing to do, I know he wishes it hadn't come to that.

He's obviously not going to spit out the truth too hastily. "What gave you the impression that there was anything to determine?" he asks in his usual measured baritone.

"A few kin from Lord Tristan's pack passed through our domain not long ago," Orym pipes up. "They asked about Kellan."

Garmon nods. "They seemed surprised he wasn't with us, since he apparently hasn't been seen with you or elsewhere in some weeks. Their reactions raised my concerns." His wispy eyebrows arch. "Was I wrong to wonder?"

Tristan? An itch creeps over my skin. That fae lord poked around Sylas's former domain before. As Ambrose's second-cousin, he seems to carry out some of the arch-lord's work for him.

It's hard to believe they ran into Kellan's relatives and dropped those hints coincidentally. I'd bet they were trying to stir up more trouble for Sylas. Maybe even to justify whatever it is that's going to happen at the meeting tomorrow.

Sylas pauses with a frown. When he speaks again, his voice is lower than before. "I'm afraid this is a serious matter, one best discussed when we're both prepared for it, not just stepping off a carriage. There are guest quarters nearby. I'll have them readied quickly, and you can make yourselves comfortable there. As soon as my hands are no longer entirely full, you'll have a full accounting."

Garmon's mouth twists, but he doesn't seem to think it worth arguing. "I'll await that accounting then."

He turns back toward the carriage, but his great-grandson's gaze has drifted to me. Orym eyes me for long enough that my back goes rigid. Sylas clears his throat and steps forward, and the young man shakes himself.

"That's her, isn't it?" he says. "The human girl you've taken. The one whose blood makes the tonic for the curse."

Those words only make my muscles tighten more. A muscle twitches in Sylas's jaw. "I suppose Tristan's kin mentioned that to you as well?"

Orym gives him a narrow look, one with enough spite in it to rattle my nerves all over again. "Yes, they made a few comments. And his cadre-chosen said that soon enough his lord will be the one taking care of her."

The bottom of my stomach drops out. Orym saunters onto the carriage after his great-grandfather without a backward glance. Sylas's face remains impassive, but there's no way he hasn't understood that remark at least as well as I have.

So that's what Ambrose will be after tomorrow. That's how he plans to get around the oath he swore not to take me into his own custody. He isn't trying to get me for himself—he means to hand me off to his equally hostile cousin.

2

Talia

"**W**hat exactly was the wording of the agreement?" Whitt says abruptly. The other member of Sylas's cadre, his spymaster and strategist, has been pacing the length of the carriage for the entire trek toward Ambrose's castle, pausing only briefly to gaze and sometimes glare at the landscape we're soaring through. His ocean-blue eyes have only gotten stormier. He stops now by the prow of the vehicle to wait for the fae lord's answer, the wind ruffling his sunkissed-brown hair.

Sylas has been less openly restless, but he hardly looks relaxed where he's sitting on one of the thinly cushioned benches beneath the canopy across from me. He rubs his square jaw, his mouth set in a frown that seems to deepen with each passing minute.

"The arch-lords swore to stake no direct claim on Talia as long as I provided the tonic to everyone who needs it.

We've been over this. I didn't think they'd risk making an *in*direct claim and passing her off to a different lord outside their trio, but clearly Ambrose trusts his cousin more than he does me."

Whitt makes a scoffing sound. "More fool him. I've no doubt Tristan would stab him in the back the second he got an ideal opening and the results looked promising. Not much honor among that lot, only fangs and greed."

He glances at me, his expression turning pained, and then back at his lord. "We can make an argument that this is still a direct claim. He might be claiming her in order to pass her on to another, but he's still the one making the order. Tristan would have no authority to override the arch-lords' decision on his own."

"I'd imagine he has some sort of argument to counter that, or he wouldn't be pursuing this." Sylas sighs. "I don't like relying on anyone outside the pack to fight our battles, but if Donovan and Celia will speak up on our side…" He leans forward and rests one of his powerful hands on my knee. "If Ambrose won't agree to move the discussion to the Bastion of the Heart, where all three of the arch-lords can weigh in, we can simply leave."

I hug myself. All my efforts at staying calm have crumbled the closer we get to Ambrose. "He'll see that as an act of treason, though, won't he? If you ignore his orders as an arch-lord? It'll give him an excuse to attack Hearthshire or try to get you banished all over again."

"We can take that chance. He'd need the other arch-lords to agree before he imposed any further sanctions on us. I have to believe they'd understand my reluctance after the deal we made so recently."

But he'd still be risking it. And the fact that he's in this position at all is my fault. He didn't want to bring me to the attention of the arch-lords in the first place.

Of course, the alternative was letting the Unseelie wage war across the border while all the Seelie warriors stationed there were crazed in the grips of their curse. The summer fae can shift into wolves whenever they want, but for decades now they've been unable to control their shifts or their wild behavior under the full moon. The winter fae would have slaughtered them.

Something about my blood that no one has been able to understand cures the violent frenzy that comes with the curse. I insisted that Sylas use me to protect his people. He warned me that the arch-lords would want to take me for themselves, considering how valuable my blood makes me to them. I decided to take that risk.

I didn't realize that my decision might make things worse not just for me but for him and the rest of the pack too.

I'm not sure if Sylas sees something of my thoughts with his scarred eye, which always seems to observe more than any regular eye should be able to, or if he just knows me well enough by now to guess where my thoughts have gone. He crosses to the bench beside me and tucks me against his massive frame, stroking his hand over my hair.

"Let me worry about the consequences of my actions, Talia. You may not belong to me, but you're worth so much more to me beyond the magic of your blood."

It's impossible not to melt when he talks like that. I have trouble imagining the fae lord ever expressing as deep an affection as August has, but he's already proven that he cares about me more than I could have hoped for. With every gesture he makes like this, the love *I* feel for him grips my own heart harder.

I don't want to lose this strange but exhilarating relationship I've found myself in, adoring and adored by not just one but three remarkable men.

I tip my face up toward Sylas's, and he takes the invitation to claim a kiss, his fingers tracing the line of my jaw. The gentleness of his touch combined with the commanding firmness of his lips leaves me as giddy as always.

Whitt makes a mock coughing sound. "Before you get too distracted, we *are* getting rather close to the prying eyes around the castle."

His tone is typically breezy, but I think I pick up a thread of tension in it. Until just a few days ago, I was only sharing my affection with *two* remarkable men. While apparently it's not unusual for the members of a cadre to take a common lover, since they only have so much attention to offer when their lord has to be their first priority, Whitt initially balked at letting anything happen between us. I'm still not totally sure what about the arrangement made him hesitate, but he seemed almost angry when Sylas first suggested it.

After the passion he showed when he finally did give his desire free rein the other day, I know it wasn't any lack of interest.

There was a time when he was concerned that I might cause problems between Sylas and August—it *is* unusual for a lord to accept shared affections—and for a little while it seemed I might fracture the bonds of the cadre in another way, leaving Whitt on the sidelines. From some of the things he's said to me, it's sounded almost as if he's worried he isn't good enough for me, as absurd as that is when he's a magical, shape-shifting immortal with possibly the most stunning face I've ever seen.

I definitely don't want him feeling left out now, when whatever bond we've formed is still so new and potentially fragile.

"I'd better get this in fast, then," I say with a grin, and spring from the bench. Whitt blinks at me, surprise flickering through his expression when I bob up as far as my toes will take me, but he dips his head so I can plant a quick but emphatic kiss on his mouth.

When I drop back on my heels, he's smiling. He gives a strand of my hair a teasing tug. "You are certainly so much more than a pissant like Ambrose could ever conceive of."

The happiness of the moment stays with me only a matter of minutes, until the signs of a fae settlement rise up in the distance. The carriage veers up a steep slope toward thick slabs of glossy black stone that jut from the jade-green grass to points several feet higher than the carriage's awning. They form an uneven wall in layers we have to weave between, none of the openings lined up for easy passage. I guess the point is to make sure passage *isn't* easy in case the arch-lord and his pack are defending themselves from intruders.

A few wolves prowl along the open stretches between the obsidian rings, but they don't show any concern at our arrival. We're expected.

As we pass between the last of the standing stones, the

sight of the structure up ahead makes my heart sink even more.

Ambrose's castle looms three times as high as any of the stones, made out of the same darkly gleaming rock. Not blocks or tiles like you'd find in the human world if someone built a palace out of obsidian. No, this sleek structure appears to have been carved out of a solid mountain of the stuff—or else summoned in one mass out of the earth, which is more likely from what I've seen of fae magic.

The line of trampled grass we've been following turns into a more formal path of embedded stones several feet from the castle's peaked doorway. Sylas motions for the carriage to stop before we reach that point. The vehicle remains hovering over the grass, and Whitt moves to the side so Sylas can stand at the bow.

It takes a few minutes for our arrival to be acknowledged. None of us speak, so the only sound is the breeze warbling around the stones. Then the door yawns open in the vast doorway, and a mass of figures pours out.

I assume Ambrose is the portly but robust man who strides out at the head of the bunch. His sharply pointed ears and the greenish tint in his brown hair show his true-blooded fae heritage, and he holds himself with impervious assurance as if he can't imagine anyone ever challenging his authority. He's the first fae I've met other than Sylas who's mastered enough true names that their dark tattoos creep up his neck and across the edges of his face.

He's dressed like a warrior in a plate mail vest—does he expect this meeting to come to outright fighting?

The dozen or so men and women who've tramped out with him must be his cadre and some of his pack-kin, hanging back to flank him. Their intense gazes send a crawling sensation over my skin. And off to the side, standing almost abreast with the arch-lord, is a slightly younger-looking man I don't recognize but whose companion is uncomfortably familiar.

The last time I faced that woman whose heavy-lidded eyes are fixed on me, she was wearing a hooded cloak that hid her jet-black hair and well-muscled shoulders. I'd know those eyes and the full lips now curled in a satisfied smile anywhere, though. She's one of Tristan's cadre, the one who attacked me when she found me in the forests around Oakmeet. Which means the man she's with must be Tristan.

The arch-lord's second cousin looks oddly less satisfied than his cadre-chosen. Leaner than Ambrose, his neck is just a little longer than looks totally natural, his knobby chin adding to the giraffe-like impression. His mouth, almost dainty, forms a tight line that gives his whole olive-toned face a sour expression. He must have gotten some of his coloring from the side of the family he shares with Ambrose, because his hair is greenish too—a paler, mint-like green that stands out on the otherwise straw-like strands.

If we had any doubts about the comments Kellan's relatives made, Tristan's presence here dismisses them. That's the man Ambrose wants to turn me over to. The man who's studying me now like I'm a sack of gold he's deciding how best to spend.

"Have you become melded to your carriage, Lord

Sylas?" Ambrose asks, cocking his head. "Come inside; let's get on with it."

Sylas draws himself up with the lordly air that reassures me even in a dire situation like this. "We won't be coming inside, Arch-lord Ambrose. I arrived as a courtesy to fulfill your request for my presence—here I am. Here is the human. If you want to make some sort of claim on her despite the agreement we reached in the Bastion just a few days ago, I expect it to be heard before the full trio of arch-lords, not you alone."

Ambrose's beady eyes narrow. He swipes a hand across his jaw, making his grizzled jowls sway. "I'm well within my rights to call you in. I have no intention of compromising the agreement we came to. All of this can be better discussed within my home."

Sylas folds his arms over his chest. "I've been given to believe that you intend to remove the woman from my custody. Was I misinformed?"

Ambrose's gaze flicks to the side as if evaluating who might have let that detail slip. "I will make no direct claim on her myself. That was the deal we made."

"If you insist we give her over to your cousin here, that transfer would still be happening as a direct result of your authority," Sylas says. "He can't make the claim himself."

"This is all foolish semantics," Ambrose retorts. "I won't be taking her. I'm merely ensuring that she's under stable guardianship."

Guardianship. As if the man next to him would be looking out for me rather than looking to exploit me in every possible way. My fingers curl against the bench's cushion. My nerves prickle with the longing to curl up on the floor where they can't see me, where I won't have so many fae sizing me up like I'm a roast to be carved. These lords are more polite than the ones who tormented me for most of my time in the fae world, but they're just as haughty and cruel.

A movement at the corner of my eye catches my attention. More wolves are slinking past the gaps between the standing stones behind us. As I watch, I count several that appear to be gathering around the path we took to reach the castle. My pulse stutters.

Ambrose knew we might try to leave before he could get his way. He has his pack ready to stop us. This really might come to a battle if Sylas sticks to his guns.

I jerk my gaze away, and it collides with Whitt's. His mouth is set in a grim line. The assembling warriors would hardly have escaped his notice. From Sylas's brief glance over his shoulder, he's taken stock of this new development as well.

He stands firm, turning back to Ambrose. "I heard it in the Bastion that the arch-lords accepted *my* guardianship over this woman. I won't relinquish it until I hear from all three that they've retracted their faith in me. If you refuse to call them in to hold a fair discussion, I'll take my leave."

He moves to ease back from the bow, and Ambrose steps forward with a grimace so fierce it makes my stomach flip over. "Only restored in honor for a handful of days and already back to your treasonous inclinations, are you, Lord Sylas? All the more reason I should ensure this precious resource is in trusted hands."

Sylas's voice stays measured, but it hardens. "I'd say

overturning the ruling of two arch-lords is far more treasonous than refusing to do so. You've heard my position."

"And as your arch-lord, I demand you get off that carriage with the girl and behave with the loyalty you claim to value so highly. Reject my orders, and you'll have a much larger problem on your hands, I assure you."

His pack-kin approach the carriage too, and the ones among the stones emerge. In a moment, they'll have formed a ring around us. Sylas looks at Whitt, silently but with some obvious deliberation. The two men may have their differences, but they know each other well enough that they can communicate plenty without speaking.

I can't tell what they've decided, but the tensing of both their faces makes me tense up too, my heartbeat skittering at an even faster pace. They're not going to give in, and we can't just glide on out of here. They're planning some desperate measure to break past Ambrose's pack.

How easily will he be able to claim they committed treason after that? Will my pack be thrown right back to the fringes of the Mists—will Sylas face an even worse punishment for a more overt crime?

Whitt sets a hand on my shoulder, meant to look casual but with a surreptitious squeeze that urges me downward. He wants me to crouch low—so I'll be braced for whatever they're about to attempt?

Ambrose strides toward us, his teeth bared, canines gleaming in points just shy of his full fangs. "Lord Sylas, this is the last time I'll give the order—"

For a second, my heart pounds so hard it dizzies me.

It's me they want—it's all about me, just like it was with horrible Aerik and his cage.

I promised myself I wasn't going to let anyone use me again, that I'd make my own decisions about what happens to me. That I'd help Sylas and his cadre in every possible way after how they saved me. I can't let myself become their downfall.

But we have nothing to bargain with, no point of leverage here… except me.

The thought hits me with a chilling certainty, and my hand has dropped to the sheath at my hip before I've even considered exactly what I'm going to do. My fingers close around the little dagger's hilt. I jerk the blade from the leather cover and to my neck in one swift motion.

Instead of crouching, I step up on the bench so Ambrose and the others can see me better. My hand shakes, and the blade nicks my skin with a faint sting. I grit my teeth and restrain a wince when I swallow.

No one gets to take me hostage except *me*.

Ambrose and his pack-kin have already halted at my display. The arch-lord stares at me with a mix of revulsion and bemusement. "What in the skies—"

"It's me you're talking about," I say, my voice shaking but loud enough to carry. "I'm still a person. I have a say. And I'd rather die than stay with any lord other than Sylas. You won't get any more cure for your curse if I spill all my blood today."

Sylas and Whitt are staring at me too. Whitt moves an inch, and maybe he could wrench the dagger from me before I could do any real damage if he really wanted to. I cut my gaze toward him and force my hand to press the blade closer.

The pain splinters sharper through my throat. Blood ripples over my skin. I don't want anyone thinking I'm not serious about this.

How serious *am* I? Part of me wants to lie down and just sob. But another part, the part that's keeping my spine rigidly straight and my fingers tight around the hilt while my pulse rattles through my veins, knows that I absolutely would rather die than end up in Tristan or Ambrose's clutches.

I've been just a *thing* to the fae before. Never again. I can't go back. Now that I've remembered what kind of a life I could really have, I think I'd lose my mind completely.

Whitt goes still, looking queasy but resigned. Sylas's hands have clenched where he's standing by the bow, but he holds himself still too, his dark eye smoldering fiercely.

Ambrose speaks in a cajoling voice that still holds a sliver of a sneer. "Come on now, pet. You don't really want to hurt that lovely neck of yours. Do you really expect me to believe you'd slit your own throat?"

I look straight back at him, my jaw tightening. "You don't know anything about me. You have no idea what I've been through or what I'm capable of. I stay with Sylas, or you can test just how far I'm willing to go to make sure I don't end up anywhere else."

Blood is still trickling down from the incision at the edge of the blade. It streaks over my sternum and dampens the fabric of my shirt. I must *look* pretty serious, because Ambrose's tan skin turns slightly gray. His mouth flattens, but he can't seem to find any words he thinks will fix this situation.

"Let us leave," I say. "No, promise you won't try to take me from Sylas again, for anyone, and then let us leave. *Now*."

The arch-lord clearly doesn't want to take the chance that I'm willing to do it. I can only imagine how the other two Seelie rulers would react if they found out he caused their "precious resource" to destroy herself. But he obviously doesn't want to give in either.

He lets out an exasperated sigh, as if I'm simply an inconvenience, and says in a bored tone, "Since you're so adamant about it, perhaps I should consider Lord Sylas's qualifications more closely." His attention shifts back to the fae lord. "You have three weeks—until four days before the next full moon—to make a case that proves she's better off in your care than Lord Tristan's. We'll meet again then."

"In the Bastion, with the full trio, not here," Sylas says, his voice steady but rough.

"Fine, yes, in the Bastion." Ambrose makes a dismissive wave with his hand. "All these witnesses so mark it vowed. That's enough dramatics for today."

He turns on his heel, and with that gesture, the warriors pull back from the circle they were forming around us.

Sylas directs the carriage to withdraw. As it glides backward toward the erratic stone walls, he keeps watching the men we're leaving behind, while Whitt moves to the stern to monitor the warriors by the standing stones.

I hold the dagger to my throat, the shivers that ran

through my hand now rippling through the rest of my body. The pain has expanded into an ache that stretches all across my neck and up to my jaw. But I can't stop. I can't retreat until I'm sure we're safe.

Amid the rows of immense stones, Sylas swivels the carriage around. It picks up speed slowly. We leave the last row of obsidian monstrosities behind and cruise down the rest of the slope. No wolves or warriors patrol anywhere I can see.

A shudder wracks my arm, and I drop my hand.

The instant the blade leaves my throat, Sylas springs at me. He scoops me up so quickly I squeak in surprise, but before I can even start to be scared about how angry he might be, he's lowered his head by mine, murmuring the word I've heard him use before on other wounds to seal my skin. A tingle races over my throat, and the sting numbs. Then he snatches the dagger from my fingers and hurls it between the trees in the forest we've just glided into.

"Don't you *ever* hurt yourself like that again," he growls, his dark eye blazing, his arms wrapping tight around me. I think I feel a tremor of his own ripple through them. "I will never put you in a situation where death is your best option. I swear it by the Heart."

I tip my head against his chest, and he hugs me even closer, kissing my temple. Sudden tears well in my eyes— at what I had to do, at what I might have done if Ambrose hadn't backed down. At the anguish I've clearly caused this man I love. My voice comes out reedy. "I didn't want to. But I—I couldn't let them—what would you have done if I hadn't?"

It's Whitt who answers, his voice sounding strained. "We could have summoned enough magic to lift the carriage high enough and propel it fast enough to avoid Ambrose's pack. Almost certainly."

Almost. Not good enough. And besides— I glance up at him and then at Sylas, touching the fae lord's cheek. "He was already talking about treason. If you ran off like that, he'd have called you a traitor and come to attack Hearthshire to get me, wouldn't he?"

Sylas exhales, slow and ragged. "Most likely, yes. We could have still pleaded our case to the other arch-lords and hoped they'd be reasonable... But I won't deny your approach bought us more time and a better bargaining position. You just shouldn't have to—I never like seeing you put yourself at risk, Talia."

I tuck myself close to him again, hugging him back as if I can make up for the terror he felt watching me like that. "I know."

"Next time, we'll be more ready. I won't let it come to this again. You never need to go that far. Do you hear me?"

"I do," I say meekly, but that doesn't mean I agree.

It'd be nice to pretend that this, nestling in Sylas's strong arms with his rich earthy scent filling my lungs, could be all I do from now until forever. But I've seen enough to know beyond a doubt that this world doesn't work that way. My pack and my men are in danger, and as long as I can do something about that, I won't let them face it alone.

They've risked so much for me. Risking my death

might be the only way to feel I deserve all the good I've managed to find in this life.

3

Whitt

Soulstones are cryptic things. They're said to be created from the essence of the fae they came from and to mimic that essence in some ways. The stone of a cheerful fae might beam brightly at all hours, while a sulkier one would show only erratic flickers of light.

Kellan's has a whirling, churning quality to its glow that suits his volatile loyalties well enough, although he was never anywhere near this quiet. If he'd been more like his stone in that respect, I'd have liked him a little better.

Sylas wraps the soulstone back in its spider-weave cloth and tucks that into the leather pouch he's kept it in. He holds the pouch out to me. "I trust Garmon will find we conducted everything according to the proper rites. Make sure you emphasize how much we regret the delay in seeing him to his proper resting place and that we'll call on them in their own territory within the next few moons."

"And what a joyful trip that will be," I can't resist remarking, even though I anticipate the exact baleful look my half-brother gives me. I grin at him. "Naturally I'll avoid expressing *that* sentiment to our guests."

"Naturally," Sylas says, sounding more amused than anything else, and an odd little quiver shoots through my chest with the recognition of the trust he's placing in me.

It's absurd, really. I wouldn't be part of his cadre if he didn't trust me. Heart knows he wouldn't put up with my snark and my more hedonistic habits if he didn't. But still. Somehow until this past full moon, I didn't recognize or had let myself stop recognizing just how much my lord values my position in the pack.

I aim to be quick-witted at all times in honor of my name, but I've clearly let past events sour my perceptions in unfair ways. It doesn't appear Sylas noticed to any concerning extent, so all's well that ends well. I'll just ensure my judgment is never so compromised again.

I give him a jaunty bob of my head, because it wouldn't do to get *too* deferential. "I'll see to this immediately. You can consider the matter dealt with."

"I expect they'll want time to sit with the news before facing the cause of Kellan's death," my lord says, "but if they do wish to speak to me right away, let me know at once."

"Of course."

Explaining Kellan's downfall to his grandfather and whatever exact relation the pipsqueak is won't be a fun conversation. Heading down the hall from Sylas's study, I allow myself a gulp from my flask, currently topped up with absinthe. Just enough to take the edge off my nerves and let my thoughts flow smoothly. While I'm never half as drunk as I may seem, I operate best with a little lubrication to grease the wheels of my mind.

A startled gasp carries from Talia's bedroom, where the door stands half open partway down the hall. A jolt runs through my veins in the instant before August's chuckle reaches me. If he's with her, she's unlikely to be in any danger.

I pass the doorway with the stealth that comes naturally after centuries as spymaster. Talia is perched on August's lap where he's sitting cross-legged on the floor, their profiles to me, her hands raised in the air and her face as bright as the space between her palms. The glow she's conjured spills through her fingers.

They're working on her magic. He's been teaching her the true name for light—and it appears it's coming easier to her now. She's finding the happiness she said she needed to fuel that magic easier, despite everything she's been through since reaching Hearthshire.

My steps slow so I can take in her joy for just a moment longer. She was a lovely creature when she first came to us, as much as I balked at admitting it then, but she's becoming absolutely radiant as she finds her footing among us.

Talia doesn't have the ears or the nose to pick up on my presence, but August's warrior instincts are ever alert. His gaze darts my way. A quick but companionable smile crosses his face before he returns his attention to his pupil.

I move on, but the sensation that gathers behind my sternum then is far more than just a quiver. It's a blooming of warmth—what I think might be happiness of my own, as unfamiliar as that emotion has become.

It's not just our home we've regained. We've recovered everything good in our partnership, as both brothers and a cadre serving our lord. I hadn't registered just how distant I was feeling from the others until that distance closed, our habits and reactions making us a cohesive unit again.

I could blame Kellan for the initial division, but I know it started before Sylas felt obliged to welcome him into the cadre. If I'm being fully honest with myself, it probably started with me.

I thought the mite would wreck us, and instead she's strengthened our bonds. Brought us back together from wherever we were drifting off to.

And we almost lost her yesterday.

As I head down the stairs, the image flashes through my mind of Talia standing rigid on the carriage bench, her dagger pressed to her throat. The scarlet rivulet trickling down her pale skin. The desperate determination in her grass-green eyes.

The warmth inside me disappears beneath a wave of nausea. My hands curl into fists. For one white-hot moment, I'm a mere thread from unleashing my wolf and charging all the way to Ambrose's domain to tear him and Tristan to pieces.

They pushed her to that brink—they provoked that desperation—

I don't know how to convince her she'll never need to resort to a measure like that again, and I hate that I can't. The fact that Sylas is grappling with the exact same dilemma doesn't give me any comfort. She *is* precious, but for far more than the arch-lord and his crony of a cousin could conceive of. She deserves some actual peace.

But first I have to deal with our unwanted guests. Orym had better not make any more disdainful remarks about our human, or I may not be able to resist tearing *him* to pieces while he's conveniently available.

Just before I reach the front door, I allow myself another gulp of absinthe, though it's difficult to say whether it soothes my temper or inflames it more. Outside, I stretch out into wolf form and lope toward the trees. It's so short a distance to the guest houses that no one would bother with a carriage or a horse, but I have no wish to prolong this task with a leisurely stroll.

Hearthshire's accommodations for high-ranking guests include a keep only slightly smaller than the one we made do with in Oakmeet and a few smaller houses for those with a particularly large retinue. Unless Garmon has been particularly stealthy himself, he only brought his great-grandson to attend to him, so Sylas sent a few of our pack-kin over to wait on them, as is appropriate for a lord.

I wouldn't be surprised if Garmon turned up understaffed specifically to test how well Sylas would cater to him. That family has always put far too much energy into climbing the social ladder and demanding esteem from others. And look where their inclinations got them. Most of the true-blooded members of their associated packs and a great deal of the faded kin as well were slaughtered after their attempt on Ambrose's throne, those who survived were banished...

Garmon might not have been an active part of the

plotting, but his children and grandchildren learned those attitudes from somewhere.

Even though the house is technically ours, I have to treat it as their residence. I rise up from my wolf and rap my knuckles against the door, tugging at my vest to ensure it's straight. Wouldn't want to look sloppy in front of a lord.

One of our own people answers the door and ushers me inside. I find Garmon and Orym in the sitting room basking in the afternoon sun. The scent of the dinner my pack-kin are making for them, roast flame-pleasant if I'm not mistaken, laces the air. But as they get to their feet, Garmon makes a point of emphasizing the stiffness of his aging limbs as if being put up here was a hassle to them.

"Whitt, isn't it?" he says, scrutinizing me. "What are you here about? When am I finally to understand what's become of my grandson?"

I force myself to bob my head as low as I did for Sylas, not because I respect this man more, but because he'd see much less as an insult. "That's exactly what I'm here for. I'm afraid, as you must already suspect, it isn't uplifting news. Perhaps you would like to sit down?"

Garmon lets out a raspy guffaw. "No, these old bones can manage to hold me up while I hear this. Go on."

It's a matter that requires a certain amount of delicacy, which is difficult because Kellan was anything but delicate himself. I weigh my words carefully. "You may have gathered over the years while we were banished to the fringes that Kellan wasn't entirely satisfied with his position there. It wasn't the life he expected to have. Lord Sylas understood his frustrations and did what he could for him, even offered to release him from service if he preferred to seek a livelihood elsewhere, but he wasn't able to find a course that suited him."

"None of this explains where he's gone."

"I'm afraid it does." I dip my head again as if the conversation pains me—which it does if not exactly for the reasons Garmon would want it to. "My cadre-fellow began to challenge Sylas's authority in increasingly disruptive ways. Lord Sylas was running out of options. And the arrival of our human guest only brought out more rancor. Despite all she can offer to the Seelie, Kellan took a dislike to her and went out of his way to harm her."

"So he went for her blood when her blood is what she had to offer," Orym tosses out, so callously my claws itch to spring from my fingertips. "That seems reasonable."

I will my gritted teeth to unclench. "Blood that *all* our brethren need. A cure that would have been destroyed if Kellan had gone unchecked. In the end, he outright attacked her, and Lord Sylas was forced to fight him to preserve her life. He asked for Kellan's yield, but Kellan chose to make another lunge at the girl. It was a choice between a boon to all Seelie kind and a single fae in an act of undeniable mutiny. My lord did not make the decision lightly all the same, and he regrets to this day that it came to that point."

As I say the last words, I pour the spider-weave cloth from the pouch and let the folds fall open in my hand to reveal Kellan's soulstone. It flares like a tiny, muted ball of sunlight in the midst of the dark cloth.

For all his bluster, I suspect Garmon knew what was coming. I don't pick up any trace of shock in his expression as he takes the stone in. Orym, though, starts to sputter.

"Lord Sylas killed our pack-kin over some cringing dung-body? What in the—"

I cut him off before he can get any farther with his insults. "Kellan was *our* pack-kin from the moment he accepted the position in Lord Sylas's cadre, and I should hope *your* kin have taught you the proper respect that's due to one's lord."

Garmon squints at the stone and then at me. "It does seem odd that this happened so abruptly. I long suspected Lord Sylas wasn't particularly enthusiastic about taking Kellan into his service."

"If you'd been there, you wouldn't have found it abrupt at all," I say, my jaw starting to tighten all over again. "You haven't seen us in decades. And you can check for yourself that the stone shines true. He was offered a fair yield and refused it. The stone can't lie."

He peers at the soulstone again and murmurs a word. The light inside it flashes pure white before dwindling again. The huff of his breath sounds more irritated than accepting.

"And Lord Sylas saw fit to send his cadre-chosen to deliver this news rather than facing us himself?"

"He felt the news would be better delivered from an uninvolved party. Why would you want to look at the man who caused your grandson's death while processing that fact?"

"So that I could take him into account as I see fit." Garmon gives another huff and collects the stone and its trappings from me. "So I can demand to know what amends he'd make."

Sylas doesn't owe these miscreants any amends for Kellan's insubordination, but I can't imagine saying as much would win us any points. I step back. "He's ready to call on you now if you wish to see him immediately. I can—"

Garmon shakes his head with a jerk. "No. We must leave at once to see this stone finally to its proper resting place. If Lord Sylas truly has the honor you'd claim, let him travel to us to pay his respects fully. I'll expect him soon."

He turns with a swish of his cloak and motions for Orym to follow him. The young man aims a scowl at me before taking after his great-grandfather.

"Wait," I say, and hustle out of the house. I dash back to the castle as a wolf, but when I shift by the entrance, Garmon's spindly carriage is already cruising through the clearing toward the gate. Even if Sylas could catch them in time, it'd hardly do for him to race after them like a chastised whelp.

I watch them go, biting back half a dozen insults I'd like to hurl after them. Do they really think they're still so important that Sylas *needs* to care what they think of him and his respects?

But Sylas will care, which is exactly what makes him an excellent lord and why I'd be a terrible one.

The only crime anyone's ever claimed we committed, we've been absolved of. Garmon is father and grandfather to a host of traitors. He should be lucky he got even a cadre-chosen attending to him. But no, in his eyes I wasn't enough. A few drops of fae blood short. If he hasn't gotten Sylas's attention, what do any of the rest of us matter?

I stride into the castle to inform Sylas of their response with a sour flavor creeping through my mouth, wishing I couldn't so vividly remember my own experience with the same resentment Garmon expressed.

I've put that behind me now. I don't give a rat's ass what they think. Let them drift off to whatever backwater domain they've slunk to. I have a precious woman to save.

4

Talia

Every room in Hearthshire's castle is bigger—grander—than its equivalent back in Oakmeet's keep. And there are more of them: sitting rooms and a library, a third floor full of guest rooms and servant quarters, a massive ballroom in the western wing with its ceiling two floors high.

But it's laid out in pretty much the same way, with a T-shaped hallway that has the main, spiraling staircase at its base, and the atmosphere, if a little more imposing, feels familiar. I haven't lived here a week yet, and I can already call it "home." Especially when I'm sitting perched on a stool in the kitchen, kneading dough while August preps a haunch of deer for a roast.

The kitchen itself is twice the size of the one back in Oakmeet, with five islands of varying sizes and a stone oven at one end so vast you could roast an entire stag in it, but August's touch is everywhere from the organization of the utensils to the ingredients already stocked in the pantry. When I'm here working beside him, it feels impossible that I could ever be wrenched to some other castle by forces beyond these walls.

Wouldn't it be nice if that were true?

"I think it's just about ready," I tell August, judging the elasticity of the dough the way he's taught me. The purple mixture is warm and pliant against my fingers, giving off a rich nutty smell.

My lover pauses in his work to watch me stretch a section between my hands and nods with a grin that's all the praise I need. "I can take over from there."

He glances down the counter to where one of his new kitchen assistants from the pack is working. Now that he has more space and more duties to attend to, Sylas wanted to bring more of the pack-kin into the castle to help with the day-to-day chores. "How are the berries coming along?"

"Just a few more to peel!"

As the woman shoves her bowl toward August, footsteps rap against the floor outside. A call rings down the hallway. "Lord Sylas?"

Recognizing the voice as Astrid's—one of the sentries —I slip off my stool, give my hands a quick wipe on a rag, and limp over to the doorway to see what's going on. August comes up behind me, giving my shoulder a reassuring squeeze.

Astrid shoots us a quick but tight smile before turning her attention back to the staircase, where the fae lord is just coming into view. The sentry's gray hair and lined face indicate she's old even by fae standards, but her wiry frame shows no sign of weakness.

"What's the trouble?" Sylas asks, his voice as steady as always but his unscarred eye even darker than usual with concern.

"I'm not sure yet if it's trouble. There's a carriage coming this way, five passengers, faded fae. Looks like a family. No noticeable weapons or armor—they look peaceful enough. They're coming at a good clip, though. I expect they'll be here within the minute. I didn't think we were expecting anyone."

Sylas frowns. "We weren't. Thank you for alerting me. You can return to your post."

He heads in the same direction down the hall toward the front door. I hesitate and then follow, curiosity tugging at me as much as my nerves. If there *is* more trouble on the horizon, I'd like to be able to prepare as well as I can.

"Sounds like I may need to double the meal," August says after me, sounding cheerful enough that I have to think the situation can't be *that* horrible. Maybe fae dropping in on each other happens a lot more often when you're not living in disgrace banished to the fringes. Before now, I've only seen pack life at its lowest.

When I slip outside behind Sylas, he doesn't remark on my presence. The carriage is already gliding into view between the arch of the trees. I move to the side, staying in the shadow of the castle.

The five figures who come into focus as the carriage draws nearer do look like a family. There's a couple who appear to be middle-aged by fae standards and three young women who'd pass for twenty-somethings in human terms—the youngest maybe not quite out of her teens. They all have glossy brown hair ranging from chestnut on the mother and the youngest daughter to tawny on father and the eldest, and the girls all share their mother's sharply pointed nose.

Their clothes are close to the simple tunics and dresses most of our pack-kin usually wear, just a little fancier with glinting embroidery along the collars and the cuffs of the sleeves. The middle daughter's hair swirls around her head to where it's pinned in place by a gold clip that sparkles with emeralds.

As the carriage slows, Sylas steps forward to meet the newcomers. "Hello there. What brings you to Hearthshire?"

"Greeted by the lord himself," the man says with a little chuckle and a bow so casual it immediately raises my hackles. "We're honored. I don't expect you'd necessarily remember me: I'm Namior of Dusk-by-the-Heart, and this is my wife, Tesfira, and our daughters, Lili, Irabel, and Toraine. Tesfira and I attended more than one ball and banquet here when Hearthshire was at its height. When we heard it was being restored to its former glory, we couldn't resist stopping by and seeing if there was any way we could assist in exchange for your hospitality."

While he speaks, his gaze roves over the castle, the surrounding buildings, and the forest beyond. Dusk-by-the-Heart, he said his domain was called. I'm just wondering whether that's one of the arch-lord's domains in their cluster around the Heart of the Mists when Sylas says, "Ambrose felt he could spare you?"

My stance tenses even more. These are Ambrose's pack-kin, then.

Understanding clicks in my head with a chill that ripples down my spine. They can't really be here to help and admire the rebuilding efforts. The arch-lord must have sent them to look for any proof they could find that Sylas isn't fit to keep me in his pack.

Spies. That's the word for it. Where's Whitt? A spymaster should know how to deal with intruders like these.

Fae rules of hospitality must mean Sylas can't send them right off, even though from the set of his shoulders I suspect he'd like to. He makes a broad motion toward them. "I appreciate your consideration. We've been settling in quite well as it is—and I'd hardly want to put guests to work. If you'd like to join us for dinner tonight and see how the renovations are coming together, my pack would be happy to see you to the guest buildings."

Tesfira offers a coy smile. "No need to go to that much trouble, Lord Sylas. We'd be perfectly happy with the visitor quarters in the castle, and then we can be closer at hand to offer our service."

Closer at hand to lurk around and observe us, she means.

Thankfully, Sylas isn't any more inclined to accept that proposal than I would be. He shakes his head emphatically. "I certainly couldn't set you up there when the outer buildings are free, especially when it comes to esteemed kin of the arch-lord. Let me see you there myself."

He sets off without waiting for a response. The

husband and wife exchange a glance, the daughters murmuring discontentedly, but they direct their carriage to glide behind the fae lord, maybe intending to argue more once they catch up with him.

Hopefully he'll be able to get rid of them completely before too long. Even watching them drifting away, uneasiness creeps over my skin. We haven't figured out a solid strategy yet for convincing the arch-lords that I *do* belong here, especially when we don't know anything about what arguments Ambrose will make other than that he isn't likely to play fair.

I could go back to helping August in the kitchen, but a restless itch tickles through my limbs. I look toward the pack village, where several of the fae had stopped to check out the visitors and have now gone back to their usual pursuits.

If I can show I really *am* a member of the pack, not just an object that Sylas keeps around for my blood, surely that would work toward convincing the other arch-lords that I should stay here? How could it be a good thing to uproot a "precious resource" from a home where I'm respected and protected by the entire pack?

I've made a few tentative forays into joining their activities—maybe it's time I do a little more.

A few of the pack-kin who were watching the newcomers have gathered closer in conversation. I recognize a couple of them by name: Elliot, whose family tends to the sheep and who supplies the pack with milk and cheese, and Brigit, a woman who always wears brightly colored dresses and who's a regular fixture at Whitt's nighttime revels. As quickly as my warped foot allows, I hurry over to them, grateful for the boots that make my feet at least look normal even if my steps are a bit uneven despite the built-in brace.

"Hey," I say as I reach the group of three, feeling abruptly awkward. "I guess the pack is a lot more popular now that we're back at Hearthshire."

Elliot smiles crookedly. "Seems that way. But maybe not the kind of 'popularity' we'd prefer." He turns to the others. "We should get on with gathering the shy-caps before they're gone."

I try to hold myself in a stance that looks capable and enthusiastic. "Is that something you could use a hand with?"

The three of them look me over, and then Brigit shrugs. "The more hands we have, the more chance we'll grab them all. Do you know shy-caps?"

"Ah, no," I admit, limping along with them as they head toward the forest, hoping shy-caps aren't anything ferocious.

"They're mushrooms," explains the other woman, whose name I haven't caught. "Elliot spotted a patch of them coming back from the pasture. They got their name because they don't show themselves for long—you get about an hour and then they fade away."

They stop to pick up reed baskets from a storage shed near the edge of the forest, and I take one too. Harper darts over to us and snatches one for herself. She taps me teasingly with her elbow. "No going off on your first adventures without me."

I smile back at her. "I don't know how much of an

adventure picking mushrooms will be, but it sounds like everyone's welcome."

It turns out collecting the shy-caps isn't all that simple after all. The little mushrooms, all of them smaller than my thumb, glimmer faintly in the streaks of sunlight that trickle between the leaves in the grove where they've sprouted. But half of the time when I reach for one, it vanishes before I can close my fingers around it. From the muttered curses of the fae around me, I gather that isn't just my problem. Elliot must have spotted them close to the one-hour deadline.

I manage to fill my basket halfway and feel pretty satisfied with that. Harper has less luck, veering this way and that and then sighing in exasperation when yet another slips from her grasp. She swings her basket and ambles closer to me. "More guests—and from one of the domains of the Heart! You went out with Lord Sylas to Dusk-by-the-Heart, didn't you? I suppose it's even grander than Hearthshire?"

Even as I smile at the eagerness in her voice, my chest tightens at the memory. "The castle is very... imposing. I only saw the outside. We weren't there for very long."

My voice probably gives away my discomfort. Harper hesitates, ducking her head. She doesn't know exactly what went on during that visit, but the tensions between Sylas and Ambrose aren't a total secret. "Of course. Perhaps that's why they've come here instead. I wonder if we'll have a ball soon, now that more packs are taking an interest."

No doubt she's imagining showing off her dresses to them, hoping they'll want one and spread the word. "I don't know," I say. "I'm not sure what the guests are expecting."

Brigit snorts. "They expect to poke their noses where they don't belong. Meddlers."

The other woman, whose name I now know is Pomya, tips her head in agreement and pulls back her lips to show her wolfish fangs. "They'd better not meddle too much, or we'll show them how Hearthshire defends itself."

Elliot tsks at her. "A great look for us it'd be if we pounce on the first friendly guests we've gotten since returning."

"You call that bunch friendly?"

"No," he admits. "But they're playing at it, so we have to play along, don't we? You don't think I'd like to turn them out on their asses for Lord Sylas? But if he thought we could get away with that, he'd do it himself."

Brigit glances back toward the castle with an unusually pensive expression. "He's done a lot for us. It's a shame the best we can offer is a bunch of mushrooms when there's still so much unsettled."

Her gaze skims over me, with a prickle down my spine at the knowledge that everyone here knows I'm the main cause of the pack's currently precarious situation.

But I'm also the main reason they were able to return to Hearthshire at all. That's got to be worth something, right? Listening to them brings a pang into my chest. Their sentiments echo my own wish to contribute more, to be more than a walking blood dispenser. I can offer something very important, but it's not really something I actually *do*.

"Maybe there are ways we can help that don't go as far as tossing them out," I venture.

Pomya cocks her head. "Like what?"

"Well, they're going to poke around and spy on us, right? So we can keep an eye on *them*. Try to catch them doing something suspicious enough that it'll give Sylas an excuse to send them away—or maybe even make Ambrose look bad so he'll be less likely to keep hassling us."

She grunts. "I'd rather tear a strip off of them like they probably deserve. No one should get to threaten our pack."

Harper twists a strand of her pale hair around her finger. "But if they aren't *acting* like a threat…"

"We know they're not here because they care so much about us," Brigit says. "If I notice them putting one foot out of line, I'm not letting them get away with it. They need to see how strong we still are."

I think back to something Whitt said to me before I faced my former captors for what I hope was the last time —about how playing to your weaknesses can be a way of being strong. "I think if they're playing games, then we can too. If we pretend we're weaker than we really are, that we don't realize what they're up to, then they'll give more away. And then we can surprise them by really getting the upper hand later."

Elliot hums to himself, and Pomya looks skeptical. I'm not sure they agree with my reasoning or even think I'm making much sense. But at least I get a vaguely impressed whistle out of Brigit when she checks my basket. "You've got quick hands, girl. I'll give you that much."

Any lingering shy-caps have vanished. We tramp back

along the overgrown path to the castle and find Sylas waiting by the village. He nods to his pack-kin, but his gaze focuses on me. A hint of a smile curves one side of his mouth. "I see you've been finding new ways to contribute around here. Can I have a word?"

As if I'd say no. I pass my basket to Brigit and meander with Sylas back toward the trees. My stomach knots. Have the guests already become a problem?

"Is everything all right?" I ask carefully, not sure how much I should say even with the village at a distance.

Sylas smiles wider but with a grim edge. "As right as it can be, I suppose. Just a complication at a time when my attention needs to be elsewhere. Kellan's grandfather wishes me to attend to him personally in his own domain, and I don't want to delay that responsibility for however long our visitors may decide to enjoy our hospitality. The more time he has to stew, the more chance he'll find some way to give our current enemies ammunition against us."

Ambrose is already plenty dangerous as it is. I nod in understanding. "So you're going right away, even with the guests?"

"Yes. Whitt and August can 'entertain' them well enough—but I'd like you to accompany me."

To the domain where the rest of Kellan's relatives now live? My shoulders stiffen automatically. "Why?"

"Because given the current circumstances, I'd rather not leave you *here* when I'm not nearby. And also because, as Kellan's intended victim, I hope your presence will help remind his family of how much we all might have lost if I hadn't intervened." Sylas's smile softens. "You do seem to have a way of adjusting the perspective of those around you. But—I know it won't be easy for you. They won't harm you, but they may not be kind either. I won't force you to come."

He won't force me, but he thinks me being there would help him. How can I say no to *that*?

After all the ways he's protected me, all the risks he's taken for me, I'm not sure there's anywhere in this world or mine I wouldn't follow Sylas to if he asked.

I drag in a breath. "You don't need to. I'll do whatever I can. When do we leave?"

5

August

If you'd asked me while we were living at Oakmeet, I'd have said I missed the chatter and companionship of visitors, which we lost almost entirely after we were banished. But guests like this family from Dusk-by-the-Heart? I could definitely do without *them*.

"You don't look all that different from a regular human," the middle daughter says to Talia, sitting next to her at the dinner table. She grabs a handful of my love's hair as if handling a doll. "Other than this. It doesn't grow this color, does it?"

Talia's face turns nearly as pink as those locks. "No. It's just brown naturally. August dyed it." She glances at me where I'm seated at her other side with a hint of worry that makes my stomach clench. So concerned that she might let us down somehow if she says the wrong thing. I want to reach for her hand to squeeze it, but the one nearest me is clamped around her fork.

The youngest daughter actually gets up out of her chair and gives Talia a sniff. "Smells like a normal human too." She giggles and flops back into her chair, glancing around at all of us like she expects us to be equally amused by her observation.

Their father waves his hand toward Sylas. "You haven't made any attempt to determine the source of her… unusual blood?"

I can tell my lord is holding himself back from a full glower. His unscarred eye shines darkly. "We've made plenty of attempts, but the answer has eluded us. It may be that it's a random natural phenomena with no specific source."

The eldest daughter pokes at the scraps remaining on her plate while eyeing Talia. "I wonder what it tastes like when it's not all mixed up in the tonic. Would you let us sample a little?"

My shoulders tense, and my gums twitch with the emerging of my fangs. I'm not sure I'd have been able to hold myself back from springing across the table at her with a chomp of my teeth to let her find out how much *she* likes offering a sample if Sylas didn't speak again, quickly and firmly. "She may contain a mystery, but she's still a person and a valued member of our pack. She bleeds enough for us when it can save us. I would not ask more from her for curiosity's sake."

He hasn't outright chided, but the rebuke in his words is obvious. The daughter—Lili, I think that one is?—ducks her head, having at least the grace to look abashed.

Talia manages to take another bite, but her nervousness shows all through her stance. Dust and doom,

I can only imagine how much worse her situation will be if Ambrose pulls off his claim. She shouldn't have to put up with being treated like a curiosity, an exotic trinket we picked up in our travels, rather than a conscious living being.

But if we bite our guests' heads off—as much as I might want to in the most literal sense—we'll look undisciplined and vindictive to the arch-lords. It isn't as if they're harming her in any observable way. Ambrose won't hesitate to point to any incident that happens during this visit when making his case. So I grit my teeth and will my claws to stay within my fingertips.

At least when dinner is over, Whitt shepherds the bunch of them outside to join in his second revel at Hearthshire, leaving the rest of us in peace. Although I suspect Talia would have liked to join in the revel if these strangers hadn't been in attendance.

I slip my hand around hers like I wanted to at the table and lean in to kiss the top of her head. "Are you all right?"

She gives herself a little shake and aims a small smile at me. "It's fine. It makes sense that they're curious. As long as I have all of you, it doesn't really matter how the other fae treat me."

It does, though. It matters to me. And she shouldn't have to put up with their disrespect.

Of course, tomorrow she might be facing even worse.

After she's gone to her bedroom for the night, I track down Sylas. He's in the gym, examining the cabinet of weaponry we brought to Oakmeet when we left and restored to its proper place just a few days ago.

He takes out a short sword and turns it over in his hands, testing its weight. Apparently he doesn't have the highest hopes for how tomorrow's visit will go either.

I wouldn't normally question my lord's judgment, but the knot of worry in my belly propels the words out. "Are you sure it's a good idea for Talia to come with you?"

Sylas raises an eyebrow at me, his gaze managing to be so penetrating even though one of those eyes can't even see. At least, it can't see anything of this world. "Do you think I'd be taking her if I hadn't decided it was?"

I grimace. "It's only—it's bad enough how Kellan treated her, how Garmon and the other one insulted her when they were here. They'll be bolder on their own terrain. She shouldn't have to hear how they'll talk to her or about her."

"I don't know. Perhaps it's useful for her to see the full span of fae attitudes—to know just how wary she needs to be of everyone outside this domain, even now that we've dealt with Aerik." Sylas's voice turns grim. "I don't think this is the last challenge we're going to face on her behalf. The more steel she can find in herself, the better. You know how strong she already is."

I do. I wish she didn't have to be that strong. I wish I could slaughter everyone who so much as points a sneer in her direction.

She's been through so much pain already, and it still weighs on her.

"And our guests here?" I ask.

"Whitt will do most of the work keeping them occupied. Give them another feast for dinner tomorrow, and if all goes well, we'll be back by nightfall." He pats my arm. "I'm sure Talia would appreciate whatever breakfast you can whip up for our travels tomorrow. Will you leave something in the cold box? I want to leave at dawn."

"Of course, my lord," I say, and head back to the kitchen to see what I can pull together that might bring Talia a little joy while she anticipates her destination.

When I wake the next morning, my lord and my love are already gone. I stalk through the halls restlessly and finally whip up a small breakfast for myself, since after last night's revel Whitt isn't likely to make an appearance in the dining room until lunch. I've just polished off an omelet and brought the plate back to the kitchen when the middle daughter—Irabel?—comes slinking in.

"Oh, are you already done with breakfast?" she says with a trace of a pout, propping herself against the nearest island.

Something about her pose and her tone makes my hackles rise. I force myself to smile. "Did my pack-kin not prepare something in the guest house this morning? I'm sure Sylas intended for your meals to be seen to."

She shrugs. "They did, but I thought it'd be much more fun to have whatever you'd come up with. A cadre-chosen who's a warrior *and* a chef—there aren't many of those."

She peeks through her eyelashes at me, and the prickling discomfort solidifies into a fuller understanding. She's flirting with me. It's been decades since any fae woman thought it worth pursuing me, and I wasn't old enough to be eligible for all that long before our disgrace —I'm out of practice at recognizing the signs.

Knowing what she's up to doesn't ease my mind at all.

She's aware that Talia and I have taken to each other—we didn't see any point in hiding that when the whole pack knows. But because Talia's only human, as far as this woman is concerned—because we aren't properly bonded as mates—she still considers me a perfectly reasonable target for her interest.

It takes all my self-control not to growl at her. Her assumptions are the same ones almost any of our brethren would make. That doesn't mean I have to cater to them, though.

"I'm afraid I didn't have any elaborate plans," I say, keeping my tone cool. "I have duties to attend to, but if you check with my pack-kin who are seeing to your stay, I'm sure one of them could put something together for you regardless of the timing."

"Hmm. If you're not the one making it, I'm not sure I'm all that hungry." She straightens up and saunters closer. "Could I help you with some of your duties? You must be very busy with so much to catch up on now that you're back in Hearthshire."

Another growl collects at the base of my throat. I smother it down, but my voice still comes out with a bit of an edge. "These duties are best carried out alone. And what needs I have for companionship in general are already well taken care of. Please don't trouble yourself."

My full meaning must be clear enough. Her face falls, and she gives another half-hearted shrug. "If you change your mind… I believe my father had something he wanted to discuss with you as soon as possible. Do you have a moment to call on him before you go off on your duties?"

I restrain a sigh. "I do. I'll find him as soon as I'm finished here."

She gives me one more lingering glance and then sashays off. I glare at the pots dangling over the counter for several seconds as I gather my temper.

Should I have been less brusque with her? Have I soured the situation in some way that will come back to bite us?

But the gall of her attempting to work her charms on me as if I'd cast aside Talia the second a woman with fae blood shot one coy glance at me…

No, maybe we haven't been firm enough. I trust Sylas's judgment, and he's seen fit to trust mine. I'll speak to Namior—and make it absolutely clear that we consider Talia a full member of the pack, and that disrespect shown to her is an insult to all of us.

I stride into the hall, heading toward the entrance. Yes. I'll simply… advise them so they recognize their rudeness. I can do that calmly, can't I? *They're* the ones who should be embarrassed of how they've offended us. It'll only—

A twitch in the shadows along the edge of the floor catches my eye. I pause, my head jerking around to try to track the movement.

I can't make out its source. When I inhale deeply, my entire body tenses.

Did I just catch a hint of *rat* in the air?

Another wavering shadow draws my attention to the foot of the stairs. I spin the rest of the way around and march toward it. If one of the filthy Murk has dared sneak into our home with Heart only knows what spiteful intent, I'll bite *its* head off, you can be sure of that.

I hustle up the stairs, taking another breath and another. The scent I thought I picked up downstairs has faded away. I don't catch sight of any creatures lurking on the stairwell or in the hallway upstairs either.

I prowl around for a few minutes until I'm forced to accept that my mind might have simply been playing tricks on me. I have been pretty keyed up since we first heard Ambrose had called for Talia.

As I turn back toward the stairs, a noise reaches my ears: a soft thump and a rustle of fabric. My ears prick. Someone's in the library.

I stalk toward the doorway just as the oldest of the visiting daughters emerges. She's patting the fabric of her skirt, which forms an odd lump by her thigh for a moment before she smooths it out. At the sight of me, she startles and then claps her hand to her chest. "Oh, I didn't realize anyone was up here. I was just returning a book Sylas said I could borrow yesterday."

I remember hearing her ask about that, but something about this encounter rubs me the wrong way, especially after her sister made a point of seeking out my attention downstairs. Why didn't this one say good morning on her way up? What was she doing with her skirt just now?

I can hardly demand she lift it up to show me. If I'm wrong, it'd be even worse than if I attacked her over Talia.

There isn't any chance that...? As I nod in acknowledgment, an absurd suspicion wriggles through me, and I step just close enough to catch her scent. She's a wolf—there's no doubt about that. It isn't as if we could have somehow missed the scent of five rats pretending to be Seelie after spending any time in close proximity anyway.

Still, I can't help taking on extra step to confirm that will both keep them busy and benefit the pack. "I thought I might propose a hunt, if you'd want to join in. Our pantry could still use some stocking."

There's no mistaking the predatory gleam that lights in her eyes with the stirring of her wolfish instincts. "I'm sure my whole family would be happy for the chance to stretch our legs," she says with a bob of her head.

"Excellent." I motion for her to continue on her way. "I was just getting something from my room. If your father asks, you can tell him I'll be there shortly, and then we'll see about the hunt."

When she's vanished down the stairwell, I enter the library instead. I've never spent much time in this part of the castle, never missed it when we went without a full library in Oakmeet. My gaze skims over the shelves of leather and leaf-bound books, the armchairs and their side tables, the objects on display here and there from Sylas's travels. There are a few gaps amid the books, but I can't tell whether anything we should be concerned about is missing.

Since no one's around to hear it, I let out the growl I've been holding in for so long. Sylas will know better than I do. As soon as he returns—let it be tonight—I'll tell him what I saw and let him decide what we should make of it.

It would be too much to hope that Ambrose's pack-kin didn't have any extra wickedness up their sleeves, wouldn't it?

6

Talia

The wind whips my hair back from my face, bringing a trace of tears into my eyes until I avert my gaze. I think I'd enjoy this journey more if Sylas hadn't set the carriage at top speed. And also if I'd found anything to like about the place we're traveling to.

Our breakfast long eaten, there hasn't been much to do but watch the landscapes go by. Even that loses its thrill as we reach a narrow, winding valley between two steep cliffs. Sylas has to slow the carriage so it can navigate without bumping the pocked stone, and the scenery quickly merges into a seemingly endless mass of orange rock and turquoise moss.

I lean back on the bench and rub my eyes, restraining a yawn. I can't say I got the greatest night's sleep anticipating this morning's trip.

Sylas monitors the carriage's movements for a few minutes longer and then, satisfied that his magic is directing it well enough that he can trust it to pilot itself, sits down next to me. He reaches beneath the stiff fabric of his formal vest and produces a leather sheath with a matching leather-wrapped hilt protruding from it.

He hands it to me. "To replace the one I threw away. You shouldn't go unarmed."

I wrap my fingers around the leather, which is warm from lying so close to his skin. A weird mix of gratitude and trepidation coils in my chest. I hadn't been sure he'd want to trust me with another blade after his reaction to my self-hostage gambit. But… "Do you think I'm going to need it where we're going?"

His mouth twists. "Better you have it and don't than go without and do. None of those once of Thistlegrove are known for kindness toward humans. They're rarely kind to *each other* unless it serves them. Given what you offer and who you're arriving with, you needn't fear for your life, but if anyone oversteps before I can intervene, I fully support you showing how unwise that is for yourself."

And this is the family he found himself tied to through marriage—through no choice of his own, since the true-blooded fae have no control over who they connect with as their soul-twined mate.

The more I learn about how things work for the purest of the fae and their love lives, the less appealing it sounds. What good is having a soul-deep bond with someone you didn't choose and maybe never would have if you'd gotten a say in it?

I fix the strap on the sheath to the belt around my fae-styled dress. A pouch with the remaining salt from the small supply Whitt gave me dangles at my other hip.

Together, those weapons make for a small protection against the physical strength and magical power of the fae, but it's something. The salt saved me from being mauled by one of my former captors a couple of weeks ago. And my old dagger had something to do with saving me from Ambrose, at least in the moment.

With the sheath secured, I look up at Sylas, taking in his pensive expression. "What *exactly* did Isleen and Kellan's family do? I know they committed some kind of treason against Ambrose. They tried to take over as arch-lords? How would that even work?"

The fae lord folds his hands together on his lap. "There are two ways an arch-lord can be displaced. The more civilized way is to prove them unfit for the job based on wrong-doing or incompetence, and then the two remaining arch-lords must agree on a lord they feel would make a fitting replacement and for whom they receive the Heart's blessing."

I'm taking a wild guess that's not what happened in Isleen's case. "And the less civilized way?"

"We are still wolves as well as fae in spirit. If a pack shows it's powerful enough to overcome another and take the lord's life or force their yield, they're granted the right over that domain. It's the same for an arch-lord as any other."

I shiver. "Your mate and a bunch of her family tried to *kill* Ambrose?"

"As near as we can determine," Sylas says. "They'd come up with a strategy combining their various magical specialities and a few rare true names that kin among them had managed to master. It appeared they'd been laying the groundwork to ensure their entry into his castle unhindered for months if not years, slowly and subtly. I've never heard a full report on what happened once they were inside the castle… I don't know how close they came to succeeding. But they didn't, and Ambrose, his cadre, and his guards tore every one of them they caught to shreds."

He pauses, and his voice turns even more grim. "There wasn't enough left of Isleen to form a soulstone, but I saw the remains to confirm they were hers."

My next shiver comes with a twinge of nausea. "She can't have been thinking *you'd* become arch-lord when she hadn't even told you the plan?"

Sylas shakes his head. "She was serving her mother, who would have taken the title. But it would have benefitted her and me too, having a familial connection by the Heart."

"Kellan was part of Isleen's cadre, wasn't he? Why wasn't he punished?"

"He wasn't part of the attack. I think perhaps he was meant to provide some sort of alibi if the attempt went wrong but she was able to escape unhindered. And he *was* punished—by being banished alongside me. If I hadn't taken him into my cadre, he'd have been sent off with his grandfather and the other stragglers from the family and their packs to the other end of the fringes. I thought I owed it to him to give him a chance… If I'd understood how far she meant to go with her plotting and how soon, maybe it all could have been averted."

He lapses into somber silence. He's told me before that he feels responsible for the attack and his pack's banishing even though he wasn't directly involved in the treason.

Soul-twined mates share thoughts and emotions, and he'd shut Isleen's out as well as he could after she betrayed him by sleeping with another man.

"Even if you'd figured it out, you might not have been able to stop her," I have to say. "You'd already argued with her about the parts you did know, and it didn't make any difference."

"There was more I could have done if I'd known more. But it's true we can't be sure of how the past would have unfolded regardless." He lets his stance relax against the side of the carriage and brushes a strand of my hair back from my cheek with a gentle graze of his fingers. His expression softens. "I have my pack where they belong in the present, and that's what truly matters. And I'll endeavour to ensure you *never* have need of that dagger. I certainly hope you won't put it to the same use as you did the last one."

I swallow hard. "I wouldn't want to. I don't *want* to die. I just—if it comes to that or going back to the kind of torture I faced with Aerik— I've got to have some kind of control over my own life." I lean against his shoulder, soaking up more of the heat that emanates from his body. "I don't like the thought of abandoning you all to the curse. It'd only be if I didn't see any other way—and even then I'm not totally sure I'd have the guts to go through with it."

Sylas wraps his arm right around me. "I've said it before, and I'll keep saying it: what happens with our curse isn't your responsibility. You're a *person*, not just a cure. We need to find a proper solution that actually solves the problem, not this stop-gap measure that relies on your sacrifice. You shouldn't make any of your choices based on the idea that you'd be abandoning us. You've already given so much of yourself."

A sharper pang of affection fills my chest. Wanting all the comfort I can take from his embrace, I slip my legs over his and nestle myself right against his chest.

Sylas makes an encouraging rumble and hugs me to him, his chin coming to rest against my forehead. The tickle of his hot breath over my skin rouses more heat everywhere our bodies touch. Desire unfurls low in my belly.

The fae lord's keen senses have become highly attuned to my emotional state. He shifts me against him and kisses my temple with a lingering tenderness. His voice comes out even lower than usual, with a hungry note that sends a tingle straight to my core. "I wish I had more time to be with you as a man rather than as a lord. Perhaps once we've dealt with this difficulty and with Ambrose's scheme, we'll have enough peace for me to offer you the attention the lady of Hearthshire deserves."

His open expression of longing gives me the courage to look up at him with a sly boldness I hadn't known I had in me. "What would you do if you had that time?"

The corners of his mouth curl upward. He ducks his head to trail his lips down the side of my face, nipping my earlobe and then claiming the crook of my neck with a swipe of his tongue.

My head sways to the side to give him more access, every part of me lighting up at just this brief intimacy. For a moment, the carriage around us and all thought of the confrontation ahead fade away.

But *only* for a moment. Sylas lifts his head, and I realize the mossy cliffs have given way to flatter rocky terrain. He brushes one last kiss to my cheek and eases me off of his lap.

"We'll cross the borders of Garmon's new domain soon. Best that his sentries don't discover just how much you mean to me."

Even though it was short, the interlude leaves me steadier than I felt before. I can face these fae. Why should I be intimidated by them? The only person here whose opinion I care about is the lord beside me. I have to help him win them over whatever way I can so that they won't make the problems we're already grappling with even worse.

I'm not sure what message Sylas sent ahead of us, but Garmon and his pack are clearly ready for our arrival. As we come up on a sprawl of low metal buildings, several fae emerge to meet us, their expressions solemn but unsurprised. The smooth walls shine with a coppery sheen, close enough to the color of bronze to make my pulse stutter. I can't help imagining being shut up in a box with solid sides, not even the glimpses beyond that the bars of Aerik's cage allowed me.

The carriage stops, and Garmon steps out of the largest of the buildings, only one story high but stretching across the sparse grass to the width of several of any of the smaller structures. His great-grandson flanks him. Looking at his wizened face and then his companion's, it occurs to me that nearly all of the fae here are either so young they could pass for teenagers or elderly enough that their old age shows in their skin and hair.

When Isleen and her mother made their assault on Ambrose's castle, they must have taken nearly all their family's capable pack-kin with them. And none of those made it back.

"So," Garmon says in an imperious if raspy voice, "the great Lord Sylas finally graces us with his presence."

Sylas doesn't wait for him to go on. He steps out of the carriage and immediately dips into a bow so low it startles me. Orym's eyes widen; even Garmon blinks at the sight.

"Forgive me, Lord Garmon, kin-of-my-mate," Sylas says. "I wished to spare you the pain of looking on the one who caused the loss of your grandson while hearing the news of that loss, but clearly I was mistaken in my priorities. I give you my apologies and my deepest regrets for the fate Kellan met."

Garmon hesitates, his mouth twitching with uncertainty. "And yet you bring what I understand to be the true source of that fate with you." He cuts his gaze to me.

Sylas straightens up and beckons me out of the carriage. I scramble over the side as gracefully as my warped foot and his helping hand allow, which isn't much. Standing next to him, I bob my head in a poor imitation of his bow, hoping that'll curry me a little favor.

Sylas touches my back. "Talia was the greatest victim in this situation. Despite how Kellan meant to harm her, she has come to offer her condolences as well."

"I'm sorry for your loss," I say quickly, willing my voice not to squeak. "I never wanted anything like this to happen."

"And yet it did, thanks to a dung-body," Orym mutters just loud enough for me to hear.

Several of his companions murmur amongst themselves in a tone that echoes his. My stance tenses.

Sylas casts a stern look at the young fae man. "Thanks to this human woman, we were able to fend off a horrific attack by the Unseelie just days ago. Kellan deserves respect for the service he gave and the ways he supported me in my cadre, but I could not stand by while he jeopardized all our futures in a way that could have far greater consequences than we've already faced."

He turns to Garmon. "You're old enough to have seen much, to have had to make many hard decisions. I hope you can understand how a lord may need to carry out acts he wishes were otherwise."

Garmon sighs. "Well, will you pay your respects or not? We have given him his proper place in the mausoleum."

Sylas gives him another, smaller bow. "Lead the way."

We trek across the uneven terrain to a narrower cliffside that rises from the ground like the hull of a capsized ship. A copper door is embedded in its jagged face. Garmon speaks a few syllables to open it and ushers us inside. Orym and a few of the other pack members, possibly Garmon's cadre, trail behind us.

The space inside looks more like how I'd picture a bank vault than like a cave. Metal walls gleam all around us. Ridges of the same metal jut out at random intervals, each holding a nest of cloth dappled with dried leaves and flowers in a ring around a soulstone. Those stones provide the room's only light: a pulsing, wavering glow that reflects of the surfaces all around us. The copper scent in the air gives me the impression that I've bitten my tongue to the point of bleeding.

I don't think I could have picked out Kellan's stone from memory, but Sylas walks right to one of the protrusions and inclines his head. "I'm glad to see his soul finally at rest. Be at peace, my cadre-chosen. Shine a light for your kin that outlasts any darkness."

Someone gives me a swift prod. "Haven't *you* got anything to say?"

Sylas swivels, his good eye darkening, but I raise my hand slightly to hold off any complaint he'd make. These people want to see that I regret Kellan's death too. How can I show that in a way they'll believe? *I* have to believe it too.

The fae man hated me from the moment he saw me. He threatened me, pushed me around—he would have blinded me and smashed my other foot if he'd gotten the chance. Never having to see him again is a relief.

But I still meant it when I said I hadn't wanted anyone to die.

I glance at his few remaining relatives. The hostility has faded from Garmon's face. Now he only looks tired. So much of his family was destroyed, and he's watching yet another of the younger generation laid to rest here.

I know how that feels, don't I? I've lost every part of my family, some of them right in front of me in a mess of gore and screams. This fae lord must have had to identify several of the torn-up bodies like Sylas did with his mate.

A lump rises in my throat. The image of blood streaking across darkened grass flashes through my mind.

So much death around me, all because of the power *my* blood holds. So many lives lost.

I'm almost getting to a place where I don't blame myself, but I never wanted *any* of it.

"I'm sorry," I say. My voice comes out quieter than I meant to, almost hoarse. Holding Garmon's gaze, unexpected tears well up behind my eyes. Before I can will them away, one spills down my cheek. I swipe at it, embarrassed, but watching me, his expression softens even more.

"You'd cry for the fae who would have savaged you?"

"I cry for everyone who's died to bring or keep me here," I say. "He meant something to you, and that means something to me. I'm sorry for your loss."

The words come out awkwardly, but I must have gotten something right. Garmon's face tightens, and then he nods, motioning us toward the door. "It was good of you to come and good of you to speak so."

During the lunch we're offered and the conversation afterward, I stay on the fringes of the discussion, watching and listening and preferring not to draw attention. The talk turns from somber remarks about the war to increasingly fond recollections of Kellan's better moments, and by the time we head back to the carriage, even Orym has stopped frowning, though he hasn't quite managed a smile yet.

"We still have some time yet before Hearthshire is ready for balls and banquets again," Sylas says. "But once we are, we'll host you in honor of the ways our families were once joined. You have my word on that, and every respect I can offer along with my condolences."

"I would that it had been another way," Garmon says enigmatically, but he gives me the slightest dip of his head in recognition after he bows to Sylas.

It isn't just them, I think as I take my seat in the carriage. All of our enemies are still people behind the bluster, the insults, the threats, or the outright violence. Ambrose is a person. Even Aerik is, as much of a monster as he's made himself at the same time.

It'd be easier to remember that if they were all willing to see the same in me.

7

Talia

Night has fallen over the land like a blanket of darkness by the time we return to Hearthshire. Only a couple of orbs still glow behind the castle's windows, the pack houses mostly dark too.

I stretch my limbs in the cooling air, stiff from two long journeys in close succession, and let Sylas help me out of the carriage. When we come into the castle's entrance room, Whitt is already stalking over to meet us. August appears a moment later. No one else seems to be around—the pack-kin who've been helping around the castle have gone back to their own homes, I assume.

"Our guests didn't run you too ragged?" Sylas asks Whitt.

The spymaster smirks. "We *did* give them a pretty good run. The whelp here had them pitch in on a hunt." He gives August a playful smack to the shoulder. "They've retired to their accommodations for the night. I have a couple of my people keeping an eye on the guest buildings to alert us if they decide to sneak off on some business after hours. How was your turn as guests?" His gaze slides to me with an evaluating air, as if making sure I haven't been traumatized by the experience.

"I think that matter is settled to everyone's satisfaction." Sylas glances at me too, with a reserved but warm smile that makes my heart glow like the lanterns. "Talia played a large role in that."

Whitt clucks his tongue in amusement. "Making friends wherever you go, even among those miscreants, are you, mighty one?" He strokes his fingers down the side of my face in a brief, unexpected gesture of affection. He hasn't generally initiated any public displays in front of his brothers.

"I just told them the truth," I say. "And left out the parts that I didn't think they'd want to hear." Like what a jerk I think Kellan was.

"So wise already." Whitt seems to hesitate and then dips in to give me a kiss that's even more unexpected, so fleeting you'd think he was hoping he could get it in without the other two noticing. Even that swift brush of his lips makes my heart skip a beat.

He straights up immediately, returning his attention to Sylas with a breezy tone but a pleased glint in his ocean-blue eyes. "I should give you a full accounting of today's happenings—including an interesting observation Auggie made and our invitation to a banquet at Donovan's home. Shall we take this to your study?"

As they head off, August's gaze follows them for a moment. Then he swoops in with a near-crushing hug as if not to be outdone by his older brother's demonstration.

I snuggle close to him, a smile springing to my lips. "Missed me?"

"Always," he murmurs.

"If you need to talk to Sylas—"

He shakes his head. "I already went over it thoroughly with Whitt. You're really all right after the talk with Garmon?"

"Yeah, just tired."

He presses a kiss to the corner of my jaw, waking my whole body out of its travel fatigue. I feel too wound up from the confrontation with Kellan's family and Ambrose's threat hanging over me to fully relax into the moment. I think my nerves need a little pampering, if that's available.

I look up at August. "Has the castle's sauna been fixed up yet? I could use a soak in the pool about now."

He beams down at me. "It's all ready. Let's get you a bath."

He scoops me up, ignoring my squeak of surprise, and carries me to the stairs that lead to the basement. "I *can* still walk," I inform him, giving him a mock-glower that the smile I can't restrain must totally undermine.

"But why should you have to?" He grins wider and bounds down the stairs.

Like most of the castle's rooms, the sauna here is like a larger, grander version of the one back in Oakmeet. There are not one but two pools, a smaller one like an oversized hot tub with heat radiating from the water and one closer in size to a real swimming pool beyond it. The marble tiles on the floor and the polished wood walls gleam from their recent cleaning.

A familiar mineral scent laces the humid air. As August sets me down, I inhale it deep into my lungs and let out a happy sigh.

A folding screen with solid wooden panels has been set up in one corner of the room, also just like in Oakmeet. August moves toward it just like he always did there, to give me privacy while I bathe but ensure my safety at the same time.

I pause where I've crouched to slip off my boots. At the thought that passes through my mind, my pulse thumps a little harder with a nervous hitch—but what do I have to be nervous about? I just held my ground in front of a whole pack that dismisses humans like me. August *loves* me. There's nothing to be ashamed of in wanting something like this or admitting to wanting it, is there?

My voice comes out quiet anyway. "August? I—I think I'm steady enough now that you don't need to worry about me drowning. You don't have to be on guard duty whenever I take a bath."

He catches himself with a chuckle that sounds mildly embarrassed. "Of course you are. I just—habit. I'll leave you to yourself then. If you do need me, I'll be down the hall in the entertainment room. I'll still be able to hear if you call."

He swivels to head for the door, which isn't what I intended at all. I force myself to blurt the words out, my face flushing. "No, I was actually thinking— If you wanted, you could join me?"

August stops in his tracks. Desire sparks in his golden

eyes so hot my cheeks outright burn. "Join you… in the pool?" he asks, careful but with undisguised eagerness.

That eagerness might be the only thing stopping me from melting into a puddle of embarrassment after all. My gaze darts to the floor and then back up to meet his. "Yes. I mean—it might be… fun?"

His smile then could light up an entire galaxy. He walks over to me, his eyes molten but his expression so gentle it prompts no regrets at all about my invitation. His voice goes husky. "Yes, I think it could be."

Suddenly I have no idea what to do with myself. Well, if I'm getting in the pool, whether alone or with company, there are some pretty obvious steps to take first unless I want my clothes drenched. I busy myself with undoing the laces on my boots and the buckle on my belt.

August shucks off his own shoes and then reaches for his shirt, every movement smooth and methodical, as if he's giving me plenty of time to change my mind. But each bit of him unveiled only makes *me* more eager. I can't help watching the flex of his muscular chest as he pulls off the shirt, the way the motion ripples through his brawny shoulders and arms, how his multitude of tattoos play across his skin in response.

My own skin heats beneath my dress, reminding me that I still have work to do. I push myself back to my feet, favoring the good one, and grasp the dress's hem. Without giving myself a chance to balk, I tug the flowing fabric right over my head and drop it on the floor.

The warm air wraps around my bare breasts and legs. August makes a rough sound and peels off his trousers much faster than the rest.

We've seen each other naked before, but in the heat of the moment, not quite so deliberately. A quiver of anticipation that's still a little nervous runs through me. I strip off my panties and wobble to the steps that lead into the pool without waiting to take in August's reaction.

The heated water closing over my limbs soothes the burst of anxiety. I sink in down to my shoulders and glide around, just as August removes his last bit of clothing.

Oh. The sight of him fully naked sends a tingle straight to my core. Every part of him is taut with sculpted muscle, full of coiled strength I know can offer such tenderness as well. And the impressive shaft between his legs is half-erect already.

I jerk my attention from it to his face. At this point, it's a miracle my cheeks haven't scalded right off.

August looks anything but offended by my interest. He prowls into the water with a wolfish air and circles me before catching me in his arms from behind. His lips brush the shell of my ear. "What did you have in mind next?"

I hadn't thought that far, but with his solid arms around me and the currents in the water rippling over my skin, longing throbs down below. We've done a lot together in the past several weeks, exploring each other's bodies, but we haven't actually had sex yet. It felt so good with Sylas while August caressed me too. I want to know what it could be like with this sweet, unearthly man who loves me just as I love him.

The time we came close, he stopped things because he could tell I was, as he put it, "fertile." I reach to trail my fingers along his neck. "Is there any reason to worry about — Can we do everything tonight?"

He tucks his head close to my shoulder and inhales, followed by a teasing flick of his tongue. "Anything you want, Sweetness."

I lean back into him, thrilled by the hard length that nudges my hip. "Then I want everything."

With a hungry growl, he whips me around. The instant I'm close enough, he cups my jaw and claims my mouth as if he was starving for me.

I cling to him, losing myself in the passionate melding of our mouths, the slide of our skin turned slick in the water. My breasts graze his chest, my nipples stiffening at the contact. I loop my arms around August's neck and kiss him back just as hard.

"My Sweetness," he murmurs in the brief breaths before our mouths collide again. "My love. My Talia."

I have no interest in arguing. He might not be the only man in this castle who's won my heart, but he does own it. And I want to be his in every possible way.

He adjusts me against him, one arm around my waist, the other easing higher. His hand glides through the water, stroking over my curves until it reaches one pebbled peak. At the swipe of his thumb, I gasp against his mouth. My fingers curl into the short, dampened strands of his hair.

My legs have splayed around August's waist. His erection, fully hardened now, presses against my inner thigh and then skims the spot where I'm most sensitive. A giddy jolt races through me.

I arch toward him instinctively, already aching with

need, and August groans. His next kiss sears against my lips.

"Not yet," he mumbles. "Don't want to rush this. You deserve better than that."

Part of me wants to say I deserve him inside me *right now*, but just the thought of saying that dizzies me. And then he's kissing me again, fondling my breasts, letting the head of his shaft tease over the nub between my legs, and it's all I can do to keep my head at all.

Whimpers quiver up my throat alongside the flood of pleasure. My fingernails dig into his scalp before I realize what I'm doing, but if they hurt August at all, it only provokes an even more heated growl.

He pushes us through the water until I'm braced against the tiled side of the pool, my breasts rising just above the surface. With a fiery gleam in his eyes, August lowers his head and laps his tongue over one of my nipples. He sucks it into his mouth and swirls his tongue around it, nips it and lavishes it until I'm squirming with need at the rush of bliss coursing through my chest. Then he moves to the other, worshiping it with the same intensity.

I run my fingers over his hair and across his shoulders, hoping my touch feels at least half as good to him as his does to me. I'm still half-submerged, but I'm on fire all the same, desire flaring through every nerve.

One of his hands slips between my legs, stroking over the delicate folds there. The need swells so sharp and heady I cry out.

"I want to be in you so badly," August rasps, his lips trailing up my sternum.

A shaky noise of agreement tumbles from my mouth. He kisses me there again, deeply and passionately, and shifts me against the pool wall. The stream of one of the jets spills across my thigh, and a shiver of excitement tingles through me with the memory of how he encouraged me to put those to use in the pool back in Oakmeet.

August clearly remembers that moment well too. He pauses, testing the current with his hand, and nuzzles my cheek. "You enjoyed the jets before, didn't you?"

"Not as much as I'm enjoying you."

"But what if you could have both?"

He turns me in his hands, quick but careful, so I'm facing the wall. My arms fold over the edge of the pool instinctively. He places me right in front of the jet, and the gush of propelled water hits me right where I'm aching most.

I moan, my head drooping toward the tiles. August dapples kisses up my spine to the nape of my neck. His erection settles between my legs, teasing over my opening from behind as the jet massages the nub above.

How can my body possibly contain this much pleasure? Every time I think I've found the pinnacle of it, it turns out it can soar even higher.

August loops his arm around my waist. His lips graze my shoulder blade. "Ready, Sweetness?" he asks in a tone both so tender and blazing hot.

My voice spills out in a gasp. "Yes. Please. *Now*."

His ragged chuckle reverberates from his chest. He slides into me, just the head, and another moan reverberates out of me.

August rumbles in answer, hugging me tight, his mouth clamped on my shoulder. My inner walls tingle and relax around him.

It's easier this second time, my muscles melting in anticipation of the ecstasy to come. He pushes deeper into me with one smooth thrust, the current of water stutters against my core, and that's all it takes.

I clench with a crackling of a release that quivers through me from my center to the top of my head and the tips of my toes. August growls encouragingly and begins to pump in and out of me, slowly at first but picking up speed and force.

Between his hardness filling me and the jet pulsing against my sex, the wave of my orgasm has barely rolled through me before I find myself racing toward a new peak. My breath shudders out of me. I feel as though I'm going to shatter apart in the most delicious way.

August buries his face in the crook of my neck, his own breath shaky, his mouth branding my skin. His hand closes over my breast and massages it in time with the rhythm of his thrusts. The water laps around us, licking our skin, the current below pulsing on against me.

I'm flung higher and higher, so much bliss rushing through me I can barely breathe at all, and then I come with another cry. The ecstasy of the moment sizzles through every inch of me even more brilliantly than before.

"Oh, Talia." August's chest hitches. He presses deeper, his muscles tensing, and the heat inside me expands as he reaches his own release.

August rocks into me gently for another few minutes,

clutching me to him. His kisses on my neck and back are so tender they make my heart ache.

I push away from the wall so I can turn to face him. He holds me to him, capturing my lips with the same fierce passion as when we started. After, I let my head fall against his shoulder and press a kiss to his collarbone. "I love you. So much."

His arms tighten around you. "And I love you. No one is taking you away from us—not now, not ever. I swear it."

My throat constricts. I tuck my face against him as if I can hide from the flicker of doubt. I wish moments like this were all the future held. I wish I could believe nothing in this world existed that might force him to break that promise.

8

Talia

ℋarper bobs on her feet, clutching the edge of the immense carriage Sylas summoned for this trip and peering avidly over the side. "A banquet. My first real one—at an *arch-lord's* castle."

Next to her, Astrid offers a mild smile. "Speaking from experience, that only means more politics and less merry-making. But I'd imagine there'll be plenty of merry to make as well."

I run my hands over the soft planes of the spider-weave dress Harper gave me for the occasion, apparently unwilling to let me go out in the one she gifted me before even though most of the fae where we're going have never seen the first one. The overlapping strips of mauve, indigo, and crimson with the speckling of gold embroidery come together like the most vivid of sunsets. Possibly even more magical is the fact that somehow none of the colors clash with my dark pink hair.

"There'd better be partying when we've dressed up like this," I say, shooting a grin at Harper. I know how much this moment means to her. Born into the pack's disgrace in Oakmeet, she's been longing to see more of the world her whole life—and she's hoping her skill with fashion design will get her invites to domains all across the Summer realm.

Her own dress is a breathtaking riot of color, vibrant green with painstakingly crafted flowers of scarlet, violet, sunshine-yellow, and sky-blue swirling all across the skirt and the base of the bodice. When she moves, they create a faint rustling sound that perfectly mimics a light breeze ruffling through a forest glade.

She clasps my hand for a second, her large eyes gleaming—and not just with excitement. "What if I say the wrong thing—or dance badly—" She lets out a strangled sound. "I have no idea what I'm doing. I don't want to make a fool of myself."

I squeeze her fingers with as much reassurance as I can convey. "I don't think you have anything to worry about, but even if you make a little mistake, I bet everyone will be too busy admiring that gorgeous dress to notice. That's what I'm counting on for myself."

She flashes a smile at me. "I'm glad you're going to be there too. We'll take it on together."

At the stern of the carriage, Harper's mother watches us with a smile of her own that brings a twinkle to her eyes. Both her parents, the musicians of Sylas's pack, are coming along to add to tonight's entertainments. I'm not totally sure how Sylas decided who else would join in, other than that the two other pack-kin I'm most familiar with, Brigit and her mate Charce, are regulars at Whitt's revels, so presumably they enjoy a good party too.

Brigit doesn't look all that enthusiastic right now, though. She bounded onto the carriage with plenty of energy when we first set off, but now she's sitting on the bench opposite us with an unusually pensive set to her mouth.

As I notice that, she glances my way and catches me looking at her. She hesitates. When Harper moves a little farther away to ask one of the others a question, Brigit gets to her feet to cross the carriage.

My body tenses with the worry that I've offended her somehow. I'm still getting my footing with the rest of the pack. But there's no accusation in her expression. If anything, she looks hopeful.

She studies her hands for a second before meeting my gaze again. Her voice comes out hushed. "Elliot and I thought about what you said the other day when we were gathering the shy-caps. We've been keeping an eye on our guests when we can. Today when everyone was getting ready, I thought I overheard something that sounded… odd."

I'm instantly twice as alert. "What's that? If you think there's reason to worry, you should let Sylas know."

Her attention shifts to the fae lord and his cadre at the bow of the carriage, dressed in the most formal finery I've seen on them so far. Sylas is eyeing the landscape pensively, the breeze tickling through his dark hair. Whitt appears to be telling August a wry anecdote, which at this moment includes a quick gesture I'm pretty sure is obscene. August gives his older brother a light punch, but he's chuckling at the same time.

Brigit turns back to me. "I could be wrong. I don't want to create a problem where there isn't one. What if Lord Sylas is upset that I was nosing around the guest quarters on my own initiative?"

"I don't think he would be, but if he is, you can blame it on me," I say. Apparently too casually, because her eyes widen. "Why don't you tell me what you heard, and I'll see if it sounds like something we should bring to him?" I add quickly.

She tugs nervously at her hair and lowers her voice even more. "It was just one of the daughters talking to her mother. I couldn't hear very much because I wasn't that close—I didn't want them to notice me lurking around. But she laughed and said something about, 'When Donovan looks the thief.' Why would she think it was amusing for an arch-lord to appear to be a thief? How would she know he's going to if there isn't something strange going on?"

Exactly the questions I'm wondering now too. I pat Brigit's arm tentatively in what I hope is an encouraging way. "That definitely sounds suspicious. We should tell Sylas and the others about it before we get to Donovan's castle. I can handle most of it, since it was my idea that you keep an eye on the guests—but will you come with me so you can confirm and in case they have any questions?"

I must seem confident enough to ease her nerves. Brigit nods, even offering me a small smile that lifts my spirits despite her report. She trusted me enough to listen to me before and to reach out to me now. I'm making at least a little progress at becoming a real part of the pack.

We ease around the other passengers to reach the trio at the bow. Sylas turns, his gaze immediately intent when he marks my approach. Whitt and August fall silent, August looking concerned and Whitt curious.

I swipe my hand across my mouth, abruptly less sure of myself than I was speaking about this from a distance. Maybe Sylas won't be pleased about the suggestion I made to his pack. But it's done now, and hopefully it's uncovered information we'll be glad we have.

"What's on your mind, Talia?" he asks, mildly enough that my throat unlocks.

"I was talking with some of the pack the other day about the visitors, and I suggested that—that since they were probably in Hearthshire to spy on us and try to make a case for why it wasn't a good place for me to stay, it might be good to watch them more carefully than regular guests and see if they'd give anything away about their plans."

Whitt's eyebrows arch with amusement. "Taking over my job now, mite?"

I shoot a mock glower at him and go on. "Brigit overheard them talking by the guest house this morning— they were saying something about how Donovan was going to look like a thief, and seemed happy about it. I thought you'd want to know."

Sylas nods, his mouth flattening into a grim line. He focuses on Brigit. "It's good that you came to us with this. I assume your presence wasn't noticed?"

"No, my lord," Brigit says with a respectful bob of her

head. "I was always careful that they didn't notice I was nearby, and I had an excuse ready in case those precautions weren't enough."

"Then you've served our pack well. Would you tell me exactly what you saw and heard?"

Brigit recounts the same story she told me with a little more detail this time. The three men listen thoughtfully.

When she's finished, August glances at Sylas. "You know I thought the one daughter might have been stealing from *us*. Could that be related?"

Sylas grimaces. "I suspect so. I did discover that a couple of objects are missing from the library—items that were tucked away where I wouldn't have checked on them for some time if you hadn't raised suspicions. The sorts of things you might steal if you wanted to avoid an immediate investigation. It's possible that despite our precautions, they managed to pass those on to their pack-kin so that Ambrose can frame Donovan for the theft."

"Why would they want to do that?" I ask.

He shakes his head. "I don't know. I can't see how it would factor into Ambrose's campaign to remove you from our care, and he hasn't shown any specific animosity against Donovan. We'll simply have to stay on our guard and watch how the situation plays out." He studies Brigit again. "Thank you for your concern for our pack. Perhaps my cadre-chosen here should have you on his staff." He gives Whitt a gentle nudge.

The spymaster rubs his hands together. "We could start with that tonight." He tips his head to Brigit. "You've clearly got the instincts for stealth and subterfuge. If our possessions ended up in Donovan's home, we should be able to smell them out—but the three of us can't go searching without calling attention to ourselves. Do you think you can find an excuse to slip away and attempt to track them down?"

A quiver runs through Brigit's body, but she raises her chin at the same time, clearly bolstered by his praise. "I'll do my best. What should I do if I find them?"

"Remove them from the premises if you can," Sylas says. "Return them to this carriage. If you can't, inform me as quickly as possible. I'll handle the rest."

"Yes, my lord. I'll make sure they don't get away with this." Brigit bows lower and retreats.

I linger with the three men, worry winding through my gut. "So, Ambrose might have it out for Donovan too? He'll be there tonight, won't he?"

Sylas nods. "It wouldn't do for an arch-lord to hold a banquet without inviting his colleagues and their favored pack-kin."

Whitt rests a hand on my shoulder. "You'll be safe from Ambrose for now. He gave his word not to interfere until the time limit he gave is up."

That won't help if his scheme hurts Sylas as much as it might Donovan. We don't even know what Ambrose is aiming to achieve.

Part of me wishes I wasn't coming at all—that I was holed up in my bedroom back in Hearthshire's castle with a book and a blanket and no one else around. But I wouldn't have felt all that safe even there with Ambrose's pack-kin still "visiting" and all three of my lovers hours distant. We have to show everyone else how well I'm doing with Sylas, and attending the banquet with him is part of that.

When we come up on Donovan's domain, the sun has just dipped below the horizon, sending streaks of amber light across the darkening sky. I'd know we're near the Heart of the Mists even if I wasn't aware of where the arch-lords live. Its energy tingles over my bare arms and reverberates through my chest.

How would it turn out if I tried to use a true name now, with all that power washing over me?

I can't try, not with all these witnesses. Instead, I focus on the tall building coming into view up ahead.

It looks almost like a gigantic sandcastle, the towers and spires that rise here and there a bit haphazardly, smoothed rather than sharp around the edges as if worn by water. But the walls aren't the grainy beige I'd expect from sand but rather a rich reddish brown, gleaming with the light that spills from the windows as if glazed.

"What's it made out of?" I ask quietly as the carriage glides closer.

"Fired clay," August answers. "Donovan's family has a lot of skill with fire and anything they can put it to work on."

The palace is utterly different from the cool, rigid lines of Ambrose's obsidian home—and infinitely more welcoming, at least to my mortal eyes. When we disembark amid the carriages already parked in the fields outside, rollicking music filters out to meet us. Harper swishes her skirt around her legs eagerly, looking as though she'd like to skip right to the doorway if she didn't have enough propriety to wait for her lord to lead the way.

The hall inside gleams with the same polished, ruddy clay, the glow of the orbs spaced along it turning it more red than brown. Servants usher our party through to a room so immense I almost trip over my own feet, taking it in.

Row upon row of orbs line the high ceiling, spilling brilliant light over everyone below. Several long tables have been set up beneath them, decked out with gold-trimmed, ivory-pale table cloths, gold platters, and crystal goblets. A fantastic mixture of savory and sweet scents fills the air. My mouth is watering in an instant.

Between the tables, dozens of fae men and women in fancy dress mill around, dipping into bows, offering cheerful greetings, and—more than anything—sizing each other up with a calculating air I don't need supernatural senses to pick up on. As we enter, quite a lot of them swivel to consider us. The intensity of their gazes prickles over my skin, and I fight the urge to shrink out of view behind my lovers.

I hadn't thought about how much of a spectacle we'd make just by being here. Sylas and his pack have been out of favor for decades, and this is their first appearance since the arch-lords pardoned them. Not to mention that most if not all of the other lords, ladies, and pack-kin must know what I represent to their people.

Despite the thumping of my heart, I square my shoulders and walk alongside August, doing my best impression of a woman who's attended dozens of fae banquets before. He grasps my hand, and Sylas catches my eye with a brief but meaningful nod. Knowing they're watching out for me sets my nerves a little more at ease.

Several musicians are already swaying with bows and reeds as they create the buoyant tune I heard from outside. Harper's parents hustle over to join them. Harper spins on her feet, taking in the tables and the glowing ceiling and the company, her grin stretching across her narrow face. "It's wonderful."

"Less wonderful if there's some underhanded business going on against the host," Brigit mutters under her breath. As we make our way down one of the aisles between the tables, she draws closer to me and speaks in the faintest of whispers. "I don't know what excuse to make to get away. Everyone's *watching*. They never looked at us like this before."

"We were never supposed traitors raised from disgrace before," Astrid says dryly. She doesn't appear to be disturbed by the attention, but then, I haven't seen anything disturb the hardy fae woman yet.

If there's a conspiracy underway to hurt Arch-Lord Donovan, we need to figure it out quickly. Every passing second is another when Ambrose and whoever else is involved could spring a trap.

My gaze darts over the table beside us. Servants are pouring liquid from various bottles into the goblets, some fizzing, some frothy, some letting off an iridescent steam. The platters hold only appetizers. No one has taken seats for the main meal yet, so I guess we're allowed to grab whatever we want while everyone circulates.

"I could spill some wine on myself," I murmur. I doubt the fae will think anything odd of a human being clumsy. "I don't have any magic on my dress. You could take me to a lavatory to help me wash it?" That seems like the kind of scenario one of the leading ladies would come up with in the human comedy films Sylas watches when he needs some mindless entertainment.

My hands settle on the delicate fabric of the dress, and I balk at the idea even though I've already said it out loud. I glance at Harper, who's lingered nearby and turned to listen. "I don't want to wreck it, though."

Harper's mouth twitches, and then she pats my arm quickly. "It's okay! If you need to do that to help Sylas— I've made lots of them. Maybe it'll get even more people looking at it."

Brigit makes a furtive motion toward the frothy, nearly black drink in a goblet a little farther down. "No need to even worry about it. Use the crackleberry wine. I know the true name for crackleberries—I can coax it right back out."

Somehow I'm not surprised she prioritized magic around an item that probably features in a lot of revels. Grateful that I don't have to ruin my friend's work after all, I meander along the table and scoop up the goblet Brigit indicated.

The liquid doesn't stop frothing as I raise it to my lips. Its scent trickles to my nose, tart and unnervingly heady. I don't think I should let any of this make it down my throat.

Instead of drinking, I swing around abruptly as if I've just had an urgent thought. My elbow bumps Brigit's arm; I let the goblet tip toward me. The dark liquid splashes down my front with a faint hiss.

"Oh!" I shove the goblet onto the table and clap my hand to my mouth, my cheeks flaring without any subterfuge necessary. I don't *enjoy* looking like a clumsy idiot in front of this audience, even if it works in our favor.

Brigit falls into her role as if she's played it a hundred times already. Which maybe she has when it's been needed more genuinely. She grasps my arm and ushers me back toward the entrance to the banquet hall. "It's all right, come on now. I'll fix you up."

Plenty of the other guests are staring at us again. I try to focus on Brigit and swiping at my dress as if I think I can rub the stain out. Both Harper and Astrid move to follow us, but I wave them both away, focusing on Harper. "I'm sure we can handle this ourselves. You should go let everyone chat you up about *your* dress."

The younger woman blushes and steps back, but Astrid strides along behind us all the way out into the hallway outside. "I have orders not to let you out of my sight," she informs me in an amused undertone.

Because of course it'd look odd if Sylas or his cadre-chosen were running around attending to one human girl, regardless of the power my blood holds. I'm not going to argue with her about it. "Thank you."

"Lavatory… Lavatory…" Brigit scans the hallway, and a servant points to a bend up ahead. She makes a grateful gesture to him and hustles me along. "Let's see if I can fix your dress and get us 'accidentally' lost so we need to check all kinds of rooms at the same time."

As we turn the corner, she murmurs under her breath. After a couple of iterations, the dampness against my chest fades. The black stain leaches away. Brigit smiles with obvious satisfaction and picks up her pace.

Her nostrils flare with each room we pass. My stomach knots with the thought of how little time we might have to search to find any clue, how long it might take before someone comes looking for us or stumbles on us, but we've only passed four rooms before Brigit jerks to a halt at a doorway.

The space beyond appears to be a music room. A grand piano with ornately carved legs stands in the middle of a thick rug, with a silver-gilded harp positioned closer to the wall beyond it. Clay shelves holding sheaves of sheet music and assorted smaller instruments line one wall; a broad cabinet with copper-handled drawers stands against the other, framed between two chaise lounges that I assume are for listeners to enjoy a private performance.

Brigit takes another sniff and steps tentatively into the room. Astrid follows, inhaling sharply herself.

"Yes," the older woman says. "There's something of Hearthshire in here." She drags in another breath. "And if I'm not mistaken, of Dusk-by-the-Heart as well."

Ambrose's domain? I guess that would make sense— easy to obtain his own possessions to make it look as if Donovan stole them. I venture after the two fae women, not wanting to linger alone in the hall outside.

Brigit and Astrid both narrow in on the cabinet. Tugging on one of the drawers, Brigit finds it locked, but with a quick word it slides open. She holds up a small book with a crumbling leather-bound cover. "This belongs to our lord."

"And this too," Astrid says, retrieving a gem-encrusted length of wood that I'd assume was a magic wand if I'd ever seen any of the fae use such a thing. She reaches into the drawer again and takes out a glossy, thunder-cloud-gray orb. The hues inside it whirl as if it really does contain clouds that are being stirred up by a rising storm. "And this came from Arch-Lord Ambrose's home not long ago."

Brigit looks at the object and shivers, so it mustn't be just my human instincts finding it unnerving. She pulls out a few papers and an odd feathered figurine and then shuts the drawer. "That's all of it. Now to put it where it belongs."

"Can you bring Ambrose's things to his carriage?" I ask.

She nods. "I should be able to smell it out using these." She glances at Astrid with an expression of deferral to her more experienced pack-kin. "Unless you feel you should handle this."

"No, I'm sure you can carry out this duty for our lord. I have to keep an eye on our companion here." Astrid gives me a friendly nudge. "But here, let me give you a hand in disguising them. If anyone asks where you're going when you leave, say you want to check if we have any bottles to replace the wine Talia spilled."

She intones a few syllables, weaving her fingers through the air in front of the objects Brigit has clutched to her chest. A filmy impression of a shawl wraps around the other woman's shoulders, hiding all view of them. Brigit shoots Astrid a quick smile and hurries off.

Just as we step out after her, footsteps sound in the opposite direction, far too close. We don't want to get in trouble for sneaking around.

Astrid's head snaps up. She speaks a hasty word and

flicks her fingers, and something rattles across the floor in the distance. Tugging me back toward the banquet hall, she gives me a wink. "That'll distract them a bit."

We slip into the banquet hall to find the festivities in full swing. Goblets clink in toasts, and laughter carries through the room. But it turns out we acted just in time. Before we can even make it back to where I spot Sylas in the midst of a cluster of other fae—true-blooded from the sharp points of their ears and the unusual hues in their hair—a young man bounds to the doorway we just came through.

"Donovan!" he calls out over the general murmur. "The performances so far are lovely, but I hear you've got some spectacular instruments in your music room. Will you let your guests have a look?"

A fae man who doesn't appear to be that much older than the one who summoned him emerges from the crowd, his hair springing from within his gold circlet of a crown in brilliant red and orange locks as if his head is on fire. More gold is woven into every inch of his gleaming doublet, matching the thick buckle on his belt. His smile looks much kinder than Ambrose's, but I'm not inclined to trust anyone outside my pack all that much, least of all the arch-lords who banished them in the first place.

"If you're that eager, I don't see why not," Donovan says, and sweeps his arm through the air. "Anyone who's so inclined is welcome to look upon the Harp of Olervan."

Is the first man one of Ambrose's pack-kin? Whoever he is, he must be setting up their ploy. Ambrose himself comes into view, bumping up against Sylas and saying something I can't make out. Just seeing his burly frame and haughty expression makes me tense up. I'm guessing the equally haughty woman at Ambrose's elbow is his soul-twined mate. Sylas told me Donovan hasn't found his yet and the other arch-lord, Celia, had hers pass on.

Near the fae lord, Whitt glances toward the doorway and catches sight of Astrid and me. My expression must tell him everything he needs to know. In a moment, he and Sylas are moving with the trickle of guests heading to the music room.

August comes from another direction, sliding his arm around my waist as we wander back the way I just came. I resist the urge to look toward the outer entrance. Has Brigit managed to stow the stolen objects already?

The music room is large but still crowded once the twenty or so guests who've come along pour into it. The young man who initiated the trip exclaims over the harp, Ambrose runs idle fingers over the lid of the grand piano, and the others mill about somewhat aimlessly.

A woman I think I recognize from Ambrose's entourage the other day kneels down by the cabinet, setting her face into a startled expression I'm sure is put on. She can't actually smell anything now that the objects aren't there, but she clearly knew where to look for them. I give August's arm a little squeeze to get his attention.

"What's this?" the woman says, pitching her voice to carry. "I'd swear I—"

She pulls at the drawer, which slides open easily—we forgot to re-lock it. But that doesn't matter, because there's nothing in it now. As she peers inside, her voice dies. She grasps the drawer above and tugs that open too, but what she's looking for is long gone.

Donovan approaches the cabinet, his brow furrowed. "Is something the matter?"

I notice Ambrose is studiously examining the shelves on the other side of the room as if he hasn't even realized what his underling is up to. The woman fumbles for a second and then recovers, pushing the drawer closed and standing with a casual air. "No, not at all. I thought I spotted something—I must have been mistaken." She lets out a tinkling laugh.

August twines his fingers with mine. Sylas seeks out my gaze, and I incline my head just slightly. Telling them the full story will have to wait.

But we did it. We foiled whatever accusations Ambrose hoped to make against our host. Donovan ambles back to his banquet without a hint of concern, Ambrose stalks along behind him with only a trace of frustration in his bearing, and I can't completely suppress the smile that spreads across my face.

Just this once, Sylas's pack didn't need him to protect them. We uncovered this scheme and defended everything that was at stake for him.

In the banquet hall, I spot Brigit back with Charce. I give her a thumbs up, which seems like an awkwardly human gesture as soon as I've done it, but her grin in return stops that from mattering.

"Would you show me what I can drink here without any magical effects?" I ask August, and within moments I'm sipping a beverage with a cherry-sweet flavor that's cool in both its pale blue color and its temperature.

Astrid sticks close by my side when August gets drawn away again. I linger by the corner of the room, watching the activity around me and reveling in my sense of victory. Brigit and Charce are exclaiming over morsels of some food they've taken from a platter. Harper is chattering excitedly with a couple of fae women from another pack who appear to be admiring her dress, just as she hoped. Sylas looks confident and relaxed where he's deep in conversation with a couple of other lords. Whitt—

Whitt is tapping the shoulder of a pretty fae woman who giggles in response, gazing through her eyelashes at him with unmistakeable coyness.

A jolt of possessiveness and alarm races through my chest. My hand clenches around the stem of my goblet.

If I'm right that she's flirting, he isn't encouraging her. His smile stays reserved, his expression showing no more than polite indifference. She slinks closer, and he taps her again in what I realize is a gesture meant to nudge her backward. This time, she gets the message. She twitters again, but her face falls a little. She wanders off to chat up some other gentlemen.

I'd feel relieved, but the next place my gaze lands is on August, who's currently standing between *two* fae ladies, one of whom is going as far as to prod his impressive bicep. I can read the discomfort in his stance, but either they don't know him well enough to recognize it or they're hoping he'll get over it.

A woman in an extravagant dress has sashayed over to Sylas now too. She tosses her hair to show him how conjured butterflies flutter from the coiled locks.

My sense of triumph drains away. I hadn't really thought through *every* part of what the pack's return to prominence would mean.

Sylas and his cadre are eligible bachelors now—men who not just had a distinguished history before their temporary fall from grace but who're also the heroes who provided the means to save all Seelie kind. Sylas has already had and lost his soul-twined mate, so no one needs to worry they'll be usurped that way. For any pack member who isn't already attached to a lord or cadre-chosen, the three of them offer an obvious step up in status.

My three men might not be interested in those overtures at this exact moment, but how long will it take before they come across some fae woman who *does* appeal to them—in ways I'll never be able to?

Astrid touches my arm. "Are you all right there? You look as if that drink hasn't settled well."

I pull myself together, shaking off the chill of my sudden realization as well as I can. "No, I'm okay. Just got lost in thought."

Looking at her, the answer to my fears is obvious. I've already started making a place for myself in the larger pack.

I just have to keep proving myself and showing what I can contribute, and when the day comes that I can't count on my lovers doting on me quite so devotedly, Hearthshire will still feel like home.

9

Sylas

I suspected Donovan was more the sort to keep early hours than late ones, and it appears I've gambled right. Strolling from the guest wing of his castle in the thin light just before dawn breaks, I spot him down a hallway, his steps brisk but with upbeat energy. I hope the conversation I intend to have doesn't deflate his spirits too much.

On the other hand, perhaps it should. The youngest of the arch-lords won't survive much longer if he doesn't recognize a serious threat when he encounters one.

"My lord," I call out, just loud enough for him to hear me, not wanting to disturb anyone else who's stayed overnight in his castle if I can help it.

As I stride toward Donovan, he turns my way. "Up so early, Lord Sylas? I hope my accommodations weren't displeasing."

His tone is light, but his pale brown eyes have taken

on a wary cast. Good. He knows I'm not likely to be approaching him like this if I didn't have an important subject to discuss.

"Not at all," I say with a respectful dip of my head. "I appreciate your saving my pack-kin the trip home in the middle of the night. But since I've happened upon you, could we speak in private? It's a rather urgent matter—of politics."

"Putting us to work already. I suppose I'll allow that you have some catching up to do on that score. Well, I haven't anything else to attend to at this hour." Donovan rolls his lean shoulders and motions for me to follow him. "My study should serve just fine."

He leads me up the stairs into the opposite wing of the castle and down a hall hung with portraits of past arch-lords from his line, all with the same fiery hair. The sound of our footsteps carries through the silence; no one else emerges.

He opens a door at the far end and ushers me into a room with a broad window placed perfectly so that the growing dawn light floods straight in. Its delicate warmth catches on a massive desk rather less orderly than my own with its scattering of papers and books. The built-in shelves show a similar state of disarray.

Donovan gives no sign of being embarrassed by the untidiness, so I suppose he sees it as normal. He drops into the high-backed chair behind the desk and waves me toward the few armchairs placed around the expansive space. I heft the nearest one around to fully face the desk and sink into it.

The young arch-lord may not be the neatest fae I've

ever met, but he doesn't lack keenness. He wouldn't have survived as long as he has without that. He leans his elbows onto his desk and peers at me consideringly. "What exactly did you wish to speak about?"

I've pondered the ideal way to present the subject to him for much of the night. "No doubt you noticed some oddness about the impromptu tour of your music room at the start of yesterday's festivities."

Donovan's gaze immediately sharpens. "Indeed I did. I can't say I knew what to make of it, though. Do you have insight to offer?"

"I do, as much as I hate to be the bearer of bad news. You may or may not be aware that a family of Arch-Lord Ambrose's pack-kin came to call on us in Hearthshire some days past, not long after he made a bid to transfer my human charge to his cousin Tristan's care?"

"I heard about your rather dramatic conversation with Ambrose over the girl and the deal the two of you made. Presumably he's hoping his people will turn up evidence they can use against you to build his case."

I nod. "That's been our assumption. But it's become clear that I'm not his only target. We determined that the guests stole a couple of infrequently used but distinctive and valuable objects from my home. A conversation one of my pack-kin overheard led us to suspect Ambrose's intent was to frame *you* with the theft. And indeed, we were able to discover those objects, along with a few things that appeared to belong to Ambrose, in your music room shortly before the supposed harp enthusiast led part of the gathering there."

The arch-lord has stiffened in his seat, a little of the

color fading from his normally pinkish face. "In the drawer Ambrose's cadre-chosen opened up. I wondered why she seemed confused by what she found there…"

"It was what she didn't find," I filled in. "The diversion was a set-up to reveal you as some sort of thief against both your colleague and the lords you're meant to be overseeing."

"And what became of the objects she expected to find?"

I motion toward the doorway. "My pack saw them conveyed safely to our carriage and Ambrose's. What he'll make of their return, I'm not sure, but I doubt he'll be happy about it."

Donovan pinches the bridge of his nose as if he has a headache. "Well, that is a serious accusation."

I study him, my body tensing. "I hope you believe I wouldn't have fabricated this."

"No, no, of course I wouldn't think that of you." He leans back in his chair, but his mouth stays pressed in a tight line. I ready myself to rise—chances are he'll ask me to leave and call in his cadre to consult with them—but he merely sits in silence for a span, his gaze sliding to the window.

After a few minutes, I feel I have to speak up in case he misjudges my intentions. "I understand you'd rather keep your confidences to those closest to you. I merely wanted to inform you of what I knew of the situation so you could act on it—and to let you know I'm at your disposal should you have any use of me. It does appear Ambrose's intentions toward us are somewhat intertwined."

"It does." Donovan's attention shifts back to me. He contemplates me for another long moment. "You've handled yourself honorably despite the hardships thrown at you these past several decades. Most of your pack has remained with you; you've contributed more than many along the border despite your reduced circumstances."

I'm not entirely certain where he's going with this line of thought. "I conduct myself as I believe a lord should," I say. As my father never was, not enough for me to admire *him*. "And I serve both my people and the summer realm as well as I can."

"Commendable sentiments." The arch-lord pauses again and then says, "Would you give me your word not to repeat the specifics of anything we discuss in this room beyond its walls?"

My magically-charged oath, he means. I rise a little straighter, picking up on the portent in the request. He's prepared to take *me* into his confidence—but he's shrewd enough to be cautious about it.

Just to be asked is an honor. Still, I have to consider my pack's needs as well as my ruler's.

"I'll happily give my word insofar as no information emerges that I'll need my cadre or my pack to act on for our own protection—and should such information emerge, I won't share where I obtained it."

"That seems reasonable." Donovan exhales slowly and gestures for me to go ahead.

With the thrum of the Heart's pulse so close by, I barely need to concentrate to summon magic into my oath. "I swear I will not repeat what is said in this room elsewhere, nor share information given to me, other than as necessary to protect my pack, in which case I will not reveal its source without permission granted."

Even after I've spoken, the arch-lord hesitates. Then he tips forward, returning his elbows to their original position on his desk. "I appreciate having the opportunity to speak to you with more candor. I've always held you in high esteem, and I know my mother did as well. Skies above, all of the arch-lords did before that mess with your mate."

With the formalities between us relaxed, some of the tension leaves my body. I give him a small but wry smile. "I'm glad to hear it."

"Because of that…" Donovan looks down at his desk and then back at me. "I'd value your advice. To be honest, I'm not completely sure of my cadre, especially in a matter that involves another arch-lord, and I wouldn't feel right asking some of them to keep things from the others. It's my own fault—I swore them in quickly when the arch-lordship fell on me so abruptly, and I should have taken more time to get a true measure of their dedication and loyalty."

His assessment sounds accurate to me, but there's no need to rub in what he's already realized. "I think such an oversight is understandable given the unexpected position you found yourself in." We all would have expected his mother to live centuries longer before passing on the crown to him. He was only a few decades out of his adolescence at her untimely death. "It's a credit to you that you've handled yourself as well as you have so far."

"Yes. Well." He sighs. "It's clear I can't have any word of my plans getting back to Ambrose. He's never appeared to *like* me particularly, but I hadn't thought he had so little respect he'd try to outright undermine me. Do you have any sense of what his goal might be?"

"Unfortunately, no." I run my hand across my jaw. "It could simply be that he sees you as the largest obstacle to taking control over Talia, and he wanted to have something over you for leverage to force your decision. And to sow discord between us over your apparent theft from me. But I have trouble seeing him taking the risk of attacking you over just that."

"So do I. Which makes his actions all the more concerning."

"Since the evidence couldn't be easily tied back to him anyway, there's no way to confront him," I say. "My advice at this juncture would be to stay even more on your guard, keep a close watch on anyone who enters your domain especially if they have ties to Ambrose, and take steps to evaluate your cadre now. You can see that you make one offhand remark or another in front of only one or two of them, something that might interest Ambrose but not pressing enough that it's likely a disinterested party would mention it to anyone else. If any of those remarks appear to be passed on, you'll know who's responsible."

"I can do that." Donovan shakes his head. "I just don't like testing them when I've offered my trust in them."

"You won't lie. And if that trust is well-placed, then nothing will come of it. It's less a test than simply being aware of how you speak and who you speak to."

"That's one way of looking at it. Whatever Ambrose has in mind, I suppose he's likely to make another attempt before too long. You only have a couple of weeks before the case is meant to be brought before us for judgment."

"I expect he'll either ramp up his efforts now that this attempt has failed or back off deciding it wasn't worth it." More likely the former than the latter, knowing Ambrose. I pause and allow myself to make a more openly critical remark. "It's a shame he's pursuing the matter this way when we still have the ravens to contend with."

Donovan grimaces. "Yes. At least we can be glad the Unseelie aren't making too much trouble at the moment."

"They haven't launched any further attacks on any scale?"

"Not one. I suspect they're still licking their wounds after their routing during that last full moon." The young arch-lord allows himself a tight smile. "So for the moment, Ambrose can be our main concern. Do you have any thoughts on how *you* might evaluate his intentions?"

I've already considered that question at length. "I can allow my guests from his pack to remain with us as long as they care to and attempt to discern more about his plans from their behavior. Obviously I'll be wary in any direct dealings I have with Ambrose. And if you should uncover any further plot or need my assistance in any other way, call on me however you need to. I hope I can count on your continued support when it comes to Talia in return?"

"Naturally. Heart only knows how Tristan would handle the poor creature." Donovan frowns. "There is a way we could put that conflict behind us right now, if you see fit."

Does he think he can get Celia to make a statement with him pre-emptively denying Ambrose's request? I wouldn't have expected him to extend what would likely be perceived as blatant favoritism my way. "What do you have in mind?" I ask cautiously.

"Ambrose claims he wants the woman in Tristan's care so that she's tended to by a party closer to the arch-lord's authority. You could choose to place her in *my* care, and he could hardly argue I'm not a high enough authority."

He says those words without any hint of investment, no sign that it's more than a friendly offer of aid, and yet they wrench at me. My fingers curl over the arm of my chair, claws pinching to spring free from the tips. My jaw clenches to hold back my fangs.

In that first instant, denial blares through my mind, drowning out nearly every thought, every consideration, beyond the urge to lunge at him for so much as suggesting Talia be removed from my protection.

No. She is mine. She is *hers*. I promised her as much. How could I risk it—how could I trust—

How could I walk through the castle I worked so hard to regain, the home she won for us, without feeling her absence like a sword digging into my chest?

I manage to hold myself in place and contain my fangs and claws, but my reaction was too forceful to hide completely. Donovan blinks and makes a hasty gesture. "I'd treat her well, of course. And make sure none of Ambrose's kin or Aerik's come near her. All of my pack-kin are grateful for the cure she offers."

I will my vicious defiance to simmer down. He meant nothing by it. He meant *well*. If he still speaks of her as not much more than that cure, as more of a creature to be tended to than a being with her own hopes and dreams, I can't say that's any better than I could really have expected from any of my brethren.

He doesn't know her. He hasn't spent any time around her. He hasn't seen…

He hasn't seen what a treasure she really is, in every way.

I swallow hard, unnerved by how deeply the conversation's turn has upended my emotions. My temper feels nearly as raw as when I watched Talia bleed from a knife at her own throat.

I have to think about what's best for her. What I want, which perhaps is more than I acknowledged before now, must come second to that.

"I appreciate your offer," I force myself to say. "I think for the time being she is safest on familiar territory among those she already knows and trusts. But I'll mention the possibility to her in case she would prefer the potential security of moving here. Even if not, if the situation becomes more dire, we'll revisit the idea. For now, what matters most is that both you and Celia will continue to speak for her staying in Hearthshire."

"I will certainly do that, and I've seen no reason to believe Celia will change her mind on the subject." Donovan stands. "It seems we've covered all the ground we can with what we know. Please keep me apprised—by subtle means, as much as you can—of any new discoveries you make, and I'll do the same for you. Thank you for hearing me out and for coming to me with your suspicions, Lord Sylas."

Just like that, he's become my lord rather than an equal colleague again. Well, that's how it should be.

As I stand, a pale ghost of an image flickers before my deadened eye. For an instant, I see a second version of Donovan's face partly overlaid with the first—but without its current calm. The filmy echo is twisted with apparent distress, beads of sweat gleaming on his paled skin. I take that in, and then the image had faded from my sight.

It could be some moment from his past: when he learned of his mother's death? When some other tragedy befell him? My breath halts around the hope that it's nothing more. Because it could just as easily be a glimpse of the future—a future in which Ambrose has succeeded in some vile plan.

Nothing in what I saw gives me enough specifics to warn the man in front of me. I file that image away in my mind and bow to him. "Thank you for accepting my warning and my advice."

Then I head back to the guest quarters where my pack-kin are still sleeping, wishing I knew what to do with the deeper ache still clenching my chest.

10

Talia

"Just one more left," Elliot says, squinting through the brush. "Pesky wool-for-brains."

He gives the insult an affectionate lilt, obviously fond of his animal charges even if he's frustrated that a bunch of the sheep managed to break free from their pasture.

I peer through the dappled shadows of the forest, watching for a pale tuft of fur snagged on a twig, listening for a sheepish bleat. I was chatting with Harper in the pack village when Elliot came hurrying over saying a bunch of the sheep were on the loose, and even though I know nothing about farm animals, helping the search seemed like an obvious way I could be of use to the pack. So far, I have managed to spot one of them, though I left it to Elliot to wrangle it back to the pasture.

Harper tagged along too. She cranes her neck where she's treading along next to me and swipes her hands over her dress. It's not as ornate as many of her creations, but still fancier than what most of my pack-kin wear for their daily activities, with glinting vines embroidered from shoulder to hem. She's probably worried about snagging *it* on a twig.

"Hopefully the last one won't take too long," I say. Not only for her sake. Even with the lovely boots she made for me, my warped foot is starting to throb from all the walking.

Harper shoots me a smile. "I don't think they really want to be lost in these woods. Maybe the taste of freedom will convince them to stay inside their fence from now on."

Behind us, Astrid—who I suspect joined in mainly to keep watch over me—lets out a snort. "I don't believe sheep think about much beyond what they see in front of them in that moment. If they figure they see some tasty nibbles on the other side of the fence..."

"At least they haven't gone too far." I glance at Harper. "Do you ever use wool in your dresses? I guess it's not all that practical when it's always warm here in the summer realm."

She hums to herself. "I've made a few things—shawls and cloaks for the chiller nights. It's not quite as much fun as the dresses. But maybe I should expand more. I could probably craft a good doublet with the right weave."

Her gaze slips away from me to a few of the other fae who've joined in the sheep hunt: the three daughters from our visiting family. They're picking their way through the forest gingerly, focusing more on giggling with each other than actually looking around, but I guess I can't complain about them trying to contribute. Even if I can't help suspecting it's only to bolster their claim that they came here to support Hearthshire rather than to spy on it.

It also seems a little odd that the sheep somehow broke out today even though Elliot swears he recently checked the fence for weak spots, when the daughters just happened to be taking a stroll through the village. I can't see how letting Sylas's livestock go free would further their cause, though.

Noticing Harper's glance, one of the daughters beckons her. My friend looks momentarily startled, but then she hustles over to see what they want. I'm pretty sure our guests are the reason she's been dressing up more since that banquet. She got enough compliments on her seamstress skills there that she figures she should try to impress the arch-lord pack members we have right here at home too.

They should be impressed, but I wouldn't count on it. They'd just better not gossip about Harper behind her back either. Middle-school-style cattiness is one thing I'd be glad to have left behind in the human world.

"Oh," one of the final members of our search crew says, bending low. "I think this is a hoof print. Of course, it might be from one of the others that we already caught." The woman—Shonille, I've gathered her name is—straightens up and rests a hand briefly on her belly, which is starting to show the visible swell of pregnancy.

Her mate touches her arm and points deeper into the forest. "We might as well look the way it was going."

Watching them, I remember how Sylas beamed as he congratulated her on the impending baby. I've rarely seen him show joy so openly. Having kids is a big deal to the fae… which doesn't totally fit with the stories told about them back in the world I came from.

Scanning the trees as I figure out how to ask this question, I slow my uneven steps so that Astrid draws up next to me. "Astrid, in the human world, there are lots of stories about faerie changelings—the fae stealing human kids and leaving fae babies behind. Does that ever actually happen? It doesn't seem like any fae would *want* to give up their own kids." And definitely not to swap it for what most of them would see as an inferior being.

Astrid gives a short guffaw. "No, they certainly wouldn't. But your people didn't come up with that idea out of nowhere. Proper fae know the value of family. The Murk don't have the same morals or qualms. And they have a lot more children because most of them are so mixed with humans already. I understand quite a few of their offspring come out… badly, so they might see such a trade as worthwhile."

I shiver. With every scrap I hear about the Murk, the rat-shifting fae who have no realm of their own and only lurk furtively around both the fae and human worlds, the less I want to ever meet one. Thankfully, it sounds like they're generally not bold enough to challenge any of the "proper" fae directly. If they didn't see Sylas's pack as an ideal target out on the fringes, I don't see why they'd bother us here.

Astrid studies me and adds, "If you're wondering about yourself with the nature of your blood, I can assure you that you couldn't be a changeling regardless. It doesn't take much fae heritage to leave a mark in your scent or your features, and everything about you appears human to me."

Sylas said as much before, but hearing her confirm it makes me oddly relieved. It'd be easier if we had a simple explanation like a fae ancestor to explain my powers, both my blood and my minor magical capability that Astrid doesn't even know about. But on the other hand, I'd rather not have any ties to the Murk the other fae seem to disdain even more than they do humans.

"I guess that's a good thing," I say with a little laugh, and tramp on through the underbrush, sweeping aside the creeping tendrils of a tall, softly-furred fern.

When I end up looking toward our guests again, Harper is saying something to them with a quick gesture. The other women chuckle. Then one of them glances my way, her eyes so piercing I jerk my gaze away.

The humidity of the dense forest settles more heavily on my skin. I was enjoying this hunt and acting as one of the pack when we started out, but my enthusiasm is dwindling fast.

"There it is!" Shonille cries in a victorious tone. There's a rapid rustling as her mate and Elliot converge on the final sheep. It baas defiantly when Elliot fastens a thin cord to its neck, but it trots after him at his tug toward the pasture.

"Thank you for your help!" he calls over his shoulder to us, and I recover most of my good mood.

Harper had been talking about another excursion we could go on before Elliot roped us into this quest. I wait until she meanders apart from the visiting daughters and then draw up beside her as we make our way back to the village. "Did you still want to show me the spot you found for collecting spider-silk?"

Harper opens her mouth and then closes it again without a sound. For a second, I almost think she's *upset* that I asked, which doesn't make any sense when she's the one who suggested the venture in the first place just a couple of hours ago. But then she smiles at me and makes a casual wave of her hand. "Nah, I think that's enough hiking for me today. We can do that another time. Your foot must be getting tired anyway, isn't it?"

True. I'd tuned the discomfort out, but it's getting harder to ignore the pain building in the arch and spreading up my ankle. I hope I'm not limping too badly now. What would Ambrose's pack-kin report to him about that?

Before I can contemplate that unnerving question for very long, a distant crash in the woods behind us draws me up short. As I turn, the racket of a body hurtling through the brush gets louder. Harper yelps, and Shonille lets out a shout of warning. I scramble backward with no idea of what's coming.

A beast leaps from the nearby foliage, glossy tusks jutting from its boar-like head, tail lashing against its leonine haunches. It charges straight toward me.

I throw myself to the side into a clump of ferns, but the creature veers after me. It shoves me over, one of its tusks gouging through my arm with a searing pain so deep a cry breaks from my throat.

I tumble into a tree trunk, scrambling to find my footing, my hand smacking against the wound it's far too small to cover. Blood wells up beneath my fingers.

The boar-lion beast whirls around. Its beady eyes fix on me again.

With a yell, two of our guests come running, one with a dagger raised in her hand. But before she's crossed the short distance between us, Astrid leaps into view clutching a sharp-ended branch. She plunges it like a spear into the creature's chest.

The beast slumps to the ground with a groan. Astrid hustles to my side, a breath hissing through her teeth at the sight of my wound. The searing sensation is prickling up through my arm and into my shoulder now. I squeeze my eyes shut, willing back tears.

Another crackle of broken twigs and battered leaves makes my heart lurch, but when I open my eyes, I see two much more welcome shapes racing into view: Sylas's and August's wolves. They barrel into our midst, August transforming in mid-spring to land as a man beside me. His golden eyes are wide, his teeth baring in a protective growl at the sight of me.

"I've got you," he reassures me in a softer but still taut voice, kneeling next to me.

As August murmurs the true words for muscle and skin to bind my arm back together as well as he can, the pain numbs in the wake of the magic. Sylas turns on his heel, taking in me, the beast, Astrid, and the rest of our party. When his gaze returns to my face, his mouth has twisted at an uncomfortable angle. He doesn't need to speak for me to recognize the guilt he feels—as if I'd ever expect him to follow me around making sure I'm safe every moment of every day.

This is a dangerous world, and I've accepted that. But

his expression reminds me of a few days ago when we returned from the banquet at Donovan's castle, the roughness in his voice when he told me of Donovan's offer, the fierceness of his kiss when I told him I had no interest in joining any pack that wasn't his. He tore himself away from me afterward as if concerned that even the intensity of that show of affection might have wounded me somehow.

"She'll be all right," August tells him, squeezing my shoulder. "I've stopped the bleeding." He turns back to me. "You aren't hurt anywhere else?"

I shake my head.

Sylas glowers at the beast. "Tuskcats shouldn't be roaming this close to a village. I've never seen one in this part of the forest before."

The eldest daughter of our guests steps forward with her arms crossed forebodingly over her chest, looking so indignant you'd think the beast had savaged her rather than me. "It seems some things have changed since you were last living here. I'd have thought you'd take more precautions to keep the human girl safe."

A sickly chill curdles in my gut. I'm abruptly sure that the tuskcat didn't come here by accident.

This attack is a perfect way to prove Sylas isn't taking good enough care of me, isn't it? They probably hoped they'd even get to kill the thing before any of his pack-kin could.

My suspicion is only strengthened by Astrid's gruff apology. "I'm sorry I didn't cut it off before it got to her, my lord. A vine caught around my ankle at exactly the wrong moment."

What an awful coincidence that hardly seems like a coincidence. The look Sylas gives his guests suggests he's thinking the same thing, but I guess he can't exactly accuse them outright without any evidence, not unless he wants them to spin his hostility as another strike against him.

"Back to the village," he says more tersely than usual. "My chief warrior and I will escort you the whole way in case any other monsters descend on us."

The eldest daughter gives a disdainful sniff that leaves me wanting to hurl Astrid's makeshift spear at her. I grit my teeth and let August help me onto my feet.

They've taken one shot at me. How can I stop them from getting in another?

11

Whitt

The grimace on Astrid's wizened face reveals just how frustrated she is. She doesn't suffer fools kindly, and she suffers our enemies with even less benevolence.

"It was those young women from Dusk-by-the-Heart," she says, directing most of her attention at Sylas. "I'm sure of it. They must have compelled the tuskcat to come this way and to target Talia using their magic—and I've no doubt they coaxed that vine into snagging my ankle just as the beast charged at us too. If I hadn't managed to free myself as quickly as I had, the elder daughter, Lili, would have played the hero."

Sylas sighs and leans back in his chair behind his desk. Like every other room in our Oakmeet keep, his study there had been trimmed down to fit the building's more modest size and the lesser magic we'd have to expend on maintaining it. I'd nearly forgotten just how homey his workspace here in Hearthshire was, with the office-like area at one end and the cluster of armchairs around a small personal hearth at the other.

A subdued fire is crackling in that hearth, adding a whiff of pine smoke to the air, but those chairs are for longer, more rambling discussions—ones not quite as urgent and fraught as this one. Today, August and I are poised at either side of the desk while Astrid gives her account from in front of it.

"I'm assuming they didn't leave any evidence we could use to prove that," I say. Ambrose's pack-kin may be treacherous bastards, but so far they've been discreet about their treachery, which is both irritating and to be expected from an arch-lord's spies.

She shakes her head. If there *had* been evidence, Astrid would have spotted it. Age hasn't dulled her senses any more than it's slowed her reflexes. "I'm sorry, my lord."

Sylas dismisses her apology with a flick of his hand. "It isn't your fault. Your quick action saved the situation from becoming even more disastrous. Thank you for that."

"Should we send the guests off?" August asks. "Now that they're actively attempting to hurt Talia, we can't give them another opportunity. Ambrose won't want her *dead*, but that doesn't mean he wouldn't be perfectly fine seeing her injured more than she already is."

That thought makes my fangs twinge in my gums. "I could certainly arrange an entirely polite excuse to boot them out of our domain."

But Sylas is frowning. "We haven't determined anything more of their larger plans. Observing them while they're here is our best chance of that. We'll just have to be even more on guard. I don't want Talia going anywhere at all outside her room without one of the four of us having her in view—and in easy reach in case something goes wrong. I've added a locking spell to her door that will respond to her touch and warn me if any outside party attempts to tamper with it."

I can imagine our mighty mite will be *so* pleased about us ramping up our babysitting efforts. But I'd rather her irritated with us than wounded by these miscreants.

"I'll consult with Arch-Lord Donovan shortly and confer with him," our lord adds. "If he's uncovered more on his end, perhaps catering to the visitors won't be necessary any longer."

I'd be glad of that, but at the same time, an uneasy prickle runs down my back. It's for Donovan's sake at least as much as our own that Sylas is unwilling to run off the guests who've clearly overstayed their welcome. An alliance with an arch-lord is no small thing, true, but what in the Heart's name have any of those high-ranking pricks done to earn a smidgeon of our loyalty?

We've had enough trouble on our plate for the better part of the past century—and particularly the last few months—without drawing attention on that level of Seelie society. Frankly, I'd rather our lord put all his trust in his own pack and cadre.

The twinge of rancor settles uncomfortably in my gut after all the ways my half-brother has shown he *does* trust me in the past few weeks.

I focus my attention on matters I can actually control. "I'll add to our sentries on duty and have them lay down traps should any other unpleasant beasties become inclined to wander too close to the castle."

August draws himself up straighter. "I've already done a sweep personally to make sure nothing dangerous was skulking around nearby."

Of course he did. Only the need to ensure Talia's protection could have torn him from her side after he carried her back to the castle.

A different sort of twinge forms in my chest—the urge to show I can tend just as thoroughly as he can to the needs of the woman who's my lover as well. "You were able to fully heal her injury?"

My youngest brother nods. "The tuskcat gouged deep —I'm not skilled enough to completely mend all the damage—but the wound is sealed well enough that it shouldn't cause her more than mild pain over the next few weeks as her body finishes the job."

"In that case..." I turn back to Sylas. "I'll give my orders to our pack-kin, and then I'll see if Talia might appreciate a respite from all the politicking and threats that've come with our arrival here. She's expressed an interest in seeing the more exotic scenery our domain has to offer. I can make a day trip of it, give her a chance to relax where she doesn't have to worry about what Ambrose's people might be plotting next."

Sylas stiffens just slightly, a reaction he obviously attempted to hide. He doesn't like the idea of her being too far away for him to reach with a quick dash, does he? But he's committed to giving her as much freedom as he can. He inclines his head.

August bristles a bit more overtly. "If you face any kind of attack when it's just the two of you—"

Somehow I don't think he'd worry about his own abilities to protect her. I consider him, arching an eyebrow. "I know which parts of our domain should be safe from roaming monsters—and without any malicious parties around to call them down on us, there'll be no reason for them to venture where we'll go. But if it makes you feel better, I can lay out a general repelling spell once we're there to further ensure her safety."

To his credit, the whelp simmers down quickly enough. He's getting a better handle on those hotheaded emotions of his. "All right. I do think it'd be good for her to have a break from all the stress she's been under, but I promised the pack another combat training session this afternoon. The more of us are ready to defend our own, the better."

"Then I'm just the man for the job." I shoot a slanted smile at him and Sylas.

My lord's expression has turned pensive. For a second I think he's going to withdraw his approval, but then he glances toward the window as if contemplating something far beyond this room.

"The best thing for her would be to remove her from Ambrose's interest altogether," he says. "I need to take more steps in that direction. Now that we're in a more favored position, it's possible Nuldar will agree to a consultation."

August perks up. "The sage?"

"Yes. He may be able to glean something about her nature that will show us the way to creating a cure that doesn't require her blood. If we can separate the solution to our curse from Talia, then Ambrose will no longer have any reason to fixate on her."

I restrain a snort. "If he says anything much of use. But we don't lose anything by trying." Like all sages, Nuldar isn't in the habit of giving much clarity in his proclamations. Occasionally one can tease a bit of concrete information out of his ramblings, though. If we could free Talia from her obligations to the Seelie completely, that would be worth a trek all the way across every world there is.

For now, all I can offer her is a briefer escape. I sketch a sliver of a bow in parting and head out to pass on my instructions to my underlings as quickly as I can.

When I return to the castle and make my way up to Talia's bedroom, my hand rises to the flask in my pocket out of habit. I catch myself just before I pull it out.

I can handle my drink, and Talia has never shown any sign of taking issue with my habits. But… for this, I don't think I want any buzz taking the edges off my senses, smoothing out my thoughts. I want to experience this jaunt with her exactly as it is.

Assuming she agrees to the jaunt at all.

She calls out in answer to my knock immediately and meets my entrance with a narrow look that tells me someone has already delivered the news about our stricter new precautions. "Are you here to escort me to the dangerous regions of the dining room or the front yard?"

I can't help grinning at her understated defiance. "You take to sarcasm so well, mite. You should bring it out more often. But no, I thought we might take a trip farther afield. You still haven't gotten to see much of our world, and precious little of what you have seen has been a pleasant experience. How would you like to take in my favorite spot in all of Hearthshire? I promise it'll be utterly free of malicious lords and their nosy pack-kin."

A smile bright enough to make my heart skip a beat springs to her face, and she leaps just as quickly from her chair, dropping the book she was reading on the side table. "Of course! Right now?"

"No time like the present. Sylas and August have already given their blessing." However reluctantly.

Talia limps after me into the hall, one of the simple fae-styled dresses she's taken to wearing swishing across her calves with her uneven gait. As many times as I've seen the effects of Aerik's torments on her, knowing he's stolen her steadiness from her permanently still makes me grit my teeth.

I manage to shake that animosity away and turn my thoughts to exactly how we're going to reach my favorite spot. I've never made a joint excursion out of it before, and her being human does come with a few complications.

A spark of inspiration hits me, first with a jab of trepidation, then with a growing enthusiasm. At the edge of the clearing, I turn to Talia. "The route there is through some fairly dense forest, not ideal for a carriage or horses but an awfully long walk. If you think it wouldn't stir up any unpleasant memories, I could travel as I normally would, in my wolf form—I could carry you easily enough."

Talia blinks at me. "You want me to ride you?" An

instant later, a blush floods her cheeks as the more provocative meaning of those words must occur to her.

A flare of similar heat shoots to my groin, but I manage a smile that's not especially lecherous. "Essentially, yes. If you hold onto the ruff at the sides of my neck, that should be enough to keep your balance. I can avoid making too bumpy a ride of it." I carried my brothers that way in play now and again when they were mere cubs. Talia has put more flesh on her bones since coming to us, but she's still not much more than a slip of a thing. I suspect I'll barely feel her weight at all.

She smiles back. "I'll be fine if you will. I know *you* won't hurt me."

She says it with such confidence that I want to kiss her. Too many pack-kin are still around—that can wait for where we're going.

I shake myself and let my wolf rise to the surface, stretching my spine and limbs, rippling fur over my four-legged frame in place of my clothes. I sink as low to the ground as I can get, my belly flat on the grass, and Talia tentatively touches my back. The gentleness with which she clambers onto me and curls her fingers into my thick fur brings a pang of warmth into my chest.

August had better believe I'd tear any creature to shreds before I'd let it lay one claw or tusk on this woman.

I stand carefully, giving her a chance to adjust her position so she's completely secure. Then I set off through the trees. At first, I stick to a restrained trot, waiting until I'm sure she's comfortable. When she's stayed in place without slipping or complaint for several minutes, I speed up by increments until we're weaving through the woods at a swift lope.

Talia's fingers dig deeper into my fur, and she leans lower on my back so her head can rest against the back of mine when she wishes to, although she keeps it raised for most of the journey. The thump of her heart echoes through her chest into my muscles, soft but even. I find myself matching the rhythm of my strides to it.

My only regret is that I can't see her expression as she takes in the changes in landscape, the innocuous but unusual flora and fauna we pass, and the experience of riding a wolf in general. But that's all right. I'll get the best view when we reach our destination.

At my faster pace, it takes little more than an hour to arrive at the spot. I slow when my ears catch the faint hiss and the patter of falling drops. Just before the trees thin, I stop and sink down again so Talia can dismount.

She slides off, bracing her hand against my haunch when she wobbles. As soon as she's straightened up, I shift into my typical form. With a few quick words of casting and a sweep of my senses around us, I lay down the deflective spell I promised August. There's no sign of creeping dangers at the moment.

Turning to Talia, I offer her my hand and a smirk. "Are you fully prepared?"

Her laugh carries through the forest. "I hope so."

I lead her forward to where the trees fall away. As she gets a clear view of what awaits us, her breath catches. And she hasn't even seen the best of it yet.

This haven in the midst of the forest is pretty striking even at first glance. Stones glinting with patches of amber form a rambling path through clusters of scarlet blossoms and then up a steep hillock that rises to three times my height. An underground spring burbles beneath the rocks, its pearlescent water catching the sunlight in small gaps here and there. A warm, honeyed scent fills the air, so heady you could believe you'd get high just breathing it in.

"Wow," Talia says. "It's—"

The rocks shift, one near the base of the hill lifting up a foot into the air and hovering there, another farther up sinking down to leave a deeper dip. A jet of water spurts from a gap between them, speckling the air with a glittering mist. Talia claps her hand over her mouth.

Several seconds later, the floating stone eases back down. Another juts higher while remaining attached to the earth. A shimmering trickle of water gushes from near the top of the hill to strike the stones with its pearly sheen all the way down.

Talia takes a cautious step closer. "Is it… alive?"

I suppose that's a reasonable question given the oddities she's seen of Faerieland so far. "No. Just animated by its own innate magic. Not enough that anyone else pays this glen much mind, but it's where I most like to come when I can step away from my work for a while."

She rests her hand on a stone. When it pushes up against her palm, a giggle spills out of her. More mist gusts into the air near her feet. "So it just keeps changing here and there however it feels like."

"Essentially. That's what I like about it. It's beautiful when you see it frozen in one place, but even more so when the unpredictability comes into play. You never know quite what you'll be looking at next, what angles it'll reveal."

Talia glances over her shoulder at me, a mischievous glint in her eyes. "Like you. No wonder you appreciate it."

I have to guffaw at that remark. "Come have a seat and relax, then, so you can enjoy both me and the scenery."

"Hmm." She peers up the precarious slope. "I think I'd like to check out the view from every available angle. I'll meet you at the top."

The image of her skidding off those stones and tumbling down flashes through my mind, and my heart stutters with a flicker of panic. I reach for her shoulder automatically. "I'm not sure—unpredictability doesn't make for the easiest climb."

"You'll just have to stick close in case I need you, then, won't you?" she says teasingly, and marches right up to the slope without another word.

I find myself remembering her comments about the dreams she had in her old life, all the travels she wished to embark on through the human world. She has an adventurer's spirit, this delicate but resilient human of ours. I bite my tongue against calling her back and letting my fears crush her joyful energy, but I stalk after her so I can be sure I *will* be there if she should slip.

Despite her wounded foot, Talia clambers up the stones along one side of the hillock with a natural agility. Perhaps I put too little stock in the physical training August has been putting her through—and her natural gumption.

I keep pace without any trouble, but I hardly have to wait around for her to navigate. She keeps her gaze trained on the rocks ahead, her muscles tensed so she can brace herself if one she's touching shifts, always balancing her weight across a few so that she has something steady to lean on regardless.

The breeze ruffles through her vibrant hair. A fresh spray tickles over us, making the pink hue glisten like a dewy rose. I watch the flexing of the lean muscles in her bare arms and calves, the deftness with which she places her hands and feet. Every time I catch a glimpse of her lovely face, it's etched with eager determination. I've given her something she's been craving, even if it wasn't quite what I intended.

I could watch her haul herself up hillsides all day.

With a triumphant sound, she grasps a stone at the top and pulls herself onto the mossy plateau. Just as she heaves her knees up over a bulging rock, that rock slides to the side with a jerk. Her cheer becomes a yelp.

I lunge forward on a surge of terrified adrenaline, but my outstretched arms aren't needed. After a brief teetering, Talia yanks herself the rest of the way up. It's a bit of a scramble, but she manages it alone.

I clamber right after her, collecting her in my arms all the same. We drop down together by the edge of the plateau, her tucked against my chest, the mossy span that stretches a good twenty feet wide and long cushioning our limbs.

Talia snorts and peers up at me. "Were you worried?"

I will my momentary distress not to show on my face or in my voice. "Perhaps a tad. You looked about ready to test my tumble-prevention skills."

She trails her fingers over my cheek with a gentle smile

that holds so much affection my pulse stutters for a totally different reason. "I know I'm safe as long as you're here with me."

She tugs me closer, angling her mouth to meet mine, and there's no power in this world or hers that could stop me from claiming that kiss. Who needs absinthe when I can get drunk on this woman?

It's over far too quickly for my tastes, but Talia stays tucked next to me as she sits up. She gazes out over the glen from our new higher vantage point, her expression nothing but pleased. I remain sprawled on my side, watching her. I've enjoyed the other view plenty of times before.

She exhales in a long, slow stream and leans back on her hands. The breeze licks over us again. The sun glows off her pale face, and it occurs to me that this may be the first time I've seen her as she was really meant to be. Well, not the magically dyed hair or the fae clothes, but free and lively, making her explorations of the world, without any villains hunting her—at least not too close by for the moment.

I take it in, letting the image burn into my memory so I can hold onto it. This one thing is only mine. Sylas and August have never seen the adventurer. I've given her a gift they didn't think to.

"It's even better from up here," Talia announces, and glances down at me. "Thank you. For bringing me here. For letting me see it all. You'd normally come here alone, wouldn't you, if it's your place for getting away from responsibilities?"

A hint of concern crosses her face, tiny but perceptible

enough to make my chest clench. I clasp her hand. "Don't feel you're intruding. I don't… I don't see you as a responsibility." The truth of that statement resonates through me. My next words catch in my throat before I propel them out. "You seemed to think before that it was a misfortune that I had no one I could 'just be' around, without keeping my wits ever alert. Fitting that you've made yourself that person, isn't it?"

If I thought she glowed before, it's nothing like the way she lights up now, gazing back at me. As if she truly is overjoyed that I've found some measure of peace in her presence—and that generosity of hers is exactly why I have. Somehow she sees me in a way none of my fae companions ever have, in a way I'm not certain even I could have identified before I had it.

I didn't know I'd ever meet a person who'd want to know who I am simply for the sake of knowing and understanding me, without searching for angles or pressure points to advance some personal agenda. But Talia isn't looking to gain anything from me other than whatever happiness she takes from the time we spend together. From knowing she's earned my trust.

But then, how can that be surprising when the main thing she's wanted for herself is the freedom to simply exist as *she* is?

There are parts of me I haven't shared and that possibly I never will, but when she bends down to press her lips to mine again, those seem so unimportant they may as well have never happened. I kiss her back, finding the perfect tilt of my mouth to provoke a murmur of desire.

There's something to be said for certain types of angles and pressure points.

Tangled up in her like this, it's hard to imagine how I could ever go without this unexpectedly wondrous being, so I simply don't try to imagine it. We won't lose her. Simple as that. Between my lord, my cadre-fellow, and I, by the Heart, we'd better be able to achieve that much.

This kiss doesn't end with one. Talia settles closer against me, trailing her slim fingers into my hair as she takes her fill of me and I of her. This is a far better setting for such a tryst than the dining hall back in Oakmeet, as fondly as I remember her quivers and gasps as I showed her just how much pleasure my mouth could conjure in her body. With the sun beaming above her and the breeze catching in her hair, she looks more than human, more than fae—like some kind of goddess.

I tease my knuckles down her chest to the swell of her breast. When they skim her nipple, I earn one of those gasps.

She kisses me harder, her tongue daring to flick between my lips. I coax her mouth wider to meet it. Our tongues tangle together, the sweet tang of her saturating all my senses—and she nudges me all the way onto my back, swinging her leg over to straddle me.

Apparently my mighty one has decided to try out other ways of riding me.

My cock was plenty interested before; now it leaps straight to attention, straining against my pants. As Talia kisses me even more fervently, I keep one hand tracing over the pebble of her nipple through her dress and use the other to ease up the skirt and adjust her against me.

There. With a slight shift of my hips, my erection presses against her core. The jolt of pleasure that contact sparks must flare in her as well, because her whimper matches my groan.

Her hands run down my chest. At their tug of my shirt, I know what she's after. Our mouths break apart just long enough for me to peel the thing off me. Then we collide in another kiss.

For a long spell, heady and torturous in the most enjoyable way, we stay like that, exploring each other's mouths, her touch roaming over my chest as mine incites every bit of bliss I can in hers, our hips rocking together at an unhurried tempo that starts to feel more urgent with the growing shakiness of her breath.

She tears her lips from mine, her head dipping so they graze my cheek instead. Then she lifts up so she can meet my eyes. So much hunger has darkened hers that I could practically come just looking at her. Her voice spills out, sweet as ever but with a husky note that shoots right to my groin.

"I want—I want to be as close to you as I can get. Completely connected."

Every particle in my body reverberates with a resounding *Yes*. I denied myself the bliss of being inside her last time, but if that's what she wants, what good would it do either of us to say no? Her scent holds a tang that tells me her monthly bleed is only a day or two off—there's no risk of compromising her freedom with unintended consequences.

And while we may never connect as closely as the

highest of fae do, having seen one soul-twined mating crash and burn from a front-row seat, I can't regret that.

Perhaps Talia does, though. A shadow that looks like sorrow flickers through her expression, there and then gone, but enough to make me hesitate.

But then, it could be my hesitation is what's caused her concern. I *did* deny her last time. Is she worried that I don't want her that badly?

I push myself up on one elbow and draw her face close to mine, our noses brushing. "I can't imagine anything better than being inside you right now, Talia. This is your ride. You've got the reins. I'll take you wherever you want to go and revel in every second of it."

She sucks in a breath and kisses me hard, and then reaches to fumble with my trousers. With rather a lot of groping and some minor acrobatics, we divest me of enough clothing for my cock to spring free and remove her undergarment as well.

I skim my thumb over her clit and down across the slickness of her opening. Her eyes roll back at my touch, a shudder rippling through her body that's nothing but longing.

Bowing over me, she lowers herself onto me with a minimum of guidance. Her channel is so drenched with arousal that I slide up into her with only the slightest, most delicious of friction.

Her thighs clench against my hips, her inner muscles clamping around me and then relaxing, and a shudder of my own runs through me. My balls are already aching for release. But oh, this is good, letting her find her way, decide her own pace. My precious adventurer.

When she's taken me as deep as I'll go, she leans in to kiss me on the lips. I massage her thigh, her ass, staying still until she begins to rock against me again. Then I match the bob of her hips with gentle thrusts, holding back the urge to let loose my wildness and claim her with the full force of my desire. The slick heat of her is a high I never want to come down from.

I want to take her just as high. Few ladies find my general temperament all that pleasing, but this is one act where I've always been able to deliver. I can read the sounds that escape her throat, the twitches of her muscles, the flutter of her eyelids, to know which touch, which angle, which motion is most welcome.

Let her have everything she asked for and more.

Talia grinds into me, starting to pant, clutching my arm. "Whitt," she gasps, like a plea, one I'd love nothing more than to answer.

"What do you need?" I murmur, my own breath beginning to break.

"I just—I'm so close—please—"

I push myself a little higher so I can kiss the crook of her jaw. "Would you like to see stars or fireworks, my mighty one?"

A rough giggle tumbles out of her. "Everything. All of it."

"Mmm. So ambitious. Whatever the lady wishes…"

I pick up the pace of my thrusts, gripping her hip so I'm meeting her in the way that brought out the deepest shivers before and then slipping my fingers around to stroke her clit. With a moan, Talia presses into my touch.

Her fingernails dig into my skin, but I welcome the tiny pricks of pain amid the rising swell of pleasure.

I like her fierce; I like her demanding. Heart knows she's owed a few demands after everything she's been through in this world.

She somehow pulls me even deeper inside her, our bodies bucking together in this exquisite harmony. I feel her come apart in the tightening of her channel around my cock. Her head falls back with a blissful cry, and there's no fighting it—my release explodes through me with a flare of the sharpest ecstasy I can ever remember feeling.

I can only hope I've brought her every bit as much in return.

Talia sags over me, boneless in her release. I raise my arms automatically to reach for her, to ease her down on the moss beside me and gather her against me.

She nestles her head against my shoulder with a dreamy smile, and I know I've come through for her in at least this one way she asked for.

12

Talia

When lunchtime creeps up on us as we lounge in Whitt's glen, I don't even have to say anything. Well, I guess my stomach does the talking for me. At its grumble, the corner of Whitt's mouth quirks up.

He speaks a couple of words I can tell from his tone are true names and extends his hand. A few seconds later, a broad waxy leaf laden with berries and a large nut in a wrinkled shell fly through the air from the depths of the forest to him.

He cracks the nut shell open on the rocky edge of our perch and hands it and the berries to me with a grin. "Can't have you starving now, or Sylas will take my head."

His ease with magic still awes me. I can reshape a bit of bronze when I need to, and I'm getting a little stronger at conjuring light, but it still takes plenty of concentration and effort. But then, as a human I'm not supposed to have any magical ability at all.

Rather than dwell on that uneasy thought, I bite into the nut, trusting that Whitt won't have offered me anything inebriating. He knows how I feel about faerie drugs.

The nut's flesh is chewier than I'd have expected, with an earthy toffee-like flavor. I alternate between it and the tart berries, and my belly is full before I'm even finished that offering.

"I know it's not quite up to the standards you're used to from August's kitchen," Whitt says breezily.

I wave his remark off, watching him with a rush of renewed affection for the man who's indulged so many of my whims today, most of them spontaneously. If only life in the faerie world were always this enchanting, no awful schemes of horrible villains intruding.

He's pulled his trousers back up, but he hasn't bothered to retrieve his shirt. I lick the berry juice from my fingers and allow myself the additional indulgence of trailing my fingers over his sculpted, tattooed torso.

Whitt's muscles flex beneath the sculpted planes. I trace the lines of a few of the true-name marks idly, and he simply lets me, totally at ease in his half-nakedness.

I find myself remembering things Sylas has told me about his spymaster—about the distance he's kept from just about everyone in his life, which Whitt has basically confirmed. A question itches at me. Maybe because of the tenderness with which he embraced our first full sexual encounter, I'm feeling secure enough to risk bringing up the subject.

"Sylas told me… you've never taken a mate. I mean, a regular one—I know you wouldn't have a soul-twined one. I guess August never had much of a chance before the pack was banished to the fringes, but you would have."

He raises an eyebrow at me. "Do you object to my unattached status?"

He should know very well that I don't. I wouldn't have this closeness with him—in every possible way—if he was committed to another woman.

I give him a playful shove. "I just wondered why. It seems like most of the fae in the pack are paired off. Or is it unusual for cadre-chosen to settle down because of the whole commitment-to-the-lord thing?" That non-romantic commitment is one of the reasons sharing a lover isn't uncommon among cadres.

Whitt catches my hand before I can retract it from the shove and runs his thumb lightly over my knuckles, considering our entwined fingers. "I wouldn't say it's unusual. Plenty of cadre-chosen do take on a mate, just one who's tolerant of their divided attention. But I never met any woman I wanted that enduring an association with."

I think of the fae women who fluttered around him and his colleagues at Donovan's banquet. "You must have had lots who'd have volunteered for the spot, back before the banishment when Sylas was considered one of the more prominent lords. So, basically, you're just picky?"

He snorts. "I'd put it more as, I have enough self-respect to be sparing in who I devote my attention to."

"They were all that bad?" I tease.

I'd thought we were bantering, but his expression goes

oddly serious. His fingers still against mine, and then he tugs my hand to his lips to press a kiss to its back.

He gazes off over the landscape ahead of us. "There's a reason I stay on my guard around all of my kind, mite. My fae brethren rarely do anything without at least a little calculation in the mix. When it came to ladies aiming to tempt me as a suitor, I always had to consider whether they were more interested in me or my proximity to a prominent lord."

Oh. My gut twists at the thought. "And a lot of them only cared about the status?"

Do I even need to ask that? I've seen how the other summer fae treated my pack while they lived on the fringes. No one from any other domain cared enough about Whitt to seek out his company there.

He shrugs. "Ah, I'm sure at least a few of them liked me somewhat. But I have no interest in being a stepping stone to social eminence on any scale. By the time I was old enough to be considered eligible, Sylas had been born, and it was known I'd be serving him when he was of age. There was never a time when it wouldn't have been a consideration."

He speaks casually enough, but his grasp tightens a little where he's still holding my hand. The tension in my gut turns into a pang that echoes up through my chest.

I never thought before about what it'd have been like for him. His entire adult life, he's had his role decided for him. His wants and hopes were superseded from the moment of Sylas's birth.

"Did you have any choice?" I ask. "If you didn't like

the idea of dedicating yourself to service in Sylas's cadre, could you have said no?"

"Of course. No lord wants an unwilling cadre. But it was that or spend my entire life idle. There wasn't any *other* lord I'd have cared to pledge myself to."

He pauses, running his other fingers over his ear with its pointed tip—not as sharp as Sylas's but obvious all the same. "I was just shy of being true-blooded myself, you know. There's a spell to test it that's conducted at birth. A few percentage more in the right direction, and I'd have a domain of my own."

I squeeze his hand. "That seems so unfair."

"It is what it is," he says, but the darkening of his eyes suggests he's not so unaffected. He shakes himself and offers me a wry smile, the first time he's really looked at me since this conversation started. "It's ridiculous, really. I have no interest at all in ruling over a pack. I'd have to behave myself and shoulder ten times as many responsibilities, and I'd find the job an excruciating bore. I doubt I'd be any good at it either. So it shouldn't bother me in the slightest that no one would ever have considered offering me the position."

The pang rises to my throat. My voice comes out quiet. "But it does."

His smile falters. His gaze slips away from me again, toward the distant trees. His silence is enough of an answer. After a moment, he grimaces. "It's just a faint niggling every now and then. I ignore it easily enough. I'd rather you never mention it to him."

Sylas, he means. I scoot closer to him, wanting to offer him whatever I can of myself, even if it wouldn't come close to making up for how much he's been denied over a tiny difference in his blood.

"Do you think he doesn't already know?" I ask. The fae lord has struck me as awfully perceptive.

Whitt lets out a dry chuckle that holds little humor. "It's become apparent to me that there are a few things that've managed to escape even our glorious leader's notice."

I grope for the right words. My thoughts trip back over the past couple of months, over the way Whitt has held me at a distance even though I know now it wasn't for lack of interest, of the way he balked when I first made it clear *I* was attracted to him. I grip his hand with enough strength that he glances at me.

"You know, it wasn't on purpose that I got close to Sylas and August first," I say. "That was just how it happened. It doesn't mean I love or want you any less than I do them. Because I don't. Less. Er…"

Whitt is staring at me with such a startled expression that I lose track of my words completely. His lips part, but it takes a second before any sound passes from them. "*What?*" he says.

My cheeks heat. Did I phrase my attempt at reassuring him badly and now I've made him feel worse? "I was just saying—even though out of the three of you I came to you last, I—"

Wait. I halt, realizing which part he probably wasn't expecting. What I haven't actually said to him before, even though the emotion has been as obvious to me as one of the castle orbs, glowing inside me whenever I'm near him. "I love you. Just as much."

Maybe even more. When he looks at me like that, like I've chiseled open a crack right through the center of his being, something inside me rises up with more determination and devotion than I know what to do with. Something that longs to flood out and fill every place hollowed with loss or loneliness behind his cocky exterior.

The sense of how much I'd give to seal the wounds he tries to hide knocks the breath out of me. It *scares* me. But only a little, because I know he'd never ask me to try.

"Talia," he says with a rasp in his voice, and I lie back down, tucking my head against his shoulder.

"I don't expect you to say it back. That's just how I feel. You don't have to do anything about it. I love you, and I'm glad that I do." For as long as I get to love him before the expectations of this world intervene.

He makes a rough sound and tips my face up so he can kiss me. The sear of his mouth makes me tingle right down to my toes.

As his lips move against mine, his hands travel over my body, kindling more heat. I'm abruptly also glad that I hadn't bothered to put my panties back on yet, because I'm not sure I want to wait even those few extra seconds before I get to feel him filling me again.

But none of it compares to the deepest, giddying burn around my heart. *I love you*, I think into every kiss, every caress. *I love you. I love you.* As if, if I can pour enough of that emotion into him now, I might extend the time before I'll have to give it up and say good-bye.

13

Talia

I shift restlessly in my carriage seat, peering over the side toward the other vehicles tagging along behind us across a plain dappled with cottony flowers. "I wish we didn't have to bring this much of an audience."

Sylas follows my gaze with an apologetic slanting of his mouth. "I would have prevented it if I could have. But it may be to our benefit in the long run. Ambrose won't be able to deny or misconstrue anything that happens when all three of the arch-lords are here to witness it."

The arch-lord who wants to claim me for his own purposes insisted that the rulers of the summer realm come along for this audience with the great sage. From the way Sylas told it, Ambrose made it sound as if he didn't trust us to give an accurate account of what happens. I hope the other arch-lords noticed how petty that sounds when Sylas has been nothing but candid with them.

"Do you really think this fae will be able to figure out why I am… the way I am?" I ask.

Whitt leans back on the bench where he's sitting across from me. "They say Nuldar knows all things. He's been around long enough to, if he really is the oldest fae still living, which I have no reason to doubt. He may even be fully true-blooded, which adds to his magical prowess. The trouble is getting him to say anything in a way you can decipher into something useful. There's a reason he wasn't our first stop in untangling this riddle. The arch-lords have consulted with him before about the curse and gotten nowhere."

He's stretched out his legs, his crossed ankles resting next to mine—closer than he'd get if many of our pack-kin were around to observe, not quite as close as he might if Astrid weren't joining the four of us on this excursion. Sylas may think having the arch-lords around could be a good thing, but he's clearly prepared for something to go wrong if he thought we needed another warrior along.

The fae woman, the oldest by far in my present company, inclines her head with a wry smile. "I've heard it said that Nuldar is as likely to muddle matters more as to shed light on them."

"But we haven't figured out anything at all about why your blood has this effect on our curse," August points out, dropping onto the bench beside me. "*Any* information should be better than none, even if we have to puzzle over what he means."

"My thoughts exactly." Sylas turns toward the bow to gaze out over the landscape ahead. "And the moment we have a source for the cure that doesn't rely on you,

Ambrose will have no grounds at all to demand Tristan take custody of you."

A shiver of hope tickles through my chest. Wouldn't that be lovely? To just *be* with these three men and their pack, however that plays out across the years ahead—to no longer exist as a bargaining chip or a tool but simply a human woman making a life for myself among the fae.

If only it could happen that easily.

The fae lord points to what looks like a silvery haze up ahead. "We're almost there."

I limp up to the bow and lean my hands against the polished wood with its tangy juniper scent. The wind teases through my hair.

As we glide closer, the mist sharpens into the more solid shapes of trees, all of them tall and elegant with gracefully drooping branches like weeping willows in the human world. Except the leaves on our willows never sparkled like this. There's a whole forest of them, stretching out maybe half a mile in front of us before darker treetops take over on either side.

"They're beautiful," I say, staring. After everything I've seen in the faerie world already, it can still amaze me.

"Starfall willows," Whitt says from behind me. "So named for the twinkling leaves and also the fact that they heat up like they've got little suns inside them by night. Much safer to visit now during daylight hours when we won't get burned."

That's something else I've learned more than once about the faerie world. There are as many deadly things here as beautiful things, and quite a few are both.

Our carriage eases to a halt at the edge of the

forest. A whispering sound drifts out to meet us. Sylas springs out first and offers his hand to help me leap the side. "Stick close to us. The trees won't hurt you during the day, but they can be somewhat... unnerving."

Wonderful. I resist the urge to shrink inside my skin and force myself to limp alongside him with my head high, ignoring the arch-lords and the few kin they've had join them disembarking around us. August stays at my other side, Whitt venturing just a couple of steps ahead, Astrid bringing up the rear.

I see what Sylas means as soon as we enter the forest. The drooping branches with their long, thin leaves had been swaying slightly with what I took to be the movements of a breeze. The moment we walk between them, it's as if they come to life.

One branch lifts to trail its tendril-like leaves over August's shoulder. Another taps the top of Sylas's head. The ones ahead of Whitt twist and rise as if peering at him. I hear a rustle behind me and a muttered objection from Astrid. "Nosy things."

"Patience," Sylas says evenly. He glances down at me. "As Nuldar has aged, he's become more and more immersed in his magical affinities. He has strong ties to trees and other plant life, as I do, although on an even deeper scale. Though he's a lord, he lives alone here now... and he's merged somewhat with the forest. The trees act through his will."

"He's making them all move like that?" I peer around us, restraining a shudder as a branch winds snake-like past August to lick its leaves down my arm.

Whitt chuckles. "We should consider ourselves lucky he doesn't insist on an even more thorough inspection."

I expect us to reach a castle or at least a house not so different from the ones Sylas has created, grown out of trees, with this Nuldar living inside it. When Whitt stops in his tracks and dips into a low bow, I realize that the "merging" is much more thorough than that.

What stands before us isn't a building but another tree —but not *just* another tree. Its sloping branches splay to either side to give a clear view within. Protruding from the trunk is the form of a man: bone-thin and wizened to the point that it's hard to tell where his wrinkled skin stops and the crinkles of tree bark begin.

One of his hands, the impressions of the fingertips just barely visible, lifts toward the upper branches. The other stretches toward the roots. The bit of cloth around the figure's hips and the crinkled hair sprouting from his head and chin are a light gray the same shade as the bark.

The man's skin holds only a trace more color than that, a faint peachy hue mostly absorbed into the trunk's pale silver. Then his eyes blink and open fully, and I'm struck by the vivid midnight-blue of the irises, so stark amid the rest of him and the tree he's become at one with.

All the fae around me—my lovers and Astrid and the arch-lord delegates who've caught up—bow just as low as Whitt did, including the arch-lords themselves. Apparently even Ambrose can recognize this sage as a higher power than his own.

I bend at the waist as low as I can while keeping my balance, not wanting to offend the being we're hoping to get answers from. When I straighten back up, it takes my best efforts not to outright stare.

"Great Nuldar," Sylas says, his deep voice resonating through the woods, "we come before you to seek your wisdom. Are you still willing to speak with us today?"

The sage's answer rasps like leaves rubbing together, his beard twitching just a smidge with the movement of his lips. "Ask what you will and I will tell what I see, Lord Sylas."

Sylas puts his arm around my shoulders and guides me forward so that I'm fully in Nuldar's view. I stand there awkwardly, not sure what to do with my hands or if I should even smile.

"There is a quality in this human woman's blood that dispels the curse we Seelie have suffered under the full moon," the fae lord says. "We wish to understand how that quality came to be and anything you can inform us of its nature."

The sage's gaze fixes on me. I find I can't tear my eyes away from his. Neither of us moves, but I feel as if I'm falling toward those dark eyes, farther and farther, into a void with no end.

My thoughts slip away; my sense of the world around me fades. All I know is the deep dark blue and a quivering sensation racing through my head and down through my chest.

When Nuldar looks away, I sway, catching my breath with a gasp. Sylas's hold on me tightens. Without him, I think I might have stumbled. My whole body is quivering on the inside now, my thoughts spinning.

But the sage is starting to speak. I focus on his words

as well as I can.

"She started in darkness," Nuldar intones in a tone that's as distant as the space I tumbled into within his eyes. "Then she came out into the light. The mother of her mother of her mother met one of the Mists who planted the seed. The seed came into bloom alongside our curse, entwined from that point forward, growing more so with the passing of generations. That is what I see." His eyes close again.

"Great Nuldar," Sylas starts, but the sage gives no response, no sign that he's even heard. I guess his abrupt withdrawal isn't that unusual, because Sylas doesn't push for more. He turns, his expression pensive, and motions for the small crowd gathered around us to go back the way we came.

I hurry along with him and August, relieved that we're not going to stick around among these creepy trees while hashing out Nuldar's proclamation. As Whitt suggested, the sage wasn't exactly clear in his statements, but I can see the obvious metaphors. The first bit especially—don't all people start in darkness and then come into the light? That's a fancy way of saying I was born. I'm not sure how helpful the rest will be if that's what he started with.

The trees prod and tug at us with their branches, but they don't stop us from leaving the forest. We all come to a stop on the flowery plain where we left the carriages.

"Well?" Ambrose demands before any of us can do more than take a breath. "You've spoken with the girl the most. What do *you* make of that?"

He has two regal-looking fae with him who I believe are from his cadre, as well as a woman in plainer though still fine clothes who's hanging back—can he not go anywhere without a servant along?

But then, it looks like Donovan has brought a couple of servants himself. They trail behind the arch-lord as he steps closer to hear Sylas's answer. Celia, who appears to have brought only a single cadre member as her companion, eyes them with a disdainful curl of her lip I don't totally understand.

Sylas folds his arms over his chest. "I'd say for Nuldar, that was an impressively straightforward answer, given what we all already know about Talia and our curse. The mother of her mother of her mother would be her great-grandmother. Planting the seed presumably refers to a pregnancy. Her great-grandmother's mate was a man with at least a little fae blood—one of the Mists."

Whitt nods. "It must have been only a very small heritage, increasingly diluted before it reached Talia, because she shows no physical signs of that ancestry. It sounds as though there was an intersection in the timing. Coming into bloom—perhaps her grandmother was born just as the curse took hold, and that synchronicity connected the two despite the weakness of the fae element in her."

He's frowning, though. Could all that also explain why I have a little magical ability? And would a curse really latch onto a random baby that was essentially human, just because it happened to be born at the same time? I don't have enough idea of how fae magic works to know how plausible those assumptions are.

In front of the arch-lords, I hesitate to ask anything that'll make me sound ignorant—or throw doubt onto

Sylas's and Whitt's explanations—though, so I keep my mouth shut. Another, more discomforting thought strikes me.

If the specialness in me that allows my blood to cure the curse is something I inherited because of an unintentional coincidence... then there may be nothing else in either world that could have the same effect. Rather than giving us a way out of our problem, this trip may have made it even clearer how valuable I am to all the Seelie.

Ambrose rubs his mouth. "What of her other relatives, then? Is this grandmother still above the dust? Perhaps a human closer to the source would provide stronger results."

My heart lurches, and August gives the arch-lord a fierce look. "We're not dragging her family here to be bled."

"There wouldn't be any point," Whitt puts in before Ambrose can argue. "The sage said the connection between the family line and the curse *strengthened* across the generations. Unless this is opposite day, that means the generations before Talia's would have a weaker effect."

Would they have had any effect at all? Aerik and his cadre didn't seem to notice anything special about Jamie's blood when they—when they tore my brother apart. The memory makes me cringe inwardly, my pulse skittering faster. I reach for August's hand, and he squeezes mine in return.

Maybe it was something only passed on to the women? I'm not sure why that would be the case. Or something only to the oldest child?

Not that it matters. Both Jamie and my mother died almost a decade ago.

"I suppose this venture was somewhat informative," Celia says in a cool voice. "But it seems to change the situation very little. Some miniscule trace of fae influence over her line doesn't make this girl anything more than a human, and the cure remains tied to her blood."

It's true—nothing's different except that I have even more questions and uncertainties. I glance back toward the forest, wondering if Nuldar would say anything else if I marched up to him and demanded answers. Somehow I doubt it.

Ambrose has turned away from the rest of us. Another carriage has come into view in the distance. He shoots the others a narrow smile. "I had a brief bit of business to carry out, and this was a convenient mid-point. Allow me a moment, and then we can discuss whatever else we need to."

Celia huffs as if she doesn't think there *is* anything else to discuss. She walks over to her carriage with her cadre-chosen, and Sylas moves to confer with Donovan. Ambrose strolls a little away from our cluster but then stops, rocking on his heels as he waits for the newcomers to arrive.

August turns to Whitt. "If all that was needed is fae influence and timing, surely there could be other beings affected. If we could find plants or animals of the Mists that came into being at that same moment…"

Whitt grimaces. "Perhaps it needs to be actual fae ancestry, not simply of this realm. You know there are barely enough Seelie offspring to count on one being born across the whole realm in any given year, let alone on a specific day."

Something Astrid mentioned to me tickles up through my thoughts. "Maybe—" I begin, and then my voice withers in my throat, because I've just seen who's stepping out of the newly arrived carriage to meet Ambrose.

The sunlight glares off Aerik's daffodil-yellow hair—and off the icy blue-white of the sharp-edged man emerging behind him. I freeze.

For a second, I think I've conjured my former captors out of my imagination after remembering their attack on my family, but no, they're really here. Aerik strides over to Ambrose, Cole sauntering behind him. He cuts a quick look my way, and his expression is all ice too.

If my pulse was skittering before, it's outright rattling through my limbs now. I suck in a breath and find my lungs have constricted. I wrench my gaze away, blinking hard, fighting to control my emotions while so many powerful fae are here to witness it if I break down.

I shouldn't be affected by those monsters anymore. We defeated them—all four of us together. Sylas forced their yield. They *can't* hurt me now.

But I wasn't prepared, and I have nine years of torment lodged in my brain that isn't erased that easily. Slivers of memories stab up through my mind: the slam of an elbow into my ribs, the cold sheen of bronze bars around me. A sound like a wheeze escapes my throat. I squeeze my hands into fists, focusing on the pressure of my fingernails against my palms, on the solidness of the ground beneath my feet.

"Talia," August says, hushed but urgent. He tucks his

arm around me, sheltering me.

I can feel the tension in his stance. He won't want to draw attention to my weakness either. Ambrose will find some way to spin it against my pack.

The arch-lord must have known I'd have some kind of reaction to seeing Aerik. Sylas said he didn't give the trio any details of my treatment, but they know that Aerik and his cadre are the ones who dragged me into this realm from my home, who broke my foot, who brought me to such a sorry state that Sylas would never have agreed to handing me back to them.

I'm not hiding my panic as well as I wish I could. Whitt steps closer with a flash of his teeth and a remark under his breath. "They won't get anywhere near you. I'd like to see them try." Astrid plants herself nearby between me and the new arrivals so I can't see them even if I look that way.

And—oh, no—Sylas and Donovan are approaching too. "Is she all right?" I hear the fiery-haired man say, and while he seems to be a much kinder ruler than his colleague, we still need him on our side. We need him to believe that I'm safe and well in Sylas's care.

"This is all a little overwhelming," I manage to say, hating the way my voice wobbles. "I'll just…" I sink down in demonstration rather than trying to force out more words, sitting on the grass and pulling my knees up in front of my chest.

There. It'll look as if I just needed a little rest. August crouches with me, rubbing my back, and with his touch and the stronger sense of being grounded, my inner turmoil starts to retreat.

They're all watching me. I can't exactly tell them to go away. I find myself staring through the gap between Sylas and Donovan where they're standing over me. At first my focus is hazy, but then a movement catches my attention.

One of the servants Donovan brought with him is shaking his head. He doesn't seem to be talking to anyone, though. He's standing there on his own, closing his eyes and opening them again with another jerk of his head from side to side. His mouth twists as if in distress.

As I'm distracted by him, my own anxiety fades even more. Is something wrong with him?

He touches his hip, adjusting something in his pocket —I catch a glint of a metal edge—and then he walks out of my view in the direction of Celia's carriage.

An uneasy tremor races through me that has nothing to do with Aerik. Something's wrong.

The last time Ambrose struck at us in a gathering of the fae, it wasn't just at me and Sylas. He had other plans, bigger plans. Why would this time be any different? He hasn't just shaken my nerves—he's ensured nearly everyone else's attention is on me instead of... wherever he doesn't want it to be.

I open my mouth, but my throat has gone so dry I only croak. My men draw closer with looks of concern.

It's not me they need to worry about right now, I don't think. My eyes dart and lock with Astrid's.

I make a frantic gesture in the direction the servant appeared to go. A furrow digs into her brow, but she looks around despite her confusion.

"Arch-Lord Donovan," she says quickly. "Does your servant have some business with your colleagues?"

"What?" The arch-lord swivels and swears softly. As he hustles away, I relax into August's embrace.

There's a thump and a yelp. Everyone around me turns to look, and so does Ambrose. "Whatever is going on over there, Donovan?" he asks sneeringly.

Donovan is standing over the servant, one hand pressed to the man's forehead, the other gripping his wrists, just a few steps from Celia's carriage. She's watching too, knitting her brow.

Donovan speaks a few low words, and the man stops struggling. He shakes his head, but in a looser motion than I saw before. "I—I'm sorry, my lord. I don't know—"

"It's all right," the arch-lord interrupts, and nudges him back towards his own carriage. Donovan casts a wary glance Ambrose's way. "Something about this place appears to have affected my servant badly. I've dealt with it."

"Humans are never quite as resilient as we'd hope, are they?" Ambrose says, and returns his attention to Aerik.

The servant was human? I guess there wasn't any way for me to tell when he was dressed in fae clothes. The fae can clearly pick up on some difference, but there's no visible sign that I can pick up on between the fae with a smaller portion of true blood and a human.

As I manage to get back to my feet, Sylas looks me over. "All right, little scrap?" he says, warmly enough for the old nickname to sound affectionate rather than belittling. When I nod, he hurries over to Donovan, no doubt wanting a more detailed account of what went on there.

Whatever Ambrose had planned, he doesn't let any

disappointment show. After a few minutes, he waves off Aerik and Cole, his supposed business with them concluded, and the arch-lords gather with Sylas and his cadre again. It doesn't take long to determine that there really isn't anything more they can glean from the sage's metaphors.

"If anything else occurs to you or it leads you to a new revelation, I expect you to report on that to us immediately," Ambrose declares, and marches off. The other two arch-lords follow suit, but not before Donovan exchanges a meaningful look with Sylas.

We hang back while the others set off. When they're far enough that my men must be sure they won't be overheard, Whitt turns to Sylas. "What was that about?"

Sylas lets out a ragged sigh. "It seems one of Donovan's human servants got himself under an enchantment. One that appeared to be propelling him toward Celia with a knife. And Donovan only brought those servants along because he got an anonymous warning that they'd be under threat in the castle today. He was manipulated into having them here."

I can fill in at least one of the blanks. "Ambrose must have enchanted him. I guess it's a lot easier to do that to a human than a fae servant?"

"Unfortunately, yes. And whether it was Ambrose himself or one of his underlings, we strongly suspect he was involved." He turns to Astrid. "Thank you for your vigilance. If you hadn't noticed the servant's odd behavior, he might have carried out his attack."

The warrior woman tips her head toward me. "It was

Talia who spotted him. She managed to convey enough to alert me even in her distress."

"Really." Sylas's gaze comes back to me, impressed but still grim. "Protecting us when we're meant to be protecting you."

"You protected me plenty," I say.

August growls. "First the thefts and now this—on top of throwing Talia into a panic. What's Ambrose's end-game?"

Whitt arches an eyebrow. I don't think the edge in his voice is really directed at his brother. "Can't you guess? As we explained to Talia not long ago, there are two ways to displace an arch-lord. Ambrose doesn't expect he could get away with killing Donovan in cold blood."

The conversation comes back to me. "The other way is to show the arch-lord isn't good enough—because of wrong-doings? Would Donovan get kicked out over stealing a few artefacts?"

"Probably not that alone," Sylas says. "But I doubt that was meant to be the only blow. And while his servant wouldn't have had a hope of dealing much real damage to Celia, instigating the attempted murder of a fellow arch-lord would certainly be grounds for dismissal. I believe we can now say with reasonable certainty that Ambrose is looking to not just put you in his cousin's grasp but to set Tristan on a throne as well."

Whitt winces. "And if that happens, good-bye to balance in the Bastion. Ambrose and Tristan will carry the vote. Whatever the two of them want from all Seelie kind, they'll get."

14

August

I've only just started to doze when the faint click of my bedroom door brings me back to full alertness. I jerk upright, but before my defensive instincts have kicked in any more than that, I've already recognized the whiff of scent that's reached me.

Talia peeks inside. She'd look like a wraith with her pale skin and her white nightgown if it wasn't for the rich pink of her hair, unmistakeable even in the dim moonlight that seeps through my window. She hesitates on the threshold. "I hope I didn't wake you up? It sounded like you just came to bed."

I've known this woman too long now to be surprised that she's canny enough to pick up on our movements around the castle. It wasn't *that* long ago she must have felt her survival and potential escape depended on knowing when we'd turned in for the night.

I don't have the words to express how glad I am that

164

she's using that awareness to come to me rather than running away now, so I settle for smiling and holding out my hand. "It wouldn't matter if you had, but you didn't. Come in. Is something wrong?"

As she limps across the floor to me, she shakes her head and then seems to amend that gesture. "Not exactly. I—After seeing Aerik and Cole today, I think the nightmares might come again. If I'm sleeping on my own, anyway. I don't seem to have them when I know I'm with someone who could protect me."

A faint blush colors her cheeks, as if there's anything embarrassing in that admission. The joy I already took in having her here spreads through my chest with a headier warmth.

I know Sylas has comforted her through her night terrors before, but this is the first time she's sought me out. I don't mind that she appreciates my brothers' attentions as well as my own, but I can't help reveling in the fact that she wanted me rather than either of them tonight.

Although I wish she didn't have to worry about nightmares at all.

I scoot over on the bed and lift the covers to make room for her. "You're always welcome here, Sweetness. I'll do my best to scare off those mangy villains even if they're only in your head."

With a relieved smile in return, she crawls under the sheets and cuddles up next to me, so easily it makes my heart sing. I wrap my arm around her torso and nuzzle her hair.

A more heated hunger stirs in my chest and lower, my wolfish instincts rising to the surface with the urge to taste and take her, but she didn't come to me for that. The whole reason Sylas set up a separate room for those sorts of encounters was so that Talia could seek us out at night without any expectations of greater intimacy.

We'll have plenty of other occasions for that. And it's not as if getting to hold her against me like this, guarding over her while she sleeps, doesn't feel plenty intimate in itself.

After the trip to the sage and all the surprises and stress that came with it, it's no wonder Talia is exhausted. Her breaths slow after only a few minutes in my embrace, her muscles slackening. I press a light kiss to the top of her head and rest my own against the pillow, but sleep doesn't come to me as quickly.

I love this woman so much. So much that seeing her in pain is like a dagger through my heart. So much that the emotion pulses through me with each beat of that heart as she lies here with me. Every moment she's near me, my body balks at the thought of letting her go.

If she were fae—fae enough that any of my brethren would count her as one—I'd ask her to be my mate. But regardless of Nuldar's comments, she's so human I'm not sure such an official bond would sit right even with our own pack-kin.

By my life, I'm not sure I'd even care about that if the tiny fae influence on her blood didn't make so much difference. For me to claim her as a mate when she's the only known cure for our curse would have political ramifications I can't even begin to imagine.

And that's without even getting into what my lord and my cadre-fellow would have to say on the subject. Would they accept a shared relationship where Talia had a more official tie to me than to them? Would *Talia* accept a mate bond knowing it would skew the tentative balance we've only just achieved between the three of us?

More questions I don't know the answer to. As much as I want her to feel cherished in every way, suggesting that step could cause more problems than happiness. I'm content with what I have for now.

Maybe I shouldn't be thinking about keeping her closer to me at all. Ambrose and his pack-kin have already managed to traumatize her, wound her… We haven't been enough to keep her safe. How can I say I'd do anything to protect her when I haven't actually managed to keep her out of his clutches?

That uneasy question leaves my thoughts spinning for a while longer before I finally drift off. When I wake up to Talia snuggling closer in the dawn light, I try to put the conclusions I've drawn out of my head. I hold her while she dozes a little longer, and then whip up a quick breakfast with her help in the kitchen. Every pleased glance she sends my way, every brilliant smile, I treasure and commit to my memory.

After we've all eaten, Sylas leaves to speak with Whitt about something, and Talia gives me a quick kiss before heading off with Astrid to find something to occupy herself with among the pack. I start cleaning the kitchen out of habit until the pack-kin who've been assisting me since we returned to Hearthshire shoo me—respectfully— out of the way. If I hadn't honed my cooking skills as much as I have, they'd probably tell me it isn't for a cadre-chosen to bother with anything in the kitchen at all.

I go up to Sylas's study expecting to join his conversation with Whitt, but when my lord calls me in, the spymaster is already gone. As I enter, Sylas stands.

"I was just about to summon you," he says. "I've arranged an audience with Ambrose. I'd like you to join me."

I blink, momentarily thrown off my purpose. "Me? Last time you took Whitt." Political negotiations are definitely not my area of expertise.

Sylas smiles and motions for me to follow him. "I wouldn't want the arch-lords to get the impression that I favor either of my cadre-chosen over the other. And Whitt will be there too, just more surreptitiously. I don't expect Ambrose to react well to this conversation. Our brother will be watching to see how he responds in the orders he gives his pack."

I walk with Sylas out of the castle, glancing toward our pack village. "Then none of us will be here with Talia—"

"Astrid has proven herself more than up to that task. I don't anticipate any major moves from our guests, but she has my orders just in case." He considers me for a second before beckoning the carriage he never bothered to revert to its natural form after yesterday's trip. Had he already known then that he'd need one again so soon? "What we do today may protect her better than anything we could accomplish here by her side."

We set off at a faster pace than he'd take if Talia were with us. I don't think he wants to leave her without our protection for any longer than he has to despite the confidence in Astrid he expressed. The wind warbles over the canopy and ruffles my hair. Sylas has tied his back in a short ponytail, but a few stray strands whip across his temples.

When we reach a stretch where he doesn't need to navigate closely, he comes to sit on the bench across from me, angling his body as I have so the wind doesn't buffet his face. I push myself to say what I've been thinking about since last night. If I don't speak up about it now, I might lose my nerve.

"I think there's something more we can do for Talia, at least until things are settled with the arch-lords and we're sure Ambrose has backed off on his intent to have Tristan take her."

Sylas raises a curious eyebrow. "Well, you know I'll want to hear your thoughts on that. Go ahead."

I open my mouth and hesitate. I don't think he's going to like this plan, not at first anyway. A large part of *me* doesn't like it. But it's a selfish part, and Talia deserves better. She deserves so much more security and certainty than we've been able to give her.

"No matter where we've been—our own domain, Donovan's, Nuldar's—Ambrose has found ways to reach her, to hurt her. But now that we have more information from the sage, and the arch-lords have even suggested we should look deeper into her heritage if we can... we could reasonably do this."

"Do *what*?" Sylas prods, his tone mild.

I inhale sharply. "We could arrange to send her back to the human world. Aerik and his cadre can't chase her there because of their yield vow. Ambrose would have trouble searching the entire place for her. We can send Astrid with her for protection, say it's to investigate her family, but really Astrid can just take her wherever they're least likely to be disturbed and give her as comfortable a time of it as possible until things are safer here."

Sylas contemplates the proposal for quite a while. I can't read his expression, but my gut knots with the sense that his evaluation might not be completely positive. Finally, he says, "You're suggesting that we send her so far away we'd have no hope of intervening if grave danger came upon her?"

"I think she's a lot more likely to face grave danger in this world than that one, and we have a responsibility to do whatever's best for her."

Sylas frowns, his gaze moving to the blurred landscape we're racing past. After another long silence, he returns his attention to me. "I'll keep that strategy under advisement should our situation become worse. I'd rather not take such extreme measures unnecessarily. For now… Ambrose may be conniving, but he isn't dim-witted. We can hope he'll see some sort of reason."

He doesn't sound all that hopeful. I grimace. "What exactly are we going to be talking to him about?"

Sylas's lips curve into a grim smile. "I think he should know that his treachery hasn't gone unnoticed. Ousting Donovan from his position will only work if Ambrose can't be charged with a crime as well—and it's unlikely to work at all if he feels he'll be watched too closely from here on out."

"We don't have definite proof, though."

"We won't be able to accuse him outright, no. But by the end of the discussion, I expect we'll all at least know where we stand better than before."

He obviously doesn't believe Ambrose will necessarily back down completely, or he wouldn't have asked Whitt to keep watch from farther afield. I resist the urge to pace the carriage, knowing the wind will make the movement more uncomfortable than nerve-settling.

Going up against other lords was one thing. Facing off against an arch-lord… I don't like it. I don't like any of this.

Our return to Hearthshire was meant to be a triumph, and Ambrose's duplicity is ruining it more with every day.

No one comes out to greet us when we approach the gleaming obsidian palace of Dusk-by-the-Heart today. Though Ambrose knows we're coming, either he hasn't notified his staff, or he's instructed them to wait for us to knock before admitting us. The fae servant who opens the door for us ushers us a short distance down a hall so dark it gives the sensation of swallowing us whole. The room she points us to isn't much better, but at least the pale upholstered furniture offers some break from the dark rock.

Sylas motions for me to sit but stays standing himself. Ambrose leaves us waiting there for several minutes before he deigns to make an appearance.

He enters briskly, his ever-present plated vest clinking with his movements, his eyes already narrowed. No doubt he can guess that this is far from being a friendly call. He shuts the door to the room with a wave of his hand and folds his arms over his chest.

"Well? Have you uncovered some urgent new development in regards to your dust-destined charge?"

I bristle automatically at the insult but hold myself in

place. He isn't bothering with politeness when it comes to his opinions about humans when the other arch-lords aren't around to overhear.

"Not yet," Sylas says evenly. "I wished to speak to you about a matter even more urgent—and one best not conveyed by distant correspondence."

"And what would that be, Lord Sylas? Do enlighten me."

His disdainful tone raises my hackles even more. I can force myself to stay seated, but there's no preventing my fangs from prickling out of my gums. He's lucky I'm holding my claws in check well enough not to gouge the fine fabric covering this chair.

Sylas lays the situation out with more care than I could have managed. "It's caught our attention that certain attempts have been made to undermine one of your fellow arch-lords. As if someone were seeking to have him removed from his position."

Ambrose lets out a huff, not allowing any hint show that the accusation affects him. "Then my colleague should certainly bring that to us, not you."

"Perhaps he will as well. But as one who serves the trio of arch-lords, I feel it is my duty to express my own concerns as well."

"And what would you have *me* do about it, Lord Sylas?"

Sylas regards him with the impenetrable calm I've always admired. "Perhaps you could take steps to ensure no such treachery occurs when you or your pack-kin are in the vicinity. Since I'm sure you would never risk your own position by aiding such efforts."

A smirk crosses Ambrose's face, so thin and cool it sets my teeth on edge. "Naturally. I'll certainly take your claims into account." He studies Sylas until all my nerves are prickling. "I wonder if you've fully considered all the factors involved, though."

"What do you mean?"

Ambrose gives a seemingly careless shrug and trails his thick fingers over the back of the nearest chair. "It doesn't appear you have any proof of this treachery, or I assume you'd have presented it."

"Many are aware," Sylas says. "It'll only be a matter of time."

"For sure. Only, it is such a shame that my colleague has garnered such hostile feelings, don't you think? You can't have imagined these efforts came out of the blue. I don't condone the behavior, of course, but when a ruler refuses to budge for the good of his people, it's unsurprising that this sort of thing occurs."

"On what matter has Donovan 'refused to budge'?"

Ambrose tsks to himself. "He wants to make friends with our true enemies, do you know? To extend a branch to the Unseelie, to offer that *we* will take the oath of peace and put ourselves at their mercy to speak to them. My other colleague, at least, sees the folly in that, but she hesitates to do what we truly need to. We will never be free of their heckling until they're utterly crushed."

Sylas watches him, his stance tense. "You want to initiate a full-out war against the Unseelie."

Take the battle to the ravens. Attack them on their own ground. I shift in my seat, my wolf stirring at the thought. But I have enough instincts beyond the animal to tamp down on that eagerness.

We've struggled enough with the winter fae on our own ground. How many more Seelie will die if we press on into their own realm where they're so much more comfortable than us? How much more fiercely will they strike at us if they feel directly threatened?

I wouldn't want to speak to the Unseelie arch-lords myself, but surely *someone* should before we take the conflict to greater and bloodier heights.

"I didn't say that," Ambrose said. "Only that it seems to be the clearest avenue to the peace we'd surely all welcome. Quash them and be done with it. But that can only be achieved with a united front."

That's why he wants Tristan to replace Donovan. That's why he's so set on getting control over the rulership now. I bite back a snarl at the depths of his treason. Unity, my ass. He means to tear apart the institution he's supposed to champion.

"You know," the arch-lord goes on casually, "it might even turn out to be in your benefit if such a turn were to occur. Without the conflict with the ravens, we'd have less to lose in the grips of the curse. Securing your pet wouldn't seem quite so pressing. I'm sure in such a scenario, it wouldn't seem questionable at all to allow her to remain in your keeping."

Sylas's voice remains steady, but it comes out flat enough that I'd be wincing if the words were aimed at me. "An interesting point to raise. At the moment, I'm afraid I'm more concerned about the security of the Heart and its foremost guardians."

"Ah, as well you should be." Ambrose sweeps his arm toward the door. "You appear to have said your piece. Don't let me delay your departure."

Emotions roil in my stomach as Sylas and I return to our carriage. I have enough self-control to contain myself until we've passed beyond Ambrose's domain into an open stretch of land with no fae in sight. Then the words burst out of me.

"He tried to bargain with you to support his mutiny! He truly thought you'd turn against Arch-Lord Donovan just for a suggestion that Talia would be spared. As if a word from that mangy rat of a wolf is worth anything."

Sylas growls low in his throat. "My sentiments exactly. He certainly didn't appear to be at all put off by the fact that his intentions are no longer secret."

"You don't think he'll back down."

"No. We'll have to see what Whitt observes, but after hearing from Ambrose himself, I doubt it'll change my impressions." Sylas stares into the distance, his expression so grave it pains me. Then he meets my gaze again. "I suspect there's no way to stop *his* war than to go to war with him. See his traitorous acts exposed and his power stripped before he can topple Donovan."

I swallow hard. "And he has to know that too. He'll be twice as eager to crush *us*."

"Yes." Sylas pauses. "I believe I need to reconsider your proposal for Talia."

15

Talia

"If they bounce back when you push them, then they're ripe?" I ask to confirm, glancing up at the fae woman whose garden I've volunteered to tend.

She nods with a slanted little smile as if she finds it amusing to watch a human fumbling with fae crops, but there's nothing cruel in her expression. I just have to keep at my campaign to contribute to the pack every way I can until I graduate from amusement to real appreciation.

I only manage to identify a couple of ripe gourds before August comes ambling into the village. His pace and his stance are casual enough, but there's something serious in his golden eyes that makes me sit up straighter before he's even spoken.

"Always so eager to put yourself to work," he says, his smile all warm fondness, and then motions me up. "I'm sorry to interrupt. Come back to the castle with me?"

Whatever this is about, he doesn't want to explain the

details in front of our pack-kin. I stand up, brushing the stray bits of dirt from my hands, and dip my head to the fae woman. "I'll pitch in some more when I can."

"No need to trouble yourself," she says. "But there are always new ones coming ready if you happen to stop by."

August keeps up his relaxed pace as we walk back to the castle. I'd assume that's because he doesn't want to hurry me on my wounded foot if he wasn't so quiet as well. After we've stepped into the entrance hall, he turns me to him and cups my face. He kisses me for long enough that my knees start to wobble with the rush of heat.

I reach for him, my fingers curling around the back of his neck, as if I could pull him even closer, but he pulls back with a hint of a growl as if releasing me takes some effort. His expression has gone even more serious than before.

"Sylas wants to speak with you," he says. "He's in his study."

Is that all? Although with our treacherous guests roaming around still, maybe it makes sense that the fae lord wouldn't want them knowing he had something urgent to discuss with me, whether they realize what it was or not. I definitely have no idea.

Have the things Nuldar said changed Sylas's opinion about how to handle my presence here? About how involved I should be with his pack? No one's treated me any differently since we returned, but I know how close the fae prefer to hold their cards.

I find the door to Sylas's study open. He's sitting in his usual spot behind his desk, but he gets up at my entrance.

He closes the door behind me with a quick word of magic that must be to ensure our privacy and motions me to the armchairs by the room's small hearth.

The fire crackling there is more for superficial appeal than necessary heat. The summer warmth spills through the open window along with a mix of clover sweetness and piney tang.

Sylas sinks into a chair across from the one I pick. There's a deeper somberness to his movements, beyond his typical gravity, that makes my chest clench. After August's attitude downstairs, I can't help suspecting he's about to deliver bad news.

"Talia," he says, his voice gentle. "I've given this a lot of thought, and I believe it would be best for you to travel —escorted for your safety, of course—back to the human world to investigate your family connections to the fae, ideally right away."

Oh. That doesn't seem all that surprising or ominous. Maybe he was worried that I'd balk because of what happened to my most immediate family? I lift my chin, pushing back those horrific memories. "Of course. I don't think my grandmother has any idea about… any of this. I mean, I don't even know for sure if she's still alive, and she must think I'm dead, so it might be a bit complicated."

My chest tightens all over again at the thought of navigating that fraught territory. It won't be any real homecoming. Since my mother's parents lived overseas in Greece and were hesitant to travel, I only ever met them twice—they're practically strangers to me.

If they are still alive, what questions will they have about how I've returned, about what happened to my parents? How will they react if I start badgering my grandmother about *her* parents and anything special she might have noticed about her father? I'm not sure how that information would make any difference to our situation anyway.

I swallow hard and focus on more immediate considerations. "I assume *you* wouldn't want to leave the pack to go that far, considering everything that's going on. Will Whitt or August be coming with me?" I'd have figured August would have volunteered without hesitation, but he didn't act as if we were about to go on an expedition together.

Sylas folds his hands together in his lap. "Actually, I'd have Astrid join you. As eagerly as I'm sure either of my cadre-chosen would offer their protection beyond the Mists and as much as I understand you'd take reassurance from their company, I'm afraid I can't spare them for that long either."

That long? I was picturing something like a day trip. How much could there be to uncover about a fae heritage even my great-grandfather might not have known he had? *He's* definitely not around to ask at this point anyway.

"How long are you thinking the investigation would take?" I venture.

"I think it would be best if you focused on that until the full moon arrives."

My pulse hiccups. "But that's—that's two weeks away. I don't know if I'll be able to find anything at all." I don't *want* to be away from my new home and the men who've won my heart for so much time, especially not in a place that now feels way more unfamiliar than anything here.

I'm not sure I remember how to act, how to talk with people like a normal human being, let alone all the practical concerns... I've never navigated that world as an adult.

Sylas's tone has stayed so even, not letting a trace of emotion show. As if it doesn't bother *him* at all that I'd be gone for all that time. As if he's already moved on in his mind to plans that require I not be here.

Is this even really about digging into my history, or is it just an excuse to send me away? Has Sylas decided that having me around is more of a liability than a benefit? Does he feel like I'm getting in the way—or that Ambrose's interest in me is drawing too much conflict down on the rest of his pack?

I was preparing myself to lose these men eventually, but I never imagined they might begin disentangling me from their lives so soon and so suddenly.

"The more time you have, the more likely you'll uncover something," Sylas says as calmly as before.

Something in me refuses to give in just like that. "It doesn't seem as if we're going to find *anything* that would stop Ambrose from trying to take me. Wouldn't it be better for your case if I stay here to show how well I'm adapting?"

I catch a hint of a smolder in his dark eye. Because I'm arguing? "Do you have so little faith in my judgment?" he asks.

"No, I just—" Tears that only seem to prove my weakness prickle behind my eyes. I look down at my hands, gathering myself.

No matter what happens with my lovers, the pack will

still need me—all the Seelie do. What kind of life would it be, drifting back and forth between the worlds, not really belonging to either?

I've been working so hard to be a full member of the pack, to belong as more than just a curiosity and a burden —and a lover for however long as that part will last. I hate to think what the faded fae of the pack will think if I vanish for two weeks, leaving them to deal with the trouble my presence here has already caused.

"I want to stay," I manage to say despite the constricting sensation now winding up my throat and down to my gut. I push myself out of my chair toward Sylas, as if I can present myself to him in some way that will show how much I mean this. "I want to support the pack. I want to support *you*." I grasp his arm. "If I've made some mistake, if I've screwed something up, tell me and I'll do better. I only—"

"Talia." Sylas's voice comes out so strained it's almost a growl, the muscles in his forearm flexing beneath my fingers, and then he's tugging me the rest of the way to him, leaning forward to complete the embrace.

His hand tangles in my hair. He presses his face close to mine, the movement of his jaw brushing my cheek. "You haven't don't anything wrong, I swear it. By the Heart, if I could keep you this close to me every moment of every day, I would. But I wouldn't be any kind of lord if I refused to do what's best for you."

What's best for me. Wrapped in his arms and his earthy, smoky scent, understanding washes over me in turn.

This isn't about what I'm doing but what our enemies

might do *to* me. Ambrose has tried all kinds of tactics in the last several days. Sylas is trying to protect me, like he does so often.

And I can even understand why he didn't say that to begin with, because my first reaction after I realize that is to balk even more than before. I tuck myself tighter into his embrace, forcing myself to take a moment to consider my response and whether my resistance even makes sense.

But there's one piece of the puzzle I don't have. Sylas didn't give any indication he was thinking like this after our last clash with Ambrose. Last night everything seemed normal.

Easing back just enough to see his face, I seek out his mismatched gaze. His dark eye smolders on, but I can recognize the heat as possessive passion now.

"Why are you suggesting this now?" I ask. "Did something happen that I don't know about?"

He lets out a rough sigh and frowns at the fire. "I spoke to Ambrose this morning. He made it clear enough that he has no intention of backing down until he's replaced Donovan with Tristan as arch-lord—and then launched a full-scale war against the Unseelie. I can't stand by while that happens, and *I* made that much clear. The conflict between us is only going to worsen until it's resolved. I don't want you to be wounded in the middle of it."

"I've survived plenty of wounds already."

"I know. I know you've done much for the pack and that you can handle yourself better than I'd ever have expected from one who's been through as much as you have. But this… it might be too much even for you, mighty as Whitt rightly says you are."

He strokes his thumb across my cheek, and there's no mistaking the affection in his gaze. "We have the benefit of a reasonable excuse for you to leave this world completely. How can I not take that opportunity to remove you from the dangers ahead?"

I suck my lower lip under my teeth to worry at it for a moment. "Do you actually think anything useful could come of me looking into my family history?"

"Truthfully, no. Even if you have relatives with the same benefit in their blood, bringing more humans into this mess won't really solve our problems. I doubt there'll be any records that would shed additional light on what Nuldar already told us. As far as I'm concerned, you're welcome to see it as a vacation. Get Astrid to whisk you off to some tropical beach where you can lounge for two weeks and relax."

I waver. It obviously means a lot to Sylas to offer me this, enough that he's putting aside his own instinct to keep me close. If there's no pressure and no quest to follow, it might be nice to see the world I was born in again, to refamiliarize myself. To exist for a little while without my fears dogging me quite so closely and without the constant reminders of my weaknesses.

The fae lord offers me a quiet smile and caresses my cheek again. "Take this opportunity to relinquish the pressures of being lady of the castle for a little while. You can pretend none of the horrors of this world ever existed."

Those words make the decision for me. A pang that's all defiance reverberates through my chest.

The horrors of the fae world are real, and there is no pretending them away, especially not while people I love are still facing them. And there's so much more to this place than horrors, so many wonderful things I've found.

I may be weak in many ways, but it's here that I've also discovered just how strong I can be. I won't abandon my pack or my lovers. *Sylas* doesn't get to step away from his post, no matter how much he must hate this conflict.

"No," I say softly. "I appreciate what you're trying to do, but no. I've been able to help before. Sometimes in ways the fae pack-kin couldn't have because of the way the other fae underestimate me and the things they don't know about me. If there's any chance that I could make a difference, I want to be here. I can take whatever pain might come with that. I knew what I was risking when I revealed what my blood can do."

Sylas bares his teeth with a hint of a snarl, but it fades into a sigh of resignation. "I won't have Astrid kidnap you and carry you off against your will. Are you *sure*? No one here would think any less of you, Talia."

I drop my gaze for a second before meeting his eyes again. "I would."

He tugs me close again, and I tip my head against his shoulder. "Wretchedly stubborn woman," he murmurs, but the remark sounds more adoring than annoyed.

"I wouldn't have made it this far if I wasn't," I have to point out. The gears in my head are already whirring away. I said I wanted to stay so I could make a difference. I'd better ensure I'm as prepared as I can be to accomplish that.

I slip my hand around Sylas's elbow. "Ambrose thinks

I'm weak, just like Aerik and his cadre did, doesn't he? That gives me a bit of an advantage. Maybe there's some small magic I could learn that would help us uncover more of his plans. And if there is, I want to start learning it today."

16

Sylas

The pond doesn't look at all like the sort of place where fae of importance should meet, least of all an arch-lord. The trees surrounding it cloak the spot in even thicker darkness. With the dusk, the croaking carp have risen to the surface of the water, sending ripples out from where their gaping mouths let loose the hoarse sounds they're named for.

But I suppose its lack of grandeur is exactly why Donovan suggested this spot. No one else is likely to be visiting the pond to stumble on our clandestine meeting.

I hear the rasp of his steed's hooves through the brush before I see him. He dismounts the black gelding, murmurs a word, and walks to meet me at the pond's bank. The carp are already quieting as evening deepens into night.

"I gather you spoke with Ambrose this morning," he says, without preamble but genially enough.

I doubt the other arch-lord mentioned that himself. Donovan wouldn't stand much of a chance if he didn't have sentries keeping an eye not just on his domain but all those that surround the Heart.

I incline my head. "Yes. I thought perhaps with a warning that his traitorous intentions had been observed, he might back down. Unfortunately, he left me with no doubt that he intends to see you removed from your throne, and as quickly as he can make that happen— though of course he didn't express that in any way that he could be sanctioned for. I know we expected as much already, but I didn't want to leave you unaware of the confirmation."

Donovan gazes toward the pond with a frown, clearly unhappy but not startled. He knows his colleagues' temperaments even better than I do. My attempt at dissuading Ambrose from his goal was always a long shot.

"It's good that you told me," he says after a minute. "I'm not sure exactly how I'll respond yet, but you can be sure that if it comes down to me or Ambrose, I'll see that Ambrose falls. I just wish it didn't have to end up like this." He rubs his hand over his face, and in that moment with the weight now resting on his shoulders, he looks far older than his actual age, older than his mother ever did.

"He indicated that he's particularly keen to ramp up our efforts against the Unseelie," I say. "Have they made any further moves since we last spoke?"

Donovan shakes his head. "We've heard nothing. No attacks. I'd like to think they may be completely beaten already, but I'm not that optimistic. It does worry me that we won't know what they're up to next until they enact those plans—but the alternative of taking the fight to them will see so much blood spilled on our side as well—" He cuts himself off with another shake. "But that isn't for you to worry about. Not yet, in any case."

"If there *is* any way I can be of service…"

"Yes. I appreciate the guidance and intelligence you've offered so far." He sucks in a breath. "I have no desire to see blood shed around the Heart either. It seems to me the best way to handle this is to set some sort of trap that will entice Ambrose into acting against me and then prove his treachery, and let him be sanctioned for that."

"That sounds reasonable," I say.

The young arch-lord offers me a flicker of a smile. "The exact approach will require more thought. I'll reach out to you when my plans are more solid. If anything else urgent arises, notify me at once. We can meet here again for any matters too sensitive to be conveyed in ways that might be intercepted."

I dip my head again. "As you bid, my lord. I wish I had more hope for a peaceful resolution."

I turn to go, but Donovan clears his throat meaningfully. I glance back at him.

"I can't promise anything, and if Ambrose sees reason after all there is the chance it may not come to this," he says. "But that chance seems small enough that I feel I should encourage you to prepare yourself and your pack. If we see Ambrose stripped of his title, I'll be pushing for you to take his place."

My heart stops. I knew the removal of one arch-lord would require the promoting of another lord to the throne, and obviously Donovan wouldn't advance Tristan in his cousin's stead, but somehow it had never occurred to me that I might be in the running.

It takes me a moment to recover myself and respond with appropriate gratitude. "You honor me beyond any expectation, my lord. I wouldn't have thought—when we're so recently restored to Hearthshire—"

Donovan waves off my subdued attempt at a protest. "You've proven yourself amply, both in the dignity with which you handled your banishment and your conduct in regards to Ambrose's schemes since then. The fact that you *wouldn't* have expected it, no matter how you've helped me, is exactly why I think you're the best man for the job. I have no doubt that if it comes to pass, you'll have earned it."

I can't let the nausea winding through my stomach show. I offer an even lower bow and an emphatic murmur of thanks, and watch the arch-lord leave with only a trace of relief. His departure does nothing to change the declaration he just made.

As I return to my horse, my stomach keeps roiling. The stallion stomps uneasily when I've settled onto his back, picking up on my emotions. I turn him toward Hearthshire and set him at a canter with a press of my heels, but I barely notice the landscape falling away with each magic-charged stride.

I've hardly had a chance to truly settle back in at Hearthshire. How can I wrap my head around the idea of taking over an arch-lord's domain?

In the first moment when I ride through my home's arched-tree gate, my breath hitches and my hands jerk at the reins unbidden. A horde of ghostly carriages shows before my deadened eye, spread out across the fields. I blink, and they're gone.

My pulse keeps hammering against my ribs as I ride on toward the stable. Like so often, there's no telling what that glimpse could mean. It could be a future in which we're casting off toward another new home—or when a fleet of Ambrose's soldiers have arrived here. It could have simply been an echo of a couple of weeks past when we arrived, or decades ago when we packed up to depart for the fringes. Most of those possibilities leave me unsettled.

Music carries across the fields. The glow seeping from behind the castle tells me Whitt is hosting one of his revels tonight. He hoped he might get enough intoxicating delights into our guests to loosen their tongues.

If he hadn't been so occupied, I'd have shared Donovan's revelation and the tangled reaction it's stirred up in me with my spymaster. As it is, I leave my steed with the stable-master and enter the castle alone.

The vast entrance room looms around me, my steps echoing through it in a way that feels abruptly ominous. August is likely around if I wanted to seek him out, perhaps in the basement enjoying the larger gym or entertainment room this building has to offer. But I find myself heading upstairs instead. I haven't quite admitted to myself what—or rather who—I'm pursuing before she steps out of the lavatory into the hall ahead of me.

Talia has changed into her nightgown, her feet bare beneath. Her face glows faintly ruddy from the recent washing, a few stray hairs damp along her temple. As soon as she sees me, she smiles, so easily I know the warmth is all genuine.

"That didn't take very long," she remarks.

"No, not long at all." And yet so much has changed with that brief conversation. I hesitate, uncomfortably uncertain of what I want, what I *need*—what's even reasonable to ask for. She shoulders enough burdens as it is.

Simply seeing her smile has melted a small portion of the tension inside me. Perhaps her presence is all I require to set the turmoil inside me in better order. I walk up to her. "May I sit with you for a short while?"

She blinks at me as if puzzled that I'd even ask. As if I should know she'd give up sleep and privacy and anything else I requested the moment I say the word. "Of course."

I wish I felt more certain I'd earned that level of devotion.

It feels strange, coming into her bedroom like this, sinking onto the mattress next to her as she props a pillow against the headboard for her to lean on. How many times have I arrived here much later in the night to comfort her, waking her from nightmares and soothing her in their aftermath?

The role of protector came naturally to me. To now be the one searching for comfort doesn't sit right at all.

But I'm here, and she's slipped her hand around mine and rested her head against my shoulder as if she couldn't be happier to have me. Skies above, I can't claim that's *wrong* either.

"Was he upset?" she asks.

She means Donovan, naturally. Who else would she think has reason to be upset, when she doesn't know what news he imparted to me?

"Perhaps a little, but he wasn't surprised. The evidence has been accumulating for some time. And presumably Ambrose has made his dissatisfaction known during the meetings of the Bastion." I pause, breathing in her sap-sweet scent, absorbing the soft warmth of her body against mine. I've nearly convinced myself that this is enough, that I shouldn't interrupt her rest any longer, when she speaks, quiet but clear.

"It must be hard. For you, working with Donovan to stop Ambrose. The pack was banished because people blamed you for the attack on him—you worked so hard to prove you weren't like that, and now you might really have to fight him."

I stare down at her. I didn't say a thing to her about how I was feeling—but she's heard me talk about the past enough times. How can I be startled that she'd put the pieces together?

She knows me better than I've given her credit for.

There is one thing she doesn't know, but with her gentle words of compassion echoing through my mind, that spills out too. "It is. But more than that—Donovan has said that if Ambrose must be replaced, he wants me to become arch-lord."

Talia raises her head to meet my eyes. Her fingers tighten where they're twined with mine. "And you're not sure you'd want the responsibility?"

"I'd gladly serve my Seelie brethren however I can. And the position would come with benefits for the rest of the pack beyond anything they enjoy here. But..." I can't stop my gaze from sliding away toward the wall across from us. "Everything you said is true. I've spent decades rallying against the perception that my pack and I are tainted by association with Isleen's actions. It *horrified* me that she and her family would turn against our rulers and attempt to displace one—and now I find myself doing the same thing."

Talia makes a rough sound in her throat. "It's *not* the same thing. Had Ambrose made any move against you or their family—or anyone else—back then?"

"Not that I have any knowledge of. From what Isleen did say and show me when she was still trying to convince me to support her lesser efforts, they chose Ambrose only because one of his family's former pack-kin had joined her mother's pack and shared inside information that gave them an edge." A bitter chuckle fills my throat. "I know when Donovan's mother fell so suddenly, they were tempted to start over focusing on *him* as a potentially weaker opponent."

"Then they attacked Ambrose's pack unprovoked, because they were greedy and wanted more power for themselves. You're trying to defend another arch-lord that Ambrose is betraying. It's not as if you stepped in so that you'd win the arch-lord spot."

"No. But to others, it might appear that way, especially if Donovan is able to follow through on his promise." My deadened eye brings up no images of that possible future as I speak, but I can imagine well enough without it the wary looks and scathing remarks that would follow in my tracks.

"Well, anyone who'd think that would need to get their head checked," Talia says firmly. "What else can you do? They're both arch-lords, and you can't support both of them. Either you help Donovan and do your best to stop Ambrose from hurting him, or you refuse to help and you're making it easier for the real traitor to attack a different arch-lord. Wouldn't that be worse? It's not your fault that protecting one arch-lord means you have to go up against another."

No, the only person whose fault it is would be Ambrose, for starting this traitorous campaign to begin with. What Donovan offered doesn't change that.

It's my duty to protect the rulership of the Heart from all threats I become aware of, even if those threats come from within. I've never doubted that. Donovan's unexpected declaration simply set me so off-balance I lost track of what led me to this point.

"There isn't any choice," I agree. "I have to step up for Donovan, or I'd be going against everything I stand for."

"Exactly." Talia raises her hand to trace the line of my jaw. "You always do everything you can to make things better for your pack, for the rest of the Seelie—for everyone *except* yourself. If a pitiful human who's only known you for a few months can see that, then there shouldn't be a single fae who can't."

Her tone is light, but the insult in her words rankles me anyway. A growl creeps into my voice unbidden. "You're not pitiful. You're anything but pitiful."

If those who disdain her could see how she stood up to me this afternoon, insisting on standing by my pack—no, *our* pack, because it's hers now too. Looking for every way she could help without bowing one bit to the fear she must feel.

And now, making sense of the turmoil inside me so

deftly, cutting straight through to the heart of the matter without the preconceptions and condemnations that clouded my own thoughts. She hasn't been tainted by the twisted politics of this world, even as she's taken it in and formed such a coherent understanding.

The strength in her cuts straight through to *my* heart. It nearly tore me apart just thinking of sending her off beyond the boundaries of the Mist with Astrid. My wolf wanted to thrash Donovan for suggesting with the kindest of intentions that he take her from me. She's asked for so little in her time with me, yet she's claimed so much of my respect and devotion.

And my love.

I can admit that to myself now, can't I? This burning desire to have her with me every moment, the awe that fills my chest with every bit of might she shows, the fierceness that sears through me at the merest thought of anyone harming her... I can give it its proper name. What kind of man would I be if I denied it?

I love her. This precious, astonishing, irrepressible human woman. The truth of that fact blooms inside me with the acknowledgment of it, and a fresh twinge of uneasiness follows in its wake.

I lift Talia's chin to kiss her softly, reverently, and leave my head bowed close to hers. "Thank you. You reminded me of everything I needed to remember. Sleep well, lady of the castle."

The title brings a bright smile to her lips. As she scoots lower on the bed, pulling the covers over her, I force myself to walk away. When I've shut the door behind me, my breath courses out of me in a harsh rush. I

EVA CHASE

close my eyes, willing back the new tangle of conflicting emotions.

The last time I loved a woman, I let the anguish that came with it consume me and saw everything I care about nearly destroyed. Isleen's betrayal of our vows with that unknown man wounded me so deeply I walled off my connection to her—and failed in my duty to my pack and my rulers. If I hadn't let my heart override my sense of responsibility, I'd have known how far she meant to go. Even if I couldn't have stopped her, I might have protected my pack from decades of banishment.

Will the love I feel now for Talia do either of us any good?

If it doesn't, that's my failing, not hers. I push myself forward, away from the painful memories of the past.

Whether it somehow conspires to become my downfall or not, I'll move the stars before I let it ruin the woman it's an honor to call our lady.

17

Talia

When August asks the pack members assisting in the kitchen to fetch some more duskapples for the breakfast pastries, I can't help thinking the situation can't be quite that urgent. We haven't even started making the dough.

He waits a few beats after they've headed out the door and then says in a low voice, "Sylas told me you're wanting to learn a new true name."

Ah. I nod, grinding the cloves he gave me with a pestle. As they crumble into a fine brown powder, their crisply pungent scent tickles my nose.

August continues shelling the eggs he boiled, but I get the sense his shoulders have tensed just slightly. "Did you have anything in particular in mind?"

I hope he doesn't think my suggestion to Sylas was a complaint about the lessons he *has* been giving me. "I know I still don't have the best handle on light," I say quickly, keeping my voice similarly quiet. "It makes sense that we haven't moved on from that yet. I just thought, with everything happening—if there's something I can work on that I'm more likely to be able to use to help figure out Ambrose's plans and how to stop them, I should switch focus to that for now."

There's definitely something a little awkward about August's stance even as he smiles down at me. I can't quite put my finger on what, though, so I don't know how to ask if something's the matter without making things even more awkward. Maybe it has nothing to do with me at all; maybe he's just stressed out about the situation with Ambrose too. Why wouldn't he be?

He flicks the last egg onto the platter and cocks his head in consideration. "I'm not sure which of the simple ones would be best for that in a way it'd make sense for you to use. Why don't you give some thought to the exact strategies you think you'd want to try, and then we'll see what might enhance those?"

"Okay." My spirits deflate. I wanted to get started as soon as possible. But it *was* a bit much for me to expect him to know precisely how to teach a human with limited magic how to go up against an arch-lord effectively.

What would it have been useful for me to do when we were at Donovan's banquet, or in the forest when the tuskcat attacked, that I could have done if I'd had the right magic?

I mull that question over through the rest of the breakfast preparations, but none of the ideas that occur to me fit the two necessary criteria of being something I have any hope of actually pulling off with just a short span of training and being subtle enough that I won't give away my secret magical ability to our enemies. I'm still stewing on the subject as I sit down at the vast dining table with Sylas and August.

I don't think any of us are expecting Whitt to show up after last night's extended revel, but just after Sylas thanks the kitchen assistants for their work and they head out, the spymaster saunters into the dining room. Or maybe "sways" would be more accurate. He's not staggering, but there's a waver to his steps that gives the impression his balance isn't what it should be. He flops down into the chair across from August and rubs his weary-looking eyes.

The music from the revel was still filtering through the castle walls when I got up to use the lavatory in the early hours of the morning. He can't have had more than a couple of hours of sleep. Although, knowing Whitt, it's difficult to say how much his current state might be fatigue and how much that he hasn't yet slept off whatever drinks and drugs he enjoyed overnight.

Sylas gives him a baleful glance. "This breakfast isn't so vital that I required you crawl out of bed to attend it."

Whitt appears to restrain a yawn and plucks a duskapple pastry from its platter. "Perhaps I'm practicing better self-discipline for when I may be serving a higher authority."

A soft growl escapes Sylas, though his tone stays mild. "That's hardly enough of a certainty for us to be discussing it so casually."

The other man snorts. "I assume everyone in the room already knows about your prospective surge in prestige. I promise not to sing it from the rooftop before it's finalized."

Whitt's speaking in his usual jaunty tone, a glint dancing in his eyes, but there's a sharpness to that tone and the glint that prickles at me. Obviously Sylas told him about Donovan's offer. Is Whitt bothered that Sylas might be made arch-lord? It'd mean a major increase in prestige not just for Sylas but the whole pack, including his cadre.

But it still might have rubbed Whitt the wrong way somehow. I remember the rawness in his voice when he admitted that it bothered him sometimes that Sylas is automatically granted so many more benefits than he is. I can't blame him for that. It isn't his fault his parents didn't pass on slightly more of their fae heritage to him, that his mother didn't have as much fae blood as Sylas's did in the first place.

I've just never seen him express anything close to those feelings in front of Sylas before.

The fae lord eyes his spymaster for a moment longer, but when Whitt switches to swooning over his pastry, Sylas appears to decide there's nothing worth prodding him about, at least not right now.

I shift in my chair, the quail egg I've just swallowed dropping uncomfortably into my stomach. Is *everyone* in the castle out of sorts today? If there's something in the air, I hope a swift wind takes care of it soon.

Whitt is halfway through his third pastry when a leaf flutters in to him on a much smaller breeze than I was imagining. He plucks it out of the air, glances at whatever message it holds, and gets up while popping the rest of his breakfast into his mouth.

"Matters to attend to," he says to Sylas, the words only slightly muddled by his mouthful. "I'll report back to you as I'm able, oh extra-glorious leader."

"I look forward to it," Sylas replies dryly, but his gaze follows Whitt as the other man heads out the door. He turns back to me, taking in the plate in front of me which I haven't added any more food to for the better part of five minutes now. The subtle tensions around me dulled my appetite.

"And what will our lady be occupying herself with today?" he asks.

Brainstorming spell ideas? I'm not sure lying around on my bed or the entertainment-room sofa is going to be all that inspiring, though. I nibble at my lower lip. "I guess I'll go see what needs to be done in the village today." I can't forget my other goals. The pack still needs to see me as a real member. I might get some ideas while I'm working with them.

Sylas nods. "I'll see that Astrid is ready to accompany you."

Shadow me, he means. But considering her shadowing prevented me from taking a worse injury when the tuskcat attacked the other day, I can't really complain.

When the dishes are cleared, I give August a quick kiss —which he returns enthusiastically enough to dissolve a little of my uneasiness—and walk with Sylas to the front door, because apparently he thinks I need an escort even to cross the entrance hall.

Astrid is waiting just outside. She beckons me over, looking vaguely amused with her current duty. At least I don't get the impression *she* thinks I'm in dire need of babysitting.

"No escaped sheep or rare mushrooms to gather today," she says. "I think most of our pack-kin are taking a break."

"Well, there are always the basic daily tasks, if anyone could use a hand." I look toward the gardens around the stump-like houses. Some of them might need watering.

Water—that's one of the basic true words, isn't it? August mentioned the elements and common metals, plants, and animals as the simplest ones. Although I don't know what all is common here. And somehow I don't think drenching Ambrose with water is going to be a very useful information-gathering skill, as much as I might enjoy doing it.

As I mull that over, a patch of bright color slipping by the farthest houses catches my eye. It's one of Harper's vivid dresses. She darts across the field, passing out of my view behind the castle.

She looked like she had some business she was eager to get to. Maybe I can offer to lend a hand with that. It feels like I haven't seen her around quite as much since the day we tracked down the escaped sheep.

I limp over as quickly as I can, thankful all over again for the boots she made for me that give me the extra stability of Sylas's brace without making me stick out any more than I already do. Astrid follows a few steps behind. I come around the side of the castle just as Harper has reached the edge of the forest beyond Whitt's revel area.

She's stopped there, but I stop too, because she isn't alone now. One of the daughters from Ambrose's pack—

the middle one—is standing amid the trees. They're talking, their heads bent close, but they're too far away for me to make out even a hint of their voices, let alone what they're saying.

I stay by the edge of the castle, hidden by the wall beside me and its shadow, watching. The uneasiness inside me rises up again, though I still can't explain exactly why.

Harper hands the other woman a bundle of fabric large enough that it could contain two or three of her dresses. The middle daughter smiles thinly and makes some remark that brings Harper's shoulders up, though only for a second. Then our guest swivels on her heel and strides off toward the guest quarters.

Astrid hums to herself. "What do you make of that?"

There's a perfectly obvious explanation. "Harper must have offered them dresses as a gift. She'd be hoping they'll appreciate the gesture enough to talk up her skills to other high-ranking fae." But I don't like the way the other woman smiled or how drawn Harper's face looks as she turns away from the trees.

She doesn't look hopeful but concerned. Ambrose's pack-kin better not have said anything insulting to her.

I'm about to hurry over to make sure she's okay when a much larger commotion emerges from the far forest. A carriage drifts into view, moving sluggishly between the trees. Our guests' carriage, with the whole family on board. The middle daughter must have hurried straight to it. I hadn't realized they were leaving.

Neither had my men, I suspect, because Whitt is walking alongside the carriage, talking with the husband and wife. He looks more animated than he did at breakfast, all traces of exhaustion gone, but I think I can read a certain amount of agitation in his supposedly careless gestures.

Astrid draws closer behind me. "Hmm. Interesting timing after our lord went to see theirs yesterday."

It is. Did Ambrose decide that he doesn't trust Sylas to treat his pack-kin well after Sylas showed he's aware of the arch-lord's treachery? Or is this some new phase in his plot? Even though the summer air is warm around me, I find myself rubbing my arms.

We aren't the only ones who've noticed the family's sudden departure. Brigit and Elliot wander over, hesitating near us as if they're not sure they want to draw the guests' attention.

Brigit's mouth twists. She glances at me and then at Elliot. "We never managed to dig up any other useful info, and now they're taking off."

"We helped Lord Sylas as much as we could," Elliot says, but he's frowning too.

"What you did find out was really important," I point out. Donovan might already be on the outs if we hadn't uncovered the false thefts. "And maybe there'll be other opportunities for us to help. We just have to... to wait and see what Ambrose does next."

As I speak, my stomach coils into a knot. I don't know how *I'm* going to help if there are no leads here in our domain to follow. It's not as if I can go sneaking all the way out to Ambrose's domain on my own.

Harper has lingered by the spot where she spoke to the middle daughter. When she looks our way, Brigit waves. My friend seems to balk for a moment before heading over. She glances back to where the carriage is drifting away past the castle. I can faintly hear Sylas's low baritone where he must have come out the front to see the guests off.

"I've got to get back to work," Harper says quickly, only slowing when she reaches us, not halting. "My—my mother needs another set of hands." She hurries onward, her gaze catching mine for only an instant with a brief flash of a smile.

I wish I knew what Ambrose's pack-kin said to her. If I had fae senses, would I have been able to pick up their voices?

Is there a spell that would let me?

The thought sparks in my head with an eager jolt. As all four of us meander back around the castle to watch the carriage glide through the gate, the sense of possibility expands, lighting up my mind more and more.

Yes, that just might be it. For a start, anyway.

August is standing with Sylas and Whitt just outside the castle's main door. "Well, I may as well put the pack through their paces," he says to his brothers, and starts toward the village.

I hustle ahead of the others as quickly as I can, catching him before he's called out to his trainees. "Can I talk to you just for a second?"

His head jerks up, his gaze flicking past me and then softening when he confirms that Astrid hasn't slackened off in her guard duties. "Sure. What is it, Sweetness?"

I tug him back toward the castle, waiting until we're within its walls to speak. "Sound waves travel through the air. You said air is one of the basic true words. If I could master that, would I be able to amplify sounds—so I could overhear conversations and things like that?"

August's eyes widen. I hold myself back from fidgeting as he considers. His lips curve upward, not with quite as excited a response as I might have hoped for, but with definite approval.

He rests his hand on the top of my head with an affectionate sweep of his thumb. "I think that just might be possible. Let me give our pack-kin a good work out, and then we'll see what we can do."

18

August

"It helps if you imagine a rushing sensation, like the wind moving over you, while you're saying the word," I remind Talia. "But don't get frustrated if it takes some time. You know you'll get there eventually."

Talia nods where she's sitting on the gym's mat of moss across from me, her legs crossed and her eyes closed as she feels out the true word I gave her during our training session yesterday. A guilty sort of hope twists in my chest.

I hope it takes a *long* time for her to get any grip on this word. At least long enough that there'll no longer be a need for any of us to be working against an arch-lord.

She wants so badly to contribute, though. How could I refuse to teach her?

I can't help watching the rise of her breasts beneath her dress as she inhales slow and deep, but the instinct that rises up inside me isn't lust but protectiveness. Her collarbone juts so delicately against her pale skin. The strap of the dress doesn't cover all of the scars left by Aerik's fangs.

What kind of lover would I be to see that and even think of letting her step into harm's way again?

"*Briss-gow-aft*," she murmurs with her exhale, keeping the syllables soft and sibilant the way I modeled for her. Another twinge of guilt joins my reluctance. I taught her right, but for more than a moment there, I was tempted to say it just a little wrong so there'd be no hope of her mastering it at all.

That kind of deception would have been beneath me too. There has to be something I can do, though. Sylas said she refused to return to her world with Astrid... Is there some way *I* could leave with her without jeopardizing the pack, for long enough that she might feel comfortable staying even after I returned? Would she be willing to venture back into the realm of humans if she had me by her side instead?

Even if she would for her own sake, I know she'd ask about my duties to the pack. We're on the verge of war. I'd need a convincing argument for why I could shirk my other responsibilities. I'd need to be sure I *wasn't* shirking them.

She lets out another breath. "*Briss-gow-aft*." The true name for air slips from her lips—and the hem of her dress stirs just slightly where it's pooled over her legs.

I flinch inwardly. *No.* Not already. But Talia's eyes have popped open. She's staring down at her dress with a smile stretching her lips.

"I think I did it," she says, offering me a brilliant smile

I'm not sure I deserve right now, her lovely eyes aglow with awe. "I felt the air move, just a little."

I make myself smile back. "It's a start. Getting to the point where you can shape the air enough to propel sound waves will take a little more work."

"I know. But at least I'm getting somewhere. Yesterday nothing happened at all." She runs her hands over her knees, her gaze drifting away, her eyes going distant in thought. "Of course, I still have to figure out when I'd actually get to use the skill once I've practiced enough. I guess the banquets and balls happen pretty often? Could we host one here and invite all the arch-lords? That would be a good excuse to give *everyone* a chance to observe Ambrose and his people."

"I'm not sure he'd risk making any moves or revealing his intentions while in our territory," I say. "And Sylas may not want to give him the opportunity to do so in case he would after all."

"True. But one of the other packs might host one like Donovan did. The fae all know who I am now. His pack-kin might be less cautious talking about things when I'm around than they are with other fae since they won't expect me to be able to hear as well—or to use magic to enhance my hearing. If I can find some excuse to be kind of close to their carriage or somewhere else they might talk privately, but not close enough that they'd believe I could listen in…"

And if they caught her? My muscles have already tensed just picturing it. "You don't need to go that far," I say. "If the opportunity comes up, and you don't have to put yourself in danger to take it, that's one thing. You shouldn't go out of your way to have anything to do with Ambrose and his pack."

Talia returns her bright gaze to me. "But I might not get a chance if I don't go out of my way. I won't try anything *stupid*. They don't think I can do much of anything anyway."

"I just—" I grope for a different tactic. I love how Talia's strength and confidence have grown, but that strength and confidence are exactly what won't let her back down from a challenge, especially one that she thinks could help us. The last thing I want to do is diminish her abilities. She gets enough of that from the fae outside our domain.

"I've been training the whole pack," I continue after a moment. "Whitt already has several pack-kin who know how to slip around and gather information for him. Whatever needs to be found out, we'll find it."

"But every little bit helps, doesn't it? There've been things I could do that no one else could before."

There have—and I've hated every one of those moments. When we had to stand back and watch Aerik and his cadre saunter up to her in that cage, when she held out her arm so Sylas could collect her blood in the Oakmeet kitchen... My hands start to clench at the memories. "If something like that comes up, then of course—but *we* should be the ones taking the risks until that happens."

The joy in Talia's face dims. She studies me, a furrow creasing her brow. "You don't want me to get involved."

I grimace. "I don't want you to get hurt, Sweetness. I'd rather take a thousand blows than see one land on you."

"But I still might get hurt if we can't stop Ambrose. Everything will be so much worse."

"And that's why Sylas and Whitt and I—and the rest of the pack—will make sure it doesn't come to that. You shouldn't have to face any of those threats."

"I *want* to. I'm part of this pack too. The whole reason I stayed here is—" She halts, her posture stiffening. "You've been acting a little strange since we talked about learning a new true name. No—you were tense right before Sylas talked to me the other day too… Are you upset that I didn't leave like he tried to convince me I should?"

My throat tightens at her obvious distress. "No, of course not. You have no idea how hard it was even making the suggestion to Sylas—"

She flinches. "Wait, it was *your* idea? You told Sylas that he should figure out a way to get me away from here?"

"Talia…" I can't deny it. I'd have to lie. But she's got to understand— "I only thought it'd be safer for you that way. It's my job to protect everyone in this domain, and Ambrose has already managed to hurt you more than once even with me so close by…"

I'm bracing myself for anger, but the reaction that comes over her is far worse. Her shoulders sag, her body withdrawing in on itself with a tremble of her chin. She clenches her jaw, blinking hard against a shimmer of tears. Agony wrenches through me.

I did that. *I* hurt her. The sight of her pain makes my fangs and claws ache to emerge, as if I could defend her from this offense with them. "Talia," I say again, my voice coming out hoarse.

"I got through Ambrose's tricks all right," she says before I can go on. She swipes at her eyes. "Do you really think I'm so useless that I'm better off not even in the same *world* as the rest of you? I thought— You've been training me so that I *can* fight, whatever ways I can—"

My hand twitches toward her, but I catch it, not sure she'd even want me touching her right now, as much as every impulse in me is hollering at me to hold her. "It isn't you. I think you're amazing. Heart help me, Talia, I love you, and I can't stand the thought that something might happen to you because I let you stay in harm's way."

She stares at me. "You're not 'letting' me do anything. It isn't your choice. I decide what I do. Isn't that—isn't that how it's supposed to be? You go off on plans that could get you *killed*, and I'm scared you won't make it back, but I don't tell you that you can't do it."

"That's not— I dedicated myself—" I stop, because I don't actually have a good response. I simply hadn't thought about it the way she put it before.

I *have* risked my life more than once since Talia came into it. No doubt I will dozens of times more over the course of that life, if it lasts as long as I'd like. If she asked me to hang back, I'd have to refuse. But as much as I'd say it's because I have a duty, because I swore to defend my pack and my lord with everything I have in me… that was my choice.

How can I say she should get to live freely and then try to hold her back? How can I tell her that her choice is wrong when it's the same choice *I* made?

"I didn't mean it that way," I finish weakly.

Talia's voice drops. "Being with you, with Sylas and Whitt, and with this pack is the only good thing that's happened to me in almost ten years. I love you, and I love it here. It feels *right* to fight for that every way I can. I know I can't contribute as much as you or any of the fae can, but I think I can offer at least a little bit…"

The hesitance creeping into her voice nearly kills me. I give in to the urge unfurling inside me, pulling her into my arms and onto my lap, enfolding her with my body as if I can hug the damage I've done away.

As hurt as she was, she leans into the embrace. I'm lucky she's not pushing me away.

I nuzzle her hair, my throat constricting. "I'm sorry. You've offered a *lot*. I shouldn't have tried to stop you just because I'm worried about you. That's really all it is. I—"

No, it's more than that, isn't it? The horror that stabs through me at the thought of Ambrose or his kin getting their paws on this woman echoes that other loss I try not to think about. The image flickers through my mind of my mother's crumpled body, and I close my eyes, tucking Talia's head even closer to me.

They might both have been human, but their situations aren't the same. I need to remember that. My mother never asked to stay among the fae. No one gave her any choice about it. What happened to her is on my father and all the other fae who failed to save her.

But Talia—Talia is sticking with us by her own will, devoting herself to this pack because she wants to.

I have to respect her choice, no matter how much it

unnerves me. If I treat her like a victim, then what am I doing but turning her into one all over again?

I shift her in my arms and bring my hand to her cheek, holding her gaze. "You are so strong, so capable, and no one should make you feel like you're not, least of all me. Whatever you think of that you can do to help us against Ambrose, I'll support you. Forgive me?"

A glint of tears comes into her eyes again, but from her tentative smile, I think they're happier ones this time. "It's okay. I know you only wanted to protect me. I don't want to get in the way or make the situation worse."

"You won't do that. You wouldn't let yourself do that. I've seen how careful you are. I just have to accept that beneath all that sweetness there's quite a fighter in there." I brush my lips to hers, my voice softening. "I'm proud of you. For holding your own, for speaking up instead of giving in. I was wrong, and you had every right to say so. If I ever go off on a tangent like that again, feel free to wallop me upside the head as well."

An adorable little snort slips out of her. She runs her fingers into my hair, sending a delicious shiver over my scalp. "Somehow I don't think a wallop from me would have much impact."

I rumble and tug her mouth back to mine. "You *always* have an impact on me."

I don't know if there's any way I can melt any lingering hurt by cuddling her close and kissing her with every bit of tenderness in me, but I'm happy to try. And once I've started, it's hard to remember we had any other aims we meant to fulfill downstairs. My mind wanders to a very enjoyable time we had one other afternoon in the old gym, the first time Talia showed me she could conjure light.

Oh, right. As enjoyable as this is, I should probably get back to her practice with air. Otherwise I'll be keeping her from her intentions in a totally different way.

I kiss her once more, drawing it out and reveling in the softness of her lips, and then peck a trail across her cheek to her jaw. How can I resist taking a little nibble there? Talia's chest hitches with an eager gasp, and I nuzzle her neck, a grin crossing my mouth and the last of my guilt fading away.

"You know," I murmur against her skin, "there's probably some emotion or sensation that will help you master air, just like there was with bronze and light. Maybe we should experiment."

She hums with amusement. "An interesting plan." But she tips her head to the side to give me better access to her neck. I flick my tongue across the crook of her shoulder, feeling the giddy leap of her pulse. Unfortunately, that gives me another idea that doesn't involve staying quite this entangled.

I ease back and offer my hand to help her to her feet. "Let's see what happens if we can get you airborne —literally."

19

Talia

It turns out the best way for me to connect with my sense of the air is to take a flying leap while I speak the true name. I'm really hoping it won't be long before I get to the point that I can just recall the exhilarating sensation of soaring through the air in those few moments before I come to earth, because there aren't a whole lot of ways to get a good lift when August is otherwise occupied.

I tried a few jumps on my own, but when I'm high enough to really get some wind moving around me, I can't land all that gracefully without help. My third and final attempt making use of the chair in my bedroom resulted in a jabbing pain in my warped foot that hasn't quite subsided.

I came outside thinking that the natural wind might give me enough extra sensation that I don't have to jump far. But I have to make sure I'm not too obvious, or the pack will wonder if I've gotten into the cavaral syrup and decided I'm a bird again.

If they heard me speak the syllables, they'd know just how much August is teaching me. I've come to trust many of my pack-kin, but a human who can work true names might make a little too enticing gossip for every one of them to keep it to themselves.

I eye the shadowy line of the forest. I could probably find some logs to hop off there without being in full view. But of course while the men of the castle are busy, I have my sort-of bodyguard sticking close by, and Sylas hasn't thought it was wise to let even Astrid know just how much I'm capable of. Argh.

Can I come up with a reasonable excuse for wanting to jump off logs while muttering to myself—and is there any chance the warrior won't notice when I do provoke a little movement in the air? Or should I forget about magic for now and see how I can pitch in around the village?

I haven't quite finished my internal debate when Harper emerges from her house and heads toward me, her sleek, pale hair swaying around her face. She's hugging something to her chest, and her always over-large eyes look outright sad.

"Hey," I say when she reaches me, with a smile I hope comes across as welcoming. I was starting to get the impression that she'd decided a human friend was too boring for her adventurous tastes. It's been days since she said more than a brief greeting to me.

But then, I don't know what might have been keeping her busy. She could be getting orders for dresses from prominent fae from all across the summer realm already.

"Hi." She tugs her hair behind one softly pointed ear in a nervous gesture. "I'm sorry we haven't gotten to spend much time together lately. I—I'd still like to see more of the domain with you when we have the chance. It's just been a strange time."

Relief washes through me. "It has. That's all right. A lot's been going on."

"I made a new dress for you. I thought I should do something." Harper thrusts the folded fabric she was clutching toward me. "I hope you like it."

As I let the delicate fabric unfurl, she twists her hands together in front of her, her expression tensed as if she's afraid I'll throw it back in her face. Why would she be worried about that? Around the castle, I've been wearing plain dresses like the one I have on today—it's not as if my fashion standards are terribly high.

And her latest construction is as breathtaking as ever. Currents of aquatic teal ripple together with lacy stitching like seafoam, a line of tiny silver shell-beads ringing the neckline.

"It's gorgeous," I say. "Are you sure—you've already given me two dresses, and it's not like I'm getting that many opportunities to show them off. I know how important it is to you to catch the eye of people from other packs."

Harper shakes her head vehemently. "You deserve it. I mean, unless you don't like it…"

"I *love* it." But she still doesn't look happy. I gather the fabric in my arms, wondering if the hissing sound the silky texture makes is what ocean waves actually sound like, and study my friend. "Is everything okay? I really wasn't upset that we hadn't had much of a chance to talk lately."

"Oh, yes—yes, I'm just glad everything is good." She smiles then, wide and maybe a little tight, but I'm not sure if I'm reading too much into things now. "I'd love to see it on you whenever you want to wear it, to make sure it doesn't need any adjusting."

"Of course. I'll try it on right now." I don't have anywhere fancy to go, but if it'll reassure her that I appreciate the gesture, that doesn't matter.

I head into the castle, Astrid at my heels. She hangs back in the hallway outside my bedroom, turning to chat with one of the pack members who's been helping keep the massive building clean and orderly. At least Sylas trusts that I'm not going to meet some dire fate in my own room.

The dress shivers over my skin, cool like water too. When I turn, the skirt appears to froth around my legs. I'll definitely have to wear this the next time I do have a special occasion.

On the way back downstairs, we run into August just outside the kitchen. He takes me in with an awed widening of his eyes that makes my heart skip giddily. "Look at you," he says.

As he steps closer, Astrid draws back through a nearby doorway to give us a little more privacy. August takes the opportunity to plant a kiss on me that leaves me even giddier.

"Are you sure you're not actually a sea nymph?" he teases. "You'd put the real ones to shame." Then he kisses my cheek and drops his voice lower. "How's your practicing going?"

To my relief, he shows no hint of any of yesterday's hesitation over what I'm trying to learn and why. I think we've put that behind us.

"Slowly," I say. "But it's coming along. It's better when you can help."

"Hmm. I bet I could fit in a training session after lunch."

I beam at him. "That would be wonderful if you can."

Sylas strides down the hall, back from whatever responsibilities he was attending to this morning. He slows at the sight of us, his expression warming. "All dressed up and lovely as ever. What's the occasion?"

"There isn't one." I gesture vaguely in the direction of the pack village. "Harper made it for me. I should probably get back to her. She wanted to see how it looks on me."

But even as I say that, something in me balks. I pause, turning over my memories of my friend's strange anxiety. Of the way she looked after she talked to the women from Ambrose's pack—of the fact that she was getting friendly with them at all.

My stomach twists. I'm probably being unfair, and maybe a little jealous that she's been more interested in chatting with other fae rather than me. But still... Something felt off. It's not as if she'll ever know if I simply ask Sylas— "Is there anything odd about it? I mean, it looks fine to me, but if there's any magic in it or something, I wouldn't be able to tell."

Sylas frowns and closes the distance between us. My

face starts to heat, expecting him to say it's a completely normal dress and why would I think otherwise? But he pauses in his inspection, leaning in like he might if he were going to kiss my jaw, though his eyes are fixed on the dress's neckline.

He touches one of the silver shell-shaped beads and then another, a quiet word passing from his lips. His eyes narrow. His mismatched gaze jerks back to mine.

"What else did Harper say?"

My pulse stutters. "Not much. That she was sorry we haven't been able to spend much time together. She—She seemed like she'd been getting friendly with the daughters from that family from Ambrose's pack, but I never saw her do anything *wrong*."

A growl comes into his voice. "I suppose we'll find out how much of the wrongness she's aware of, then. First—"

He speaks another word. The shells all shiver and melt into shapeless blobs. The tension gripping his face makes my gut clench even harder. "What *is* wrong?"

"I think we'd better have the responsible party with us to get the full answers to that question." Sylas glances between me and August. "Did either of you say anything since Talia put on the dress that we wouldn't want Ambrose to know?"

I cross my arms over my chest, hugging myself. "I just came downstairs. We—" We talked about my magical training. But I knew Astrid was nearby—even though we were talking quietly, I was still careful. "We didn't say anything specific, I don't think."

August shakes his head. "It was only about the skills she's been practicing," he says to Sylas. "The self-defense?"

Which is technically true, since learning magic is part of protecting myself, and there wouldn't be any reason for Ambrose to think we meant anything else, right? I'm still not sure what's going on.

Sylas makes a brusque gesture toward the hall. "Go to the audience room, both of you. We'll have Whitt join us too—and I'd better see about Harper."

He stalks toward the entrance room, radiating lordly fury. I turn to August. "Do you have any idea what he found?"

August grasps my hand. "No, but it sounds like we'll find out soon enough. Come on. Have you seen the audience room before?"

"No. Was there one in Oakmeet?"

"We didn't bother. It's mostly for formality, and we weren't expecting to conduct much important business while we were there. If Sylas needed to speak with the pack-kin on a serious matter, he did it at their homes or in the entrance room—or in his study if he trusted them enough. But a lord is supposed to have a place that expresses his authority."

He guides me down the hall past the staircase to a room at the far end, a wing of the castle that didn't exist in Oakmeet's condensed replica. With a magic-tinged word from August, the door swings open.

I'm not sure the room has been used at all since we returned to Hearthshire, but Sylas has clearly ensured it was cleaned. The wooden walls and floor seem to gleam even more vibrantly than the rest of the castle. A thick red rug with a violet leaf pattern runs from the doorway down the length of the room to a tall seat of a darker wood. It's plated with gold panels with etchings of forest scenes, the seat covered with a layer of moss.

Crimson drapes tumble from the walls on either side of the throne-like chair. As we walk toward it, several glowing orbs gleam brighter on the high ceiling above us, set in a pattern like a petaled flower.

Several embroidered cushions like the ones Whitt sets out for his revels lie in a stack by the curtains. August grabs one and puts it on the floor near the throne's foot. He stations himself just behind it, next to the throne, and motions for me to sit on the cushion. He's put on a stern expression, but he caresses my hair as if to say he's still here with me, no matter what.

Thankfully for my nerves, it doesn't take long for the others to appear. Whitt saunters in first, shooting a quizzical glance our way, to which August offers an uncertain grimace. The spymaster takes in my dress and ambles over to the other side of the throne. He's just taken his spot there when Sylas marches through the doorway, nudging Harper ahead of him.

If my friend looked nervous before, now I'd say she's outright terrified. She's tangled her fingers in the strands of her hair just below her shoulder, and her back stays rigid as she walks along the rug to halt in front of the throne. Her eyelids twitch with frantic blinks. Any color her normally cream-pale skin used to contain has drained away. She clutches her hair tighter, watching Sylas settle himself on his seat.

The fae lord's dark eye blazes with contained ferocity. He keeps his usual steady tone, but there's an edge to it that demands answers. "Harper of Hearthshire, born of Oakmeet, do you know why I've called you here?"

"I—I'm not sure," she says faintly.

"Did you construct the dress that Talia is currently wearing?"

Her gaze skims over me. I think she stiffens even more when she must notice the misshapen shells. "I did."

"Every part of it, by your own hand? The fabric, the embellishments?"

She pauses, her mouth working. I know the fae don't lie if they can help it. It damages their connection to the Heart, the source of any magical power they wield.

Harper takes a quavering breath. "I made every part of it except—except the beads, my lord."

Sylas leans forward, his pose like a wolf about to pounce. "And where did you get the beads then, my pack-kin?"

"They were a gift. I thought they worked well with that fabric."

"A gift from whom?"

"From—from—" A quiver runs through her, and she ducks her head, covering it with her hands. Her voice spills out of her faster, just shy of a wail. "I'm sorry. They said no one would notice. They said it wouldn't really matter unless— I thought it would be fine. I didn't want to hurt anyone."

A chill trickles through me, pooling in my belly. She must have realized she *could* have hurt me. But she made the dress and gave it to me, encouraged me to wear it, despite that.

Sylas repeats his question, his tone even darker than

before. "Who gave you the beads that were shaped like shells?"

"Lili and Irabel of Dusk-by-the-Heart," Harper whispers.

I knew Ambrose's pack-kin had to be involved, but my heart sinks farther hearing her confirm it.

"Did they tell you to weave them into a dress made for Talia?" Sylas asks.

"Yes."

"Did they say what those beads would do?"

"They said—they said the magic would pick up things people said and hold it inside. To prove whether Talia really is best off with you. That if she really is as happy here as you say, then it'll show that." She presses her knuckles to her lips, but a sound like a sob escapes her. "I thought it couldn't do anything harmful, then. It might even prove that she should stay here."

My hand rises to my neckline, to the tiny melted lumps of the beads. If we hadn't figured out the trick, if Ambrose had gotten his hands on them with whatever conversations they'd absorbed—he might have found out all sorts of things that could harm us that have nothing to do with me belonging here. Things about my magical power, about whatever plans we're making against him. The chill inside me prickles deeper.

Sylas pushes to his feet, looming even taller over the young fae woman. His voice reverberates through the room. "Really? You truly believed that the people who've proven themselves our enemies would give you the full measure of their plans? That it was safe to trust them with something you'd have your supposed friend wear at her *throat*? What in the world could have possessed you to take them at their word and go through with this plan rather than bringing it straight to me?"

Harper flinches. "I didn't know what else to do. I'd talked to them about my dresses, and they promised they'd wear them and tell the other packs around the Heart how they got them as long as I'd do one thing for them. I didn't know what it was. I—I took a vow. I know I should have asked more first, but it just seemed—I never thought— And when they told me, they said if I didn't, if I told anyone about it, they'd warn everyone against me instead. Say I'd broken my word to them, betrayed them, so none of the other packs would *ever* want me traveling to their domains."

"And what were you meant to do after? Find some excuse to take the dress back from Talia and return the beads to Ambrose's kin at some social gathering?"

Her answer is so weak I barely hear it. "Yes, my lord."

"I see. So you chose selfishness and your own gain over the safety of *your* entire pack." Sylas lets out a huff with a growl to it. "*Your* pack-kin shouldn't want you around. You have betrayed every one of them, including me, by putting your faith in these traitors rather than your own lord. Now you'll find yourself with no pack at all. I can't have someone in our midst who values what she has here so little."

My former friend's posture crumples with a shudder. Her head bows low. Her hands paw at her face. But she doesn't argue. She takes several gulps of air and then forces herself to straighten up again. When she does, she's looking at me, her eyes red-rimmed.

"I'm so sorry, Talia. I didn't *want* to, so I shouldn't have, no matter how scared I was. I shouldn't have let the things they said get inside my head. You deserve a better friend than that."

She turns to Sylas. "I—I accept your judgment. I understand why you can't trust me now. I wouldn't trust me either. I hope you know I never— It wasn't that— You've always been a good lord to us, to me. I'm so sorry. What would you have me do now?"

Even knowing what she did, my heart wrenches at the miserable resignation in the question. She *sounds* truly sorry. I've seen what the fae can be like, how they can treat people they think are worth less than themselves. She had choices, and she made ones that could have ruined us, but that doesn't mean it'd have been easy for her to go the other way.

I know what it's like to feel caged, how desperate you can get, the risks you become willing to take. I can see that anguish on Harper's face. Maybe she's never been caged anywhere as literally as me, but to have her dream within her grasp only to be threatened with seeing it utterly crushed for the rest of her long, long life…

I can't hate her. I'm not sure I'm even really angry. The chill has condensed into an ache I can only call sadness.

"You will go and collect your things, as much as you can carry by your own means," Sylas says. "I'll give you an hour to prepare and say your good-byes. You must leave this domain. You may no longer claim you're of Hearthshire. If anyone asks, you will tell them you've been banished for acting against your lord. Either you'll find another domain that will accept you, or you'll have to find your own way in the gaplands in between."

If she has to say she betrayed her former lord, I can't imagine any other lord will allow her to join their pack. The droop of Harper's shoulders suggests she's come to the same conclusion. She dips her head in acknowledgment. "Yes, my lord." Without a second's hesitation, she turns and starts walking toward the doorway.

She's taken three steps when I find myself on my feet, propelled by a rush of conflicted emotion. "Wait."

Both Harper and Sylas look over their shoulders at me, Harper startled, Sylas puzzled. It's Harper's expression that solidifies my unsteady burst of resolve.

She didn't expect anyone to stand up for her. She doesn't believe she deserves it, because she understands what a huge mistake she made.

"What is it, Talia?" Sylas asks.

I inhale sharply. "I'm the one she wronged the most directly. Shouldn't I get a say in her punishment?"

The fae lord eyes me. Anger still flares in his dark eye, but it's not directed at me. His tone gentles. "What would you say, then?"

"I think… Harper has never been in a situation before where she had to deal with this kind of conflict. That she did the wrong thing because she was scared and faced with enemies much more experienced at pushing people around. I don't think *she's* our enemy. She was the first person in the pack who really welcomed me and made me feel like I could belong."

"I recognize your points. Where are you going with them?"

I swallow the lump in my throat. "If there's some way we could give her a second chance, have her prove that she can be as loyal as she needs to be, then I'd like to do that rather than sending her away."

Sylas sinks back down in his seat, rubbing his jaw pensively. "I hesitate to give her another chance to betray the pack. Do you have some idea of an appropriate test that wouldn't put us at further risk?"

Do I? I think over everything Harper told us, everything we've already dealt with from Ambrose, groping for an answer.

A glimmer of inspiration sparks. "Ambrose doesn't know that you found out about the beads. We could give him false information through Harper. You could cast the same spell yourself, couldn't you? We could decide what conversations we let them absorb, and then Harper can deliver the dress the way she was meant to. If she doesn't give away what we're doing, and Ambrose acts on the information we pass on, then we'd know she kept her word."

"In this one instance," Sylas says. "That wouldn't guarantee she couldn't turn against her kin if threatened in the future."

Harper has been gaping at me, disbelieving, this entire time. Now she spins toward Sylas. In a sudden swift movement, she throws herself forward on her knees, dropping her head so low her hair puddles on the floor.

"My lord, this is my home. I don't want anything as much as I want to stay with this pack. I'll do everything Talia said, and I'll give you my true name. You can command me never to act against you, never to even speak to anyone outside the pack, whatever you need to be sure of me—"

Sylas makes a rough sound, cutting her off. He stares down at her. "You're offering me your true name? You can never take that back."

"I know," she says, still bowed to the floor. "It would be worth it not to lose my family, my friends, everything that you provide for us. I'd offer it gladly. Nothing—nothing I ever wanted beyond this domain is worth it if I have no home to come back to."

There's a long silence. Whitt shifts on his feet but says nothing. I wonder if he's not supposed to comment unless Sylas asks for his opinion. I glance back at August, who inclines his head slightly to me as if in approval but stays quiet too.

Finally, Sylas stands again. "Up," he says, and Harper scrambles off her knees. He peers down at her, all incisive authoritative power, and in that moment it isn't hard to picture him standing among the arch-lords as one of their own.

He clears his throat meaningfully. "I don't want absolute control over you. I want pack-kin who believe in me, not forced into loyalty. But I recognize the sacrifice you were willing to make and what it says about your dedication to Hearthshire. As Talia has intervened on your behalf, I will revise my original judgment. You will deliver the beads to the conspirators according to plan without giving any sign of our awareness. You will never act in any way that could harm this pack again. My cadre and I will be keeping a close eye on you. If we see *any* sign you've betrayed your commitments again, it won't be banishment you'll face —it'll be execution. You can accept those terms, or you can leave."

Harper's face lights up as if he's handed over her greatest wish. "I accept them. Yes. Thank you, my lord. If anyone should ever ask me to act in any way that affects the pack again, I'll come straight to you."

"Then it will be so."

Sylas steps down from his seat and motions August and Whitt over to him. As the three men move off to the side to consult in lowered voices, Harper eases toward me. She snatches up my hands to clasp them in hers, and my shoulders stiffen.

"Thank you so much, Talia. I thought I'd really have to —I never wanted it to be like this—I really am sorry. The whole time after you went into the castle with the dress, I was all tangled up thinking about it—"

She moves as if to hug me, and I find that for all the compassion I've felt in the past several minutes, I've reached my limit here. I jerk back, my skin twitching. Harper blinks at me.

My voice comes out rough. "I didn't want you to have to lose everything over this. I know Ambrose's pack-kin put you in an awful situation. But you still—you could have put *me* in a situation that was so much more horrible. I think it's going to take some time before I can really be friends with you again."

Her face falls, which I guess at least means that my friendship was worth something to her. "All right," she says quietly. "That makes sense. I won't forget this—what I did or what you did. If you want someone to go roaming around with or just to talk with later on, I'll be here. I'm sorry."

She slips out of the room, leaving me wondering why, when I'm sure I did the right thing, now *I* feel all tangled up inside.

20

Talia

The faint rocking of the carriage leaves me unusually queasy. Tucking myself into the seat at the stern, apart from everyone else in the waning sunlight that reaches the uncovered spot beyond the canopy, I drag in several slow breaths.

I wasn't this nervous the last time we headed off to some fae party in another domain. Of course, last time it was at Donovan's palace, and this time we're being hosted by a lord whose allegiances Sylas isn't totally sure of. And last time I didn't know Ambrose was willing to have his people wound me and to bring my former tormenters around. I have no idea what to expect from him tonight.

At least he has no idea what we're up to either. At the other end of the carriage, Harper sits next to her mother, her own smile tight with nerves. She's carrying a small pouch at her hip containing the beads Sylas constructed that she'll say she removed from my dress after I'd worn it around the castle for a day. She's supposed to stop to chat with Irabel at this party and hand them over.

I haven't really talked to her since the confrontation in the audience room three days ago. I hope that carrying out this plan will loosen some of the tension I've been carrying in my gut. I don't *like* going around with a sense of betrayal twined through me.

Whitt drifts to the back of the carriage and props himself against the wall next to me, turning his face to the sunlight. "This is too nice a spot for you to keep it to yourself, mite."

"I wouldn't stop you from sharing it." I inhale in the crisply floral late-afternoon air and close my eyes. When I open them again, Whitt is studying me.

The question tumbles out, quiet but insistent enough that I can't hold it in. "Are you thinking that I went too soft on her? That I shouldn't have spoken up for her after what she did?"

Whitt shrugs casually enough that I believe he wasn't stewing over that subject. "No. Your compassion is part of what makes you admirable. You seemed clear-eyed enough about it—and about her." He pauses. "I do hope I won't have to act on Sylas's warning, though."

That if Harper's actions endanger the pack again, she'll be executed. A fresh jab of nausea prods my stomach. I glance toward my friend, taking in her pensive expression as she gazes at the landscape beyond the carriage. She looks as if she's taking the situation seriously enough. She offered Sylas total control over her.

But I never would have thought she'd turn against the pack in the first place, even under threat.

"What exactly happens if someone has your true name?" I find myself asking. "They can order you around, make you do whatever they want, just by saying it?"

"If the other party decides to be a tyrant about it, yes." Whitt drums his fingers lightly against the curved wood. "I've never experienced it myself. Most of us have the good sense to keep our true names to ourselves and not subject ourselves to masters who'd demand them. But from what I understand, it has some similarities to a soul-twined bond, only much more one-sided unless both parties exchange them. And not nearly as automatic, vivid, or immediate."

"But still pretty intense."

He nods. "Sylas would have had command over her entire being—he could have not just given orders but delved into her thoughts and emotions to whatever extent his magical focus allowed, cast his own thoughts into her head from afar if he wished to. Give someone your true name, and you can never escape them."

He nudges my ankle teasingly with his foot. "*You* don't have to worry about that, though, mighty one, seeing as you don't have a true name to begin with."

"Right. But I have essentially no magical defenses, so any powerful fae could probably do all of that if they really wanted to without needing any secret name."

Whitt pulls a face. "Touché. All the more reason to be grateful our lord is the type to refuse the power of a true name even over a traitor."

That's true. As my gaze slides to Sylas, who's speaking with Astrid and Brigit where most of the pack-kin joining us are gathered beneath the canopy, my queasiness retreats under a swell of affection. How incredibly lucky am I that

I ended up with him and not one of the many other fae lords who'd be much less likely to care about a human's wellbeing, let alone listen to her opinions when they conflict with his own?

Whitt steps in front of me with a small smile, his tall frame blocking my view of the rest of the carriage—and everyone else's view of his hand moving to my face. He traces my lips with his thumb in a gesture so tender it feels like a kiss. "Careful you don't look at him like that when there are hostile parties around, or someone might realize he's more than just your keeper."

His tone is teasing rather than serious. I glance up to meet his ocean-blue eyes, lost for a second in their depths. "And how am I allowed to look at you?"

A smirk curls Whitt's mouth. "I'd like to say however you wish, but it's probably best you save the besotted gazes for August while we're among other packs. The rest of the time, I'll take as many as you care to aim my way."

He pulls away from me, swiveling to consider our progress. The sun has just dropped beneath the spiky treetops to the west. A violet glow stretches across the sky, and the shadows are thickening all around us. Amber lights glint in the distance, reflecting off a castle of spires that have a metallic sheen. I'm guessing that's our destination.

The event my fae companions called a "ball" looks an awful lot like one of Whitt's revels, only with a lot more people and a little more orderly. The lords and their pack-kin want to keep a certain amount of propriety around each other, I guess.

As we draw closer, I make out several low, gleaming

tables made of what looks like the same rose gold as the nearby castle, spread with matching platters heaped with food and crystal goblets only a smidge less ornately carved than the ones at Donovan's banquet. Long velvet cushions and blankets lie across the grass around them, although no one is doing more than perching gracefully on them at a polite distance at the moment. Will the fae start to couple off into more intimate activities as the night goes on, or is that kind of merry-making reserved for private revels?

Most of the guests are still on their feet, spread out in small clusters around the tables and farther across the field. Their formal finery gleams beneath the glowing orbs. I run my fingers over my own dress—the first one Harper ever gave me, with strips of fabric melding together into what looks like a landscape of rippling treetops. Between my dyed hair and fae-styled clothes, I could almost pass for one of their own... but not quite.

Well, it doesn't matter what anyone from the other packs thinks. My men, my pack-kin—they see me as a worthy presence. They're the only ones whose opinions I care about.

The carriage stops in a row between the castle and the area set up for the ball. As August helps me scramble out, my gaze darts over the meandering guests. There's Ambrose with his soul-twined mate, Tristan with a woman I assume is his, Celia lifting a goblet in toast, Donovan laughing at something his companions have said, various cadre members and other pack-kin around I recognize as well as strangers... but no sign of Aerik's or Cole's striking hair.

I exhale, tension flowing out of me with the breath.

One small mercy. Of course, there are still a gazillion other things for me to be tense about.

I watch Harper slip into the scattered crowd and then jerk my eyes away. We have to make sure we don't look as if we're aware of what she's getting up to tonight.

Several of the other guests have already drifted over to welcome Sylas. A woman in a dress that glitters with streams of emeralds snatches Whitt's arm and tugs him toward one of the tables. Sylas beckons August, and Astrid steps into place beside me, staying within arm's reach in this company.

"Here we are," I say, suddenly wishing I wasn't. But this gambit was my idea. I should at least be here to see it through. And it looks better for Sylas's case the more I show I'm comfortable enough in his care to come with him to large gatherings like this.

I catch several of the fae peering at me and murmuring to each other, but no one approaches me directly. Whether they're more nervous of Sylas's claim to me or Ambrose's, it's hard to say. Maybe both in combination mean I at least don't have to field a bunch of prying questions.

Astrid and I meander over to one of the tables where she points out the "safest" foods for me to sample. The buoyant voices and vibrant giggles around us suggest that quite a few of the guests are getting tipsy.

Harper's parents have joined the other musicians who're attending the festivities, and within a few minutes they're playing a lilting tune that brings a bunch of the fae together in a clearer patch of field to dance, though with less abandon than I'm used to at the revels. They might be here to enjoy themselves, but they aren't going to forget themselves in the process.

I retreat to the fringes of the gathering with a pastry like a crumbly croissant clutched in my hand. At my nibbling, it dissolves on my tongue with a cloying buttery flavor. I can't see Harper now, although I don't want to search too obviously for her. I spotted Namior and Tesfira ambling by earlier, so presumably their daughters are around here somewhere too.

Astrid stands next to me, taking delicate bites of a shallow berry-filled tart that's as wide as her hand. She doesn't sway with the music winding across the field or appear the slightest bit put out to be stuck babysitting while everyone else parties.

"Do you like coming to these things?" I ask.

The warrior makes a neutral gesture with her free hand. "To be honest, I wouldn't come along if it wasn't to guard you. I'm much more comfortable in trousers and work shirts than this." She plucks at the skirt of her own dress, a subdued gray sprinkled with ivory embroidery, still way fancier than anything I've seen her wearing back in Hearthshire. "Don't worry yourself, though. It isn't any hardship. I'm happy to serve my lord, and you're not exactly difficult company."

The corner of my mouth quirks up. "So you're all work and no play?" I pause. I know she's old from the lines that have formed around the hollows of her face, but with fae, it's hard to figure out exactly what that means. "How long *have* you been working for Sylas?"

"His whole life," she says. "Well, as long as he's been established as a lord in his own right. I was part of his father's security contingent before that and his grandmother's before that."

"You left their domain to go with him?"

She nods and takes another bite of her tart. She takes her time chewing it as if chewing over the rest of her answer at the same time. "His father... wasn't happy about it. But he didn't own me. And he'd worked my mate so hard in the kitchens that he nearly lost his hand to an oven, so I wasn't all that happy with the old lord either."

The hint of snark to her voice with that last sentence speaks of a woman who's a lot more than just a devoted servant of her pack. And also— "You have a mate?"

She chuckles. "Don't look so startled. There was a time when these ancient bones had much lovelier flesh on them."

My cheeks flare. "I didn't mean—you still look totally—"

Astrid waves off my protests. "It's all right. You haven't seen me with him. That's because I *had* a mate. He was already a good century older than me, and his time under the old lord hadn't been kind on his body. I think the banishment broke something in his spirit. He passed within a few years of us going to Oakmeet."

"I'm sorry."

"Not your fault. He had a good long life. He'd have been glad to know we made it back to our rightful place." She gazes out over the crowd. "*He* liked these sorts of things. I used to come to humor him. I'm not usually the melancholy sort, but it does remind me of when he was still with us." She holds up her last bit of tart. "If he'd brought the baked goods, they'd have been twice as good."

Despite the trace of grief laced through her story, her critical tone in that last sentence brings a smile back to my lips. "He was quite the chef?"

"Oh, yes." She grins back at me. "I understand your taste in men. The ones who know their way around a kitchen are definitely keepers."

As if he's sensed that he's been mentioned, August emerges from the crowd. He beams at both of us, with a tip of his head to Astrid like a thanks for taking care of me. "You can't come with us to a ball and not dance," he says to me. "And if you're going to dance, I'd like to have the honor."

I take his hand when he holds it out to me, ignoring the nervous skip of my pulse at the thought of how many of the other guests may be watching us. "I guess I can't say no when you put it that way."

The musicians are playing a slower-paced song, which suits me just fine. August lifts our twined hands and sets my other hand on his waist, and we sway and turn with the music. I'm not anywhere near as elegant or smooth on my feet as the ladies around us, but from the way he smiles down at me, I don't think he minds.

They can speculate however they want. Right now, I'm his.

Some of the other ladies mind, though. Whenever my gaze slips away from August's, I catch narrowed eyes and subtle sneers aimed our way—and I'm sure it's not him they're resenting.

My fingers tighten around his, but I can't help wondering exactly how long I'll be his for. How long will he be mine before he finds a real partner among his equals?

A constricting sensation wraps around my lungs. A fae woman near us gives her hair a disdainful toss; one I notice farther off at the edge of the dancing area smiles but with a glint of fangs. I yank my gaze back to August's face, turned even more handsome with his fond expression, but I can't shake the impression that with every passing second I stay here in his arms, I'm painting a bigger target on my back.

My uneasiness must show. August's forehead furrows. "Are you all right, Talia?"

"Yeah. I—I think maybe I just need some space. I'm still not really used to big crowds like this."

The flash of concern in his eyes at my half-lie sends a pang of guilt through me, but he leads me through the other dancers and off across the field where I really can breathe again. When we've left the other guests far enough behind that their laughter is nothing more than a distant tinkling, my lungs relax.

I tip my head back to gaze up at the stars gleaming into view against the darkening sky. "Thank you."

August squeezes my shoulder. "Take as long as you need, Sweetness. You don't have to push yourself. No one expects you to be the belle of the ball."

No, but they wish I wasn't here at all. How many of the lovely lords and ladies and their kin back there think my proper place is in a cage?

At the hiss of boots through the grass, I turn to see Sylas and Whitt walking over to join us. "Was someone bothering Talia?" Sylas asks, his dark eye already glowering in anticipation of an appropriate target.

I can't tell them what really bothered me. It isn't even really the fae women's fault. How could they not consider me an intruder, an obstacle to their goals? They don't know me as anything other than the source of their cure.

"I was just feeling a little overwhelmed," I say, managing a smile. It does feel good standing here surrounded by my three men, even if I don't know how much longer they'll be completely mine. I feel totally sure in that moment that no matter where our romance leads or how it peters out, they won't stop caring about me. They'll still defend me and my place in their pack. That should be enough.

Whitt cocks his head with an arch of one eyebrow as if he doesn't totally believe my explanation, but before he can prod, we're joined by two much-less-welcome wanderers. Ambrose and Tristan are strolling across the field to meet us.

Away from the glowing orbs, shadows fall across the faces of the arch-lord and his cousin. The growing darkness can't disguise the menace that their every movement conveys. I force myself to keep my head up and my shoulders squared, but my hand gropes for August's again of its own accord.

Sylas and Whitt turn to face our enemies, drawing closer in the same movement so that I'm partly shielded by Sylas's brawny form. I can't imagine the arch-lord attempting an outright attack with so many witnesses nearby, but my heart thuds faster. Has he figured out our trick with the beads?

The two fae men stop a few feet away, their smiles haughty. "Where are you off to with our precious commodity?" Ambrose asks.

I'm not sure August has made any effort to disguise the growl in his voice. "She needed a moment away from the crowd."

The arch-lord hums to himself. "I suppose it's a good thing you've developed such an affection for the thing. It should make the logical next step easier. If she does end up remaining in Hearthshire, that is, which I very much doubt she will."

I'd like to bare *my* teeth at him, but I suspect he'd only laugh. I don't know what he's insinuating, though.

It seems Sylas doesn't either. "What 'logical next step' are you referring to, my lord?"

Ambrose lets out a chuckle that has a scoffing sound to it. "I would have thought you could put the pieces together yourself, Lord Sylas, with all the wisdom you claim to possess. The sage's words made it clear enough."

Whitt's smile is so sharp it could cut glass. "Why don't you pretend we're imbeciles and fill us in?"

"The largest flaw in our cure is the fact that she's dust-destined," Ambrose says in a tone that suggests he thinks both men *are* imbeciles. "But Nuldar said her connection to the curse was passed on to her from her grandmother. Indeed, that it has strengthened with each passing. In that case, she should also be able to pass it on, and her short lifespan won't be of consequence. I would recommend we breed her with fae of various status and with another human to determine the combination that results in the strongest carry-through—"

I flinch the moment he says the words "breed her," and August takes a step forward to come shoulder-to-shoulder with Whitt. The muscles in his arms have gone so taut I can see their bulge even through the thick fabric of his formal shirt. "She's not a brood-mare," he snaps.

Sylas holds up his hand to stop August from continuing, but his voice is no less harsh. "Arch-lord or not, *no one* talks about my pack-kin that way."

Ambrose snorts. "Your *pack-kin*? She's a dung-bodied human waif. And I will speak about her however I want. You know I'm right, Sylas. It's the obvious solution to all our problems, no more chasing after larger answers required."

My chest has clenched up again, my breath coming short. Dizziness whirls through my thoughts. If August wasn't still gripping my hand so tightly, I'm not sure I'd be keeping my balance.

Ambrose wants to force me to get pregnant, to have kids—kids with all different sorts of men, of *his* choosing rather than mine. Babies he'd take from me the moment they're born to test them and treat them like nothing but a container for the Seelie's cure, just like he sees me...

Every part of that idea makes me want to vomit. But even I can see the sick sort of sense it makes.

If I can pass on the cure, they *don't* need any other answers. They only need to keep my family line alive. As soon as I bear children who hold the cure in their blood too, as soon as there's more than one human with that power, none of us will be indispensable either. They won't have to worry so much about keeping me alive.

Even if the trio of arch-lords agrees to have me stay with Sylas, will they agree to order him to "breed" me?

Sylas leaves no doubt about how he'd respond to such an order. "I've claimed her as a member of my pack, and so she is. You will treat her with due respect or recognize that you insult *me* just as much as her. And I'm granted every right to defend my pack under the laws you uphold."

"I don't see why you're so offended about the proposition, Lord Sylas," Tristan says. "You'd have plenty of 'right' to her yourself. Unless you're concerned you're not up to the job, considering even your own soul-twined mate wasn't satisfied with you."

Ambrose shoots his cousin a glance as if he'd have preferred to do all the talking, but he doesn't interject. Sylas's body has gone perfectly, frighteningly still. His lips curl back, showing his full fangs. "What was that, Lord Tristan?"

A glimmer of anxiety flits through Tristan's eyes. He's not oblivious to the danger he's courting. But he appears to think getting this jab in is worth it. "Isleen got awfully restless, didn't she? Perhaps if the *right* lord had conquered her a few times as well as she needed it, she wouldn't have gone off making trouble and bringing retribution down on you all."

Sylas's stance tenses as if to lunge, and it occurs to me through my horror that Tristan might even *want* him to lash out. That would be an excellent piece of evidence for their claim that he's in no state to properly care for me, wouldn't it—if he attacks another lord over what they can say was only a little joking around?

Panic shivers through me, and my free hand flies up to clutch at the back of his padded vest. Not in any way that would look overly intimate—Whitt's warning is still floating through my mind—but enough that he has to feel the weight of my hold.

Stay with me, I plead silently. *Don't let them provoke you.* Even though I'd give anything to spring at these assholes and tear them to pieces myself if I had the ability.

Sylas shifts forward just enough to pull against my grasp, I tighten my grip with a lurch of my heart—and he stays there. His teeth are still bared, his fingers curled with the tips of claws protruding, but he must master his wolf and his temper, because no more of it shows other than a flare of anger in his dark eye.

"May maggots eat those who speak so ill of the dead," he says around a snarl, and fixes his gaze on Ambrose. "Put a muzzle on your cousin before he embarrasses your family any more by lowering himself past dust itself."

Ambrose hesitates. From his expression, I'm not sure he was in on whatever plan Tristan is carrying out. Maybe his cousin came up with that ploy in the moment. Before either of them can take it any farther, a few more of the guests wander our way, curious about what's happening.

The arch-lord doesn't want to look petty or hostile in front of impartial witnesses who might report back to his colleagues. He jerks his hand toward Tristan, and they both stalk off, leaving the four of us in shaken silence.

21

Whitt

If Ambrose and his mangy mutt of a cousin had kept their mouths shut last night, today's news would count as a victory. As it is, I walk into Sylas's study at his summons feeling like I'm approaching a crumbling wall with only a speck of plaster to mend it.

The urge to take a gulp of some sort of fermented lubrication winds through my gut, but I ignore it. I indulged plenty at the last revel and wasn't terribly pleased with the results afterward. There's no smoothing the edges off of this horrible situation we've found ourselves in. I need to experience all the barbs at their full sharpness to navigate a way through.

Our glorious leader—who's been absent since I woke until now, not even showing up for meals—is braced in front of his desk rather than sitting behind it, which already doesn't bode well for whatever he's discovered that he means to share. August and Talia have already arrived,

248

Talia perched on one of the armchairs and August next to her with a comforting hand on her shoulder. Despite the tension in the air, they both manage to smile at me on my entrance with genuine warmth.

To dust with it. I set aside thoughts of the troubles hanging over us for just a moment to walk over and steal a quick kiss from our lover. Talia grasps the front of my shirt to tug me even closer and extend the meeting of our lips, making my animalistic instincts stir more than is probably appropriate for this setting. I ease back half expecting a glower from one of the other two parties in the room, but August's smile has only widened. Even Sylas's expression has softened a tad.

At least we have this—this unity between us. A lord and his cadre and their lady. I straighten up with a little more confidence that whatever Ambrose intends, we'll crush those plans and laugh about it afterward.

"The musician's daughter fulfilled her end of the bargain satisfactorily, and our favorite arch-lord has started taking the bait," I report. "I heard from one of my people just before dinner that someone, presumably one of Ambrose's pack-kin, made a tentative foray to the spot at the edge of our domain we made a point of mentioning in the presence of those magicked shells. Nothing was done that we could pin on him as wrong-doing, but we'll see how the rest pans out."

Sylas inclines his head in recognition of that minor success. "I'm glad to hear it. He may be too cautious to extend himself far enough that we could collar him based on the false information we sent, but at the very least it should distract him for some time."

Talia looks down at her hands, now balled in her lap, and then up at Sylas. Her voice comes out steady but strained. "What he said about... about 'breeding' me." Her color turns sickly just saying the word. "Could the arch-lords force me to have kids like that?"

The fact that she even needs to ask makes my own stomach turn over. My claws itch to shoot from my fingers and then preferably sever Ambrose's head from his body. I grit my teeth, hating the answer I know Sylas has to give, wishing I had some way of shielding her from the worst the fae world would throw her way.

Sylas's face becomes utterly grim again. "I believe Donovan will stay on our side. But Celia would cast the deciding vote, and Ambrose has persuaded her on other matters. Even if I let Donovan take you in, their votes could overrule any decision he'd make for you." His tone darkens even more with a hint of a snarl. "But it doesn't matter what ruling they make. We won't let them dictate what you do with your life or your body. Whatever we have to do to stop it, we will."

It won't be pretty if we have to outright reject a direct order from the arch-lords. Everyone in this room knows that, including Talia. She sinks back in her chair, reaching to squeeze August's hand.

"I don't want you to have to defy your own rulers," she says in a small voice that tears at my heart. "They'd call you a traitor for that, won't they?"

"It doesn't matter. When a decree is unjust, the only just thing is to refuse it, regardless of who passes it down." Sylas lets out a rough breath. "But perhaps it won't matter at all. If Ambrose keeps up his attempts against Donovan

250

and we can expose his own treachery soon enough, I may be the one holding that throne, and my vote with Donovan's will stop any further talk along those lines."

The ease with which he mentions that possibility prickles over me and dredges up an even stronger desire for the wine in my flask. I bite back any of the acidic remarks that want to spring to my tongue.

Such a great honor the youngest arch-lord is dangling in front of our lord. So much more glory for Sylas—and heaps more stress for August and me if we find ourselves the sole cadre-chosen of an arch-lord, the front line between him and every other schemer out there.

But no one would bother to ask the *cadre* how they'd feel about such a promotion, would they? Our sole purpose is to support our lord's ambitions.

I know my bitter thoughts aren't even fair. Sylas didn't ask for this, and he hasn't got much choice now that the honor has been offered, not without offending the man who's currently our key ally. If he *did* ask me, I'd tell him to accept the boon with all possible enthusiasm. So I swallow down the prickling sensation and focus on what's in front of me.

I'm about to ask if our actual favorite arch-lord has made any suggestions for exposing Ambrose when Sylas goes on, with a hint of vigor coming into his pose. "And I may have an opportunity to force Ambrose's hand. Tristan said more than *he* should have last night."

The memory of that lord's sneering remarks sets my teeth on edge all over again. "What do you mean?"

Sylas folds his arms over his chest, still grim but with a determined air. "I've given a lot of thought to the wording of his insults... and I believe I have grounds to call a formal challenge against him. Wolf-to-wolf, I'm certain I could beat him. Then we'll have him at the mercy of our yield. Ambrose won't stand by and watch his planned puppet be shackled by our demands. He'll have to make a move—a major one, and with much less time to plan than would be ideal. We'll be ready to catch him at it."

Grounds for a formal challenge... The queasy sensation that ran through me earlier rises up again, the dinner I abruptly wish I'd eaten less of starting to churn. "What grounds would those be?" He can't mean—

Sylas's jaw clenches. "You know that part of the reason I didn't pick up on Isleen's full intentions when she moved with her family against Ambrose was that I'd distanced myself from our connection because of tensions between us. It didn't seem relevant to mention at the time the exact, personal nature of those tensions... She betrayed our vows as mates with another man. Based on Tristan's remarks, *he* was the one who dallied with her. Interfering with a soul-twined bond and threatening the hoped-for family line is an undeniable offense."

Ah. There it is. August is nodding, his eyes widening —he clearly didn't know about the transgression. Talia bites her lip, looking pained on Sylas's behalf but not shocked. Had he already told her?

Those thoughts pass through my mind as if it's detached itself from my body, where my stomach is still roiling around and my veins have turned to ice. I'm not sure I could work my jaw if I wanted to. Every part of me seems to have shut down except this distant sort of awareness unspooling farther from the rest of me by the second.

I should have anticipated this development. It's my job to predict every eventuality. But some wretchedly naïve particle of me kept clinging to the hope that the reckoning was actually behind us.

"I would never have wanted to air the affair in any sort of public way," Sylas continues. "But if it gives us the advantage we need, I'll go out there tomorrow—I'll call Tristan before the arch-lords and confront him, and—"

Oh, no. The ice is seeping right into my chest now with a crackling of panic. I grab a hold of myself just enough to keep down my dinner and blurt out the words, "You can't know for sure it was him."

Sylas blinks at the interruption. "He all but admitted it last night. Those comments about her getting restless, about how she needed more from another man?"

"I assumed they were the most cutting insults his feeble mind could come up with, knowing that you and she had clearly not been on the best of terms at the end."

"I considered that, which is why I've been gone today tracking down a few leads. I've been able to confirm that on the evening when it happened, Tristan had departed from his castle with only one of his cadre-chosen, with plenty of time that he could have met up with Isleen by the time it happened."

With one of his cadre-chosen. Then beyond a doubt Tristan has a witness to his whereabouts. But even if he didn't, if questioned before the Heart, it'll be clear he can't get away with lying.

I hurtle onward, scrambling for the most convincing

argument. "Nevertheless, he said nothing specific. You can't know for sure where he went that day. If you bring him before the trio and make an accusation like that, and he's able to say it *wasn't* him, think of the consequences. Ambrose will spin it so you look unstable. Celia will resent the unnecessary imposition and be less inclined to take our side."

Sylas waves his hand dismissively. "I've endured taunts across several decades in regards to our fall from favor, and this is the first time anyone has raised the specter of my mate's lack of fidelity. And he'd be exactly the sort of dalliance Isleen would have chosen. A lord I've always clashed with, who I didn't think highly of and who had a low opinion of me in return—one with closer ties to the power around the Heart—who better to try to wound me with?"

I can think of a few.

"We have to make some kind of gamble," Sylas says. "There's too much at stake and too little time left to simply stand back and hope Ambrose makes a misstep. I'm certain enough. Unless you have any other reason to think this is a poor course of action, I'll begin making arrangements."

The panic that lanced through me is melting into a frigid pool of dread that saturates my innards.

I can't let him do this. There's no avoiding it any longer. I am his cadre-chosen, and I owe it to him and our pack to prevent this mistake—not least of all because it stems from the greatest mistake of my own.

"No arrangements." My voice comes out hoarse, and

Sylas knits his brow. I force out the rest of the words I need to say. "I *know* it wasn't Tristan."

My lord frowns. "How could you possibly— Surely if you were aware of some betrayal that I hadn't acted on back then, you'd have told me before now?"

August and Talia are staring at me too. I swallow thickly. Of course there would have to be an audience for this moment. Of course it would have to be the two other people who matter most to me.

Well, why not? Perhaps they deserve to know the truth as much as the man in front of me does.

The words tumble out faster than before, a bitter pill I've been trying and failing to digest for far too long. "I know it wasn't Tristan because it was *me*. She came to me. I—"

I stop there, because the fury that flares in Sylas's dark eye is enough to kill a lesser man. Certainly my voice is no match for it. And it's not just fury but a deep, searing pain that draws the furrow of his scar deeper and twists his mouth. My wolf recoils inside me.

What a maggot-ridden fool I was to ever think I'd already faced any real reprisal for my crime. None of the coldness and the distance and the growled remarks held a candle to this. His expression flays me to the bone.

I deserve nothing less.

I've done what I need to do. I don't think it would make any of us feel any better in the long run if I stick around for him to literally flay my flesh. Feeling as tattered as if I've already been sliced open, I duck my head. My last statement scrapes my throat on the way out.

"There is no possible explanation or apology I can

offer that would make up for my transgression. I'll remove myself from your sight and this domain immediately."

Then I stride out of the room and down the hall as if the Hunt itself were at my heels, with no thought penetrating the thunder of my pulse except that I make good on my final promise.

22

Talia

After the door thumps shut in Whitt's wake, the silence that grips the room is so taut it practically pierces my skin. Sylas's hands open and close at his sides, every muscle in his body rigid. A flush has broken over his face deep enough to show against his brown skin. I've never seen him look so distressed or so furious.

"My lord," August says uncertainly, his formality revealing just how out of his depth *he* feels in this situation, and Sylas seems to snap.

"All this time—standing beside me while he—" The larger man cuts himself off with a growl fierce enough to shudder through my nerves and then lunges for the door as if to chase after Whitt.

My pulse stutters even harder than it did last night when I thought he might launch himself at Tristan. My mind is still numb with shock, but my body reacts, flinging myself off the chair and hugging his arm to hold him back. Sylas flinches at the contact, but he freezes as if afraid that if he keeps moving he might hurt me.

"No," I say raggedly, squeezing my eyes closed as I press my face to his sleeve. The past few minutes play out behind my eyelids. The agony threading through Whitt's voice as he finally made his admission, the shame written all through his stance as he fled the room…

It doesn't make sense. Maybe it explains a few things, like the occasional odd remarks the spymaster has made about Sylas's treatment of him, but I can also remember with vivid clarity that moment in his favorite glen when he told me about the envy he's struggled with over the differences in their status, the pleading note that came into his tone when he asked me not to tell his brother.

I've seen how vehemently Whitt will defend his lord and his pack. He nearly cost the entire Seelie people the cure I offer because it was more important to him to send me away when he believed my presence was wrecking the bond between Sylas and August. He might have felt resentful of Sylas's authority from time to time, but he *hates* that he feels that way. He'd rather hold it in than ever let Sylas notice.

He's held *this* secret in all this time, and he admitted it now not to save himself but to protect his lord.

I don't understand how he could ever have betrayed Sylas by sleeping with his mate, but I can't believe he just tumbled into bed with her without a thought to the consequences. There has to be more to the story.

"Talia." Sylas's voice comes out raw. He sets a careful hand on my head. "Duplicity on this scale—I can't let it go unaddressed." His bicep flexes against my cheek. He glances past me to August. "Take her to her room. No— better to the entertainment room downstairs. I don't want her to have to see or hear any of this."

The dark portent in those words only makes the alarm racing through my chest blare louder. I clutch the fae lord's arm in defiance, raising my head. "*No.* You can't charge in there all raging and tear into him. You don't even know why—he wouldn't have hurt you on purpose. You *know* that, don't you?"

Sylas sucks in a breath with a hint of a snarl. "I can hardly see how this could have occurred without him realizing the damage it would cause. I never would have thought—but I wouldn't have thought it of Isleen either until it happened."

"We have to at least find out exactly what did happen." But I don't think Sylas is in any state to sit patiently through an explanation. I meet his gaze with all the determination I can muster. "Let me talk to him first. *Promise* you'll wait until we know exactly what went on between them. If you still think he deserves whatever you want to do right now, then I—I won't stop you."

Sylas is silent for a stretch that feels like an eternity. At least my interruption has given his fury a chance to simmer down however slightly.

August speaks up hesitantly. "Whitt and I don't always get along perfectly, but I've never seen any reason at all to doubt his loyalty before this. Whatever retribution you'll have him face, you should be sure of the extent of his crime, don't you think?"

The fae lord sighs, swiping his hand over his face in a

jerking motion. He peers down at me with his mismatched gaze, his jaw tight. "All right. You can have your talk. But on one condition."

Whitt's bedroom door is tightly shut, but I know that's where he's gone from the frenetic rustles and thumps carrying through it. He hasn't bothered with the lock. The knob turns easily under my grasp, and I slip inside.

At the opening of the door, Whitt's head snaps around with a wince as if bracing for an attack. An attack he assumed would be coming from Sylas. Even as his shoulders come down when he sees me, the ache of confusion inside me grows.

He might not be afraid that I'm here to savage him, but he doesn't appear to be particularly happy about my arrival. So much fraught emotion has tensed his normally breathtaking face that he looks outright haggard. I've seen him sleep-deprived and drunk and hungover, sometimes two of those at the same time, but never anywhere close to as shattered as this.

The blue of his eyes stands out starkly against the widened whites. His gaze darts to the bed, which holds a small chest and a greater than usual disarray of clothing and other scattered objects, only some of which have actually made it *into* the chest. Then he looks back at me.

"You'd better go," he says brusquely but without much real energy. "Whatever happens next isn't likely to be pretty."

It's the voice of a man who's given up. The ache creeps

up my throat. I swallow hard and nudge the door not-quite-closed before crossing the room to the foot of the bed.

"I'm not going anywhere. I want to understand what happened."

He makes a strangled sound and returns to tossing things into the chest. "All there is to understand is that I fucked my lord's soul-twined mate, and that makes me the lowest wretch there ever was, and it'd be an immense mercy for him to even let me leave the castle alive."

He turns to grab a leather pouch off the bookshelf beside the wardrobe, and I take the opportunity to clamber onto the bed and shove the lid of the chest closed. Then I sit on it for good measure.

Whitt turns, taking me in with a wildness in his eyes that's more desperate and unsettling than I've ever seen him before. "Mite, this isn't going to—"

I hold my ground, crossing my arms in front of me. "No. Tell me what happened. Somehow I can't believe one day you just decided you had to sleep with her and then did it."

He bares his teeth slightly, and for a second I think he might lift me off the chest and chuck me back into the hall. I grip the edges of the lid, my pulse stuttering. As we stare each other down, the fierce light that momentarily flashed in Whitt's eyes fades. He steps back instead, leaning against the closed wardrobe and rubbing his forehead with the heel of his hand.

"No, it wasn't like that," he says. "But the details hardly matter."

"They matter to me."

"Fine." Somehow he sounds even more hopeless than before. He meets my gaze again, his expression hardening. "There's nothing all that complicated about it. My proclivities are far from secret, and she approached me precisely as any halfway sensible person would: coming to me with a bottle of some new vintage she offered to share while we discussed a matter she wanted to pass by me."

"What matter was that?" Had she thought she was going to convince him to join her rebellion?

"Either I don't remember, or we never got to that. It wasn't as if she typically came to me. You could never have called us friends. I'd have told her to bring whatever it was up with Sylas and leave me in peace, but I knew he'd *like* us to be friendlier, and the wine did sound excellent…" Whitt's eyes wander away from mine again. "And perhaps some small part of my ego liked that she might have thought I'd have better advice than Sylas did, or more sway with him than she had. She probably saw that in me too."

None of this sounds like a prelude to some kind of love affair. As far as I can tell, Whitt didn't like Isleen all that much more back then than he does now.

I frown. "And then…"

"I went with her, and she poured me some wine, and whatever she'd put in it was impressively potent stuff." He lets out a harsh chuckle. "I can moderate myself, but only when I know what I'm actually drinking. After that my awareness got pretty spotty, but the results were clear enough."

The ache from before contracts into something hard as

a blade digging into my chest. "You don't remember *any* of it?"

"I remember bits and pieces. Enough to have no doubt at all what we did."

The blade inside me cuts right down my center, and what explodes out of that gash is anger, so sudden and violent my shoulders shake with it. "She *raped* you."

Whitt's gaze snaps back to me. He blinks, so startled and confused that my hands tighten until my knuckles are throbbing.

"She didn't force herself on me," he says. "I was conscious; I participated." He spits the last word out.

"Because she drugged you so you were too out of your mind to fight her off."

"Talia—"

I stand up on the bed, which gives me a strange vantage point looking down at him when I'm so often looking up. "What would you call it if some lord fed me a bunch of faerie fruit, without even telling me what it was, and then had sex with me while I couldn't think straight?"

Just the suggestion brings a growl to his throat. "I'd call it someone just consigning himself to a slow and painful death. But that's not—"

"Did you *want* to sleep with her?"

"No," he bursts out. "But I didn't stop it either, did I?" His voice falters. "I wouldn't have touched her if I'd had my wits, but that doesn't mean— I can't say some small part of me didn't also take a smidgeon of satisfaction that she felt using me would hurt him the most, or that just once I had something that was supposed to be only meant for him. If it hadn't been for that, maybe it *wouldn't* have mattered what she'd put in the wine or any other way she set me up."

His head droops, and my hands ball at my sides. I haven't used my body for any meaningful violence in all the time I've been among the fae, but right now I almost wish Isleen were still alive so I could let this scream out of my lungs and throw these fists at her face.

What a horrible, vindictive piece of work she was, rampaging through this domain as if her desires were the only ones that counted, breaking Sylas's heart, destroying Whitt's faith in himself, bringing disgrace down on all of them.

I don't care what good things she might have done, what better qualities she must have had for Sylas to have even agreed to complete the mating bond. The venom she inflicted on these men and their pack left wounds that've lasted nearly a century. I don't know if there's anything I could ever do to seal them over.

But I can't shout or strike at her, and it probably wouldn't help anyone if I could anyway. So I do what I can, and slide off the bed to catch Whitt in an embrace.

The fae man stiffens as my arms come around him, but he doesn't push me away. I hug him tight and close, burrowing my head against his chest. Clutching him even harder at the shudder that runs through his tall frame.

"It wasn't your fault," I say firmly, turning my face so the words won't be muffled in his shirt. Maybe if I say them enough, in enough ways, I'll convince him. "*No one* could blame you for it, or at least no one should. She purposefully got you into a state where you couldn't make the decisions you'd have wanted to. If we have to take responsibility for every spiteful emotion we ever have, then I've become a murderer at least ten times in the last few minutes, so…"

A choked sort of laugh tumbles out of Whitt, and then he hugs me back, pressing his lips to my forehead. "Of course you would see it that way. I'm not sure Sylas would be so generous."

A low voice carries from the doorway. "Perhaps you should try me."

The door swings wide, and Sylas stalks into the room.

Whitt yanks himself away from me. I spin to face the fae lord, planting myself between him and his spymaster automatically. But as soon as I see Sylas's face, I know I'm not needed as a human shield. The rage that tensed his features earlier has waned. He looks weary and pained, but not vengeful.

Whitt steps to the side, closer to the bed, so I'm no longer shielding him anyway. He glances from Sylas to me and back again, his stance rigid. "How long have you been out there?"

An answer spills out of me before Sylas can answer. "I'm sorry. He said I could talk to you first as long as he got to listen too. At least—at least now he knows?"

The two men eye each other warily. Whitt brushes his fingers down my back as if to say he accepts my apology, but his attention stays fixed on his lord.

Sylas drags in a breath. "It seems I was even more unaware of my mate's schemes than I realized. If I'd known— Why didn't you *tell* me before now? You had to realize I didn't know it was you, that I had no idea of the full situation. If I'd set my plans today in motion before talking to you, we'd have had a wretched mess to pull ourselves out of. As your lord, as your *brother*..."

The betrayal in his tone isn't as potent as before, but the full explanation hasn't healed it completely. I guess that makes sense.

Whitt cringes. "I *didn't* realize. I thought... You kept to yourself for a few days afterward, and then you were distant and shorter with me than usual—I suppose you were with anyone, but I wasn't thinking about that. I assumed you *had* to know, what with the soul-twined bond. That you were simply making up your mind about what to do with me."

"But I didn't do anything."

"No. Because the assault on Dusk-by-the-Heart happened, and the banishing... I thought you must have decided it was better to pretend it'd never happened and keep me around to help the pack through those difficult times, despite how little you must have wanted me there. You have always been in the habit of putting their needs above your own."

"And all the times we've talked since then, all the things we've been through together, it never became obvious?" Sylas demands.

Whitt's mouth twists. "I *started* to suspect—and in the past few months, I became increasingly certain... But there were hardly a plethora of ideal times to bring it up, and there was still a chance you were intentionally sweeping it under the rug, and I—" He grimaces at the floor. "And I was a coward about it. For all the bitter little thoughts I've had about never being worthy of serving as anything higher than cadre, I couldn't bear to give that position up when I knew I might lose it. So there it is. I had no idea it would come back to haunt us like this."

Sylas's posture relaxes a little more, but his brow has furrowed. It takes him a moment to speak. "I didn't know you felt so ill-treated in your role here in general. If you *would* rather be free from my service and seek a different sort of life for yourself, I wouldn't hold you to your vow."

Whitt considers him. "Is that a polite way of ordering me to continue my packing and take my leave?"

My heart lurches, but Sylas shakes his head. "It's a roundabout way of apologizing for the crime committed against you, since the one who committed it isn't around to deliver that and so much more she'd owe you." He closes his eyes for a second. "If I hadn't shut her out to save myself pain, I'd have known how she violated you. I haven't earned as much of your trust as I should have as both your lord and your brother. If you have failed me, I can only see that I must have failed you as well."

"My lord." Whitt pauses to clear the rasp from his throat. His face has turned a fainter version of the queasy shade it took on before in Sylas's study.

He reaches out to give my hair a half-hearted tussle. "If we believe this one that I can't be held accountable for feelings I don't intend to act on, then it hardly seems fair that *you* should be held accountable for them either. And I'm not sure any of us were quite in our right minds during or after all the turmoil that led us to Oakmeet. It would continue to be my wish and my honor to serve you and this pack if that is your wish as well."

"It is." The fae lord stands there, unusually awkward. I think this is the first time I've seen him utterly uncertain of how to proceed.

The anger might be gone, but plenty of tension still thickens the air. My stomach knots at the thought of how long it might take for their comradery to recover from this fissure. What if the initial injury has been left *so* long that it's already set wrong like my foot did, doomed to always be a little misshapen and prone to pain no matter what they do?

"Perhaps we could both use some time to ourselves to settle into this new understanding," Sylas says finally. He turns to go but stops when he reaches the doorway to glance back over his shoulder. "In case it needs to be said, I've never thought you deserved less simply because your blood didn't show as true."

The moment he's gone, Whitt slumps onto the bed. I reach for him, but he catches my hand, gives it a gentle squeeze, and returns it to me. "Thank you. For whatever you said or did that's meant all my limbs are still attached to my body. I'll thank you better later. For now… I don't think I'm going to be good company."

I'd insist, but even thinking of that reminds me of how Isleen imposed on him. Nausea wraps around my gut. But even if he wants to be alone, I want him to know he doesn't need to be.

"Okay. I'll be right down the hall if you change your mind. Even if you have to wake me."

He manages a flicker of a smile, a pale shadow of his

usual grin. "Thank you for that too. Don't fret, mighty one. All's well that ends well."

As I limp down the hall, that remark sticks in my head, looming more ominously with each step.

It may very well be true. But the troubles we've been drowning in don't feel anywhere near their end.

23

Talia

"The Unseelie haven't attacked at *all* since the last full moon?" I ask August as the border comes into view ahead of our small carriage. The shimmering wall of gray fog rises from the distant grassy plain all the way up to the clear blue of the sky.

Is the sky just as clear in the winter lands on the other side where the raven shifters live? Or does everything become stormy as well as cold as soon as you cross that boundary?

August shakes his head. "Not even a small foray. At first I was glad that our response during their full moon attack made them back off, but it's starting to make me uneasy that they've been so quiet for so long. After our last clash, they might be waiting until they can launch an even stronger assault."

The summery breeze coursing over us is as warm as ever, but I shiver with a sudden chill. The Unseelie seem to be determined to slaughter as many of the summer fae as they can. They'd rather strike when they believe the Seelie can barely defend themselves than have a fair fight. But then, they clearly don't care much about fairness when they've been making grabs for land all along the border with no provocation at all from the summer realm.

It's been going on for something like thirty years, from what Whitt said, and the Unseelie have refused to even say why they've suddenly turned so aggressive. Before that, the two groups weren't friendly, but they left each other alone.

I hug myself, rubbing my arms. "*Someone* over there mustn't agree with the fighting, right? Someone who has access to the Heart on their side. The arch-lords got that note warning them about what was coming at the full moon, and only the Unseelie would have known what they were planning."

"Let's hope whoever that is can shake some sense into their companions," August says. "That note might have saved us a lot of lives lost, but I don't think a few secret warnings will be enough to end the conflict. But whoever it was might be regretting helping us now that they've seen how much bloodshed their side faced when we fought back."

My gut twists as much at that thought as at the hitch of the carriage coming to a stop by Hearthshire's camp of warriors.

The camp looks to be in better shape than when we came out to the border last month. During the lull in the fighting, the warriors stationed here have had time to fortify the rough wooden buildings they've been living in, and I can see signs that the pack's return from disgrace has made other squadrons more inclined to help out. The path between the camp and the nearby village of the lord who presides over this domain is much more trampled than before, and a greater variety of vegetables fill the storage bins than are growing in the camp's rough garden.

We've come bearing even more supplies. I stay in the carriage and hand the baskets and sacks out to August, who passes them on to the pack-kin who've emerged from their temporary homes. Seeing one of the pack's cadre-chosen brings a smile to their weary faces.

It's been a lot of work for these warriors. With the pack's numbers dwindled during their banishment, Sylas had to send everyone he could spare out to help defend the border from the Unseelie, so they've had limited opportunities to return home.

Once we've unloaded the carriage, we sit around the fire pit with the warriors currently in the camp. A couple are off on sentry duty patrolling the border. August gets our pack-kin talking about the past couple of weeks here, and I mostly sit and listen.

My gaze keeps slipping over to the ominous glower of the fog that separates summer from winter. It's far too easy to picture a horde of ravens swooping through that insubstantial boundary.

August must notice my anxiety, because he tucks his arm around mine. He wasn't all that keen on me joining him out here in the first place, but I'm not going to get any opportunities to use my fledgling skills controlling air back in Hearthshire now that our enemies on this side of the border have returned home.

Ambrose and Tristan have squadrons stationed along

the border too. The last message from our warriors mentioned that they'd noticed a few pack-kin of Tristan's visiting Aerik's camp that's just a short distance from ours. Maybe I'll get a chance to contribute something here.

"I can't wait to see Hearthshire again," a warrior named Ralyn remarks, poking at the leg of venison they've set to roast over the fire. A mild meaty scent laces the drifting smoke. "Lord Sylas must be relieved to have the pack home."

"I'm working on training up some of our other pack-kin," August tells him. "In another few weeks, we may be able to start a rotation so you all will have more of a chance to rest up where you belong. Lord Sylas will be glad to have you there as much as he can."

He pauses, a trace of a shadow crossing his face, and I suspect he's thinking about the subdued but obvious tension that's hung like a cloud over the castle since Whitt's confession a few days ago. Sylas and Whitt acknowledge each other if their paths cross but have been giving each other a lot of space. I've overheard the spymaster reporting on information his contacts have picked up—quickly and without his usual wry asides.

They're clearly still working through nearly a century's worth of hard feelings, and I don't know how much either of them has told August about what went on after Whitt left Sylas's study. Even if he knows the full story, I can't blame him for being worried. *I* am, and I was there for the whole thing.

But all of us have more pressing concerns. August leans back on the log we've been using as a seat, the muscles in his arm tightening against mine. He didn't want to launch right into an interrogation about Tristan's activities the moment we got here, since Sylas doesn't want the regular pack-kin any more caught up in that conflict than they have to be, but I can tell he's about to broach that subject before he even speaks.

"The last message we got mentioned some new activity at Lord Aerik's camp," he says carefully. "Would you fill me in on the details of that?"

One of the women grunts. "Not much to tell. We've been keeping a more careful watch on that camp since the trouble they gave Lord Sylas last time. Four days ago, I was coming back from patrol and saw a few unfamiliar soldiers just leaving; one of Lord Aerik's pack-kin told them to send his regards to Lord Tristan. We spotted the same bunch coming to visit once more since."

A man who just came back from his patrol a little while ago nods and jerks his head in the direction of the neighboring camp. "Make that twice. A couple of them are over there right now. I didn't get too close, but I'm pretty sure it's the same bunch."

August hums to himself. "And you don't know what all these visits have been about?"

"We know better than to make it too obvious we're keeping an eye on them," Ralyn says. "Don't want them finding some new reason to accuse Lord Sylas of anything. Could be nothing much, but I haven't seen Lord Tristan's kin around here before now. Second-cousin to the arch-lord's folk usually don't bother this far north."

Not until now. Ambrose and his cousin have obviously decided the enemy of their enemy makes a great friend.

They must be hoping Aerik's pack can advance their cause in other ways.

I glance in the direction he indicated. I can only just make out several white shapes that are the buildings of Aerik's camp in the distance across the tall grass. It's definitely too far for any of us to overhear their conversations from here. But if Tristan's people are there right now—if *I* could get close enough for my magic to work but not so close that they'd be worried about a human listening in...

August is watching me. He can probably guess where my mind has gone. He thanks our warriors for their input, asks a couple other questions about activity along the border, and accepts a hunk of venison when Ralyn declares it done. I take a smaller piece and follow August apart from our pack-kin.

He stops by the carriage and turns to me, not yet having taken even one bite of his lunch. "You want to try your luck with Aerik's camp." His grimace tells me how little he likes that idea.

I swallow the morsel of meat I was chewing and draw myself up as straight as I can. "That's the whole reason I've been learning... everything I've been learning. The whole reason I came out here with you. They'll recognize who I am, won't they, thanks to my hair and the limp and, well, everything? I can head over upwind of them so they'll catch my scent too. They'd know the consequences if they attack me." Whether from Sylas or Ambrose—or all the arch-lords, if they damaged the source of the Seelie's "cure" beyond repair.

"I'm not sure how they'll weigh those consequences if

they realize you're spying on them." August lets out a little growl. "I should at least be close enough to jump in if they try anything."

"If you're that close, they probably won't say anything useful in case *you* hear them with those fae ears and your magic." I reach up to tap the side of his face teasingly, but a lump has come into my throat with the memory of our argument the other day in the gym. How hesitant he was to let me take any risks at all. How willing to send me completely away from his world and him if it meant I'd be farther from our enemies' reach.

I can't live like that.

"There's got to be a spell you can put on me that would protect me at least a little, and you can watch from farther away," I say, letting my tap turn into a gentle stroke of his cheek. "I've got my dagger and my salt for a little defense too. I need to do this, August. If I find something out, it could tip the balance in whether I stay safe in the long run. And I care about keeping me—and this pack— safe just as much as you do."

August leans in to nuzzle my temple, his fingers teasing along my jaw. Reluctance radiates from his stance, but he steps back with a dip of his head, his golden eyes darkened but determined. "All right. I won't hold you back, Sweetness."

The devotion in his suddenly gruff voice brings a swell of matching emotion into my chest. I tug his face to mine and meet his lips with a kiss I pour all my affection into. August kisses me back hard with a rough sound. I grip his shirt, holding him close, not caring at all what our pack-kin might think of this display.

He might be scared for me, but he believes in me.

When our mouths part, I brush mine to his cheek. "I love you."

He hugs me tight with a murmur by my ear. "If it's even half as much as I love you, then I'm the luckiest man in the summer realm. Let's get you ready for your mission. I want to make sure anyone who comes at you will regret it."

When he steps back, his gaze travels over my body with an intentness much less heated than it'd usually get with this close an inspection. He speaks a few words, and a faint quiver of energy touches me through the fabric of my dress. Then he rubs his hands together. "That should buy you a minute or two if I need to get to you. And you remember the other training we've worked on."

"Jab 'em in the eyes, knee 'em in the balls," I say, and am rewarded for my cheekiness with a laugh.

"That's the spirit." August tugs me to him for another quick kiss and lets out a huff of breath. "You'd better get going before my wolf's protective side decides it won't be ignored."

"Hopefully I won't need to take very long."

Trying to look innocent and aimless, I wander in my limping way through the grass toward the neighboring camp, the tall strands swishing against my dress. As I run my fingers over the pale blades, I note the direction the wind ripples over them and veer so that it'll sweep over me on its way to Aerik's squadron.

Let them see a simple human girl passing the time while her keepers do the real work. A human girl whose ears couldn't possibly pick up any distant voices.

Thinner stalks jut up through the grass here and there with a sprinkling of pale blue flowers at their tips. I pluck some of them, gathering them into a small bundle. Watching how close I'm coming to the bone-white buildings from the corner of my eye.

Several figures are standing in a group next to one of those buildings, looking as though they're in the middle of an intense conversation. I start weaving the flowers' stalks together, reaching into my memory to summon the soaring sensation of leaping into August's arms and letting the rasp of the splitting stems cover the whispered syllables. "*Briss-gow-aft.*"

The air trembles but doesn't bend the way I'm willing it to. I concentrate harder on the impression of flight and the shape I want it to form, whisking the distant figures' words to my ears. "*Briss-gow-aft.*"

With a whooshing sensation, a current whirls against my cheek. Voices carry with it, faint but audible.

"—she doing here?"

"It's Sylas's pet human. Picking flowers, it looks like. His pack should keep a better eye on her. If she comes closer, we'll shoo her off."

"What were you saying about—"

The current falters, but I've heard *something* useful. They've noticed me and dismissed me like I hoped. I keep stringing the flowers together, making a necklace that would fit a giant, and murmur the true name again. The breeze swirls up.

"—whatever he needs."

"It took long enough."

"You can't hurry good work. He finished as quickly as he could. I suppose there's no point in asking—"

My effect on the wind fades like before. It sounded like they were talking about some kind of plan, but I'm missing it. Restraining a grimace, I meander a few more steps toward the camp and speak the syllables.

The voices return, but they've moved on to another subject.

"—that banquet. I'm looking forward to the next."

"Oh, he'll be hosting plenty. We'll see if your lord lets you off border duty for the occasion."

"It's about time I—"

And so the cycle repeats for several iterations. I only catch a few snippets before the current I've summoned drifts away. None of the scraps I hear tell me anything meaningful.

Frustration is starting to prickle at me by the time two of the figures step away from the others with hands raised in farewell.

Those must be Tristan's men. They're leaving. I won't have any chance at all to hear what they're up to once they're gone.

I grit my teeth for a second and risk drifting even closer to the camp, just as they also move toward me. Any moment now they'll shift into wolves and lope off. I say the true name as forcefully as I can while keeping the cadence August taught me. "*Briss-gow-aft.*"

The air tickles my hair, bringing their voices with it alongside the slightly more distant laughter from the warriors they just left.

"—sure the poison will do the trick?"

"That's why we came out here, isn't it? He's poisoned enough ravens to judge the dose. With enough on the blade, not even an arch-lord's magic could fend it off."

"That'd better be true, or Ambrose will be looking for scapegoats."

"We'll just have to point him toward the supposed expert in that—"

The sound dies, but I don't need to hear anymore. My heart is thudding so loud I'm not sure I'd be able to make out much more anyway.

I spin around and catch myself, remembering that I need to look as if I'm taking a casual stroll, not at all affected by anything Tristan's pack-kin said. No panicked thoughts racing through my mind. No swell of horror clenching around my stomach.

Just one foot in front of the other, slowly but surely back toward August where he's waiting near the edge of our camp, until the pressure in my throat aches to burst out.

When I'm only twenty feet from him, I let myself run at a lurching pace the last short distance, tuning out the pang that shoots from my warped foot.

August's eyes flash. "What?" he says before I've even reached him.

I wobble, clutching his wrist for balance. "I—I think it's even worse than we guessed. They're not just trying to frame Donovan for a crime now. They're planning to *kill* him."

24

Talia

The carriage shudders with the strain of the pace August has urged it to. Wind roars past me where I've hunched in the lowest point of the floor, where the rushing currents still manage to whip through my hair. August kneels beside me, his arm around my shoulder, only lifting his head now and then to check our course.

It feels like we've been hurtling back toward Hearthshire for hours when his stance stiffens. He straightens up with a quick word to slow the carriage. I ease up to peek over the curved juniper-wood wall.

Sylas is sitting on horseback a short distance ahead of us on the beaten track through the forest, turning his steed now with a press of his heels to face us. The bay stallion is a massive animal to match its rider, with a glitter in its dark eyes that suggests it's something a little beyond the sort of horses I'd have encountered in the human world.

The fae lord casts a quick glance around with a few

muttered words and then focuses on August. "I got called away for a hasty conference with Donovan—just returning now. We can discuss the rest once we're at the castle."

August's face pales. "I'm not sure we can wait that long. What did Donovan say?"

Sylas frowns. "Only that he's been invited to a luncheon at Ambrose's home tomorrow, one restricted to the trio of arch-lords, supposedly so they can discuss their private concerns. Celia will be there too, but no one else. Donovan suspects Ambrose will have some new gambit to try and wanted to make arrangements for me to act as a sort of witness."

My stomach flips over. This must be what Tristan's men were preparing for. I scramble to the bow of the carriage. "He isn't just going to try to trick him somehow. He's going to murder him if he can."

"*What?*" Sylas's posture goes rigid.

August nods, setting a hand on my back. "Talia was able to use her growing skill with air to make out a bit of conversation between Tristan's pack-kin and Aerik's. It sounds as though they came to Aerik's camp because he has a poisons expert there—someone who's doctored a blade that they expect to be potent enough to kill an arch-lord."

Sylas curses under his breath, and his stallion stomps its feet. "I told him it might be too much of a risk, that he should consider making excuses..."

"But if you'll be there with him, then you can help protect him, right?" I say. At least Donovan took that much of a precaution.

But Sylas shakes his head. "I won't be witnessing

closely enough to stop a murder. Ambrose made it clear even cadre-chosen weren't to attend the luncheon. Donovan has given me a token magically charged so I can watch events through his eyes, so I can speak to what happens there. It's an immense gesture of trust—but it won't allow me to save him from physical harm."

He grips the reins, his mouth slanting as he seems to grapple with his decision, and then he shifts forward in the saddle. "I'll see if I can catch him before he makes it back to Blossom-by-the-Heart and bring him up to speed on this new development. We can't leave something so urgent and sensitive to messengers or charms."

Without waiting for our response, he taps his heels against the stallion's sides. It springs forward and dashes past us so swiftly I swear I see sparks lighting beneath its hooves.

I look at August, the uneasiness that's been coiled around my gut since I overheard the mention of poison winding tighter. "What if Donovan insists on going to the luncheon anyway? What kind of excuse could he give to back out?"

August squeezes my shoulder, his handsome face unusually drawn. "I don't know. Hopefully Sylas can work something out with him. But Ambrose has final say over who enters his castle and the magic to enforce it. Even Sylas wouldn't be able to force his way in if it came to that. Maybe Donovan can come up with some sort of protection he can wear or hold that would ward off the poison."

Difficult when we don't even know what kind of poison it is. As August starts the carriage gliding toward

Hearthshire again, my hands clench. If only I'd been able to hear more details. I don't even know for sure that Ambrose *does* mean to carry out this plan tomorrow.

It's only a few more minutes before the massive gate of arcing trees comes into view in the distance. When the carriage soars through it, many of our pack-kin look up from their activities around the village. Several venture over to hear the news from the border.

The warriors out there are their friends—in some cases family. It probably bothers them that they aren't adept enough fighters to take on some of the responsibility of protecting the summer realm. I've seen how much many of them are itching to support Sylas more however they can.

That thought brings a flicker of inspiration with it. I follow August to our approaching pack-kin, turning the idea over in my head.

I can't see how it would hurt anything to simply have a discussion. Maybe Sylas will sort something out with Donovan, and whatever brainstorming we do won't matter. But I don't know how likely that is, and even if they manage to divert Ambrose's latest attempt, Donovan can't avoid him forever.

It'd be good to have a definite strategy up our sleeves. And if we're going to outthink a scheming arch-lord, the more minds we can put together, the better.

When August has finished speaking, I give a little cough before the pack-kin who've gathered can start to leave. "I think there's something important that Lord Sylas might need our help with. If there's anyone who'd be willing to talk through the problem and see what strategies we can come up with, you could join me in the entrance hall of the castle?"

I glance at August for his approval, since I don't really have any authority here, no matter what fond titles Sylas has bestowed on me. August hesitates but then tips his head. "This is important to the security of not just our pack but others too. What we do discuss can't leave those walls. And for now, it's only hypothetical."

Astrid steps up immediately. "You know you can count me in—and to see through this strategy too."

Brigit and Charce come forward, and then Elliot, Shonille and her mate, and a few others I haven't spoken to as much. August motions us all into the castle.

I limp across the thick rug and sit in the middle of the room, the others automatically sinking down around me to form a circle. All except one figure who hangs back outside that ring.

Harper's shoulders hunch when I look up at her, her body tensing as if she expects me to order her to leave. But she did come through with Ambrose the other day. She might have a better idea of his weaknesses than those who haven't had any dealings with him do. I exchange another look with August, who lifts his eyebrows as if to say, *It's your call.*

She can stay, then. I'm not going to say anything specific anyway. Sylas hasn't wanted them knowing the details of this conflict, and I can respect that. Besides, it's probably safer for all of us that way.

I set my hands in my lap and gaze around the circle. "Let's say Sylas needed to get into another lord's castle— one with magical defenses and guards so he couldn't just walk in whenever he wanted to. Because—because he needed to talk to someone inside urgently. It wouldn't have to be sneaky, just something that would let him come inside and find the right room without anyone managing to stop him before that. But he wouldn't want to hurt anyone either. Can any of you think of some magic or another sort of trick we could use to help?"

One of the men looks doubtful. "If Lord Sylas can't see a way…"

"Maybe he *will* figure it out," I say. "But he'd want to try to do it alone, because he doesn't like putting any of the rest of us in danger if he can manage it. You all want to do more than that, don't you? I want to fight for this pack and for everyone who's welcomed me, and I know some of you have wanted to step up too."

There's a moment of silence. Then Brigit speaks up tentatively. "Would all the possible entrances on the first floor—including openings like windows—be guarded?"

Astrid rubs her narrow jaw. "If this is a powerful lord, he'll have considered and secured all possible access points one way or another. The difficult part would be either getting past the guards or breaking a magical barrier where they're not around—and without alerting them so they'd come charging over right away regardless."

"If a bunch of us put our magic to work together," Elliot starts, and then pauses. "But we'd need to be close to the building to apply enough power. Maybe if we had the cover of night?"

August grimaces. "We'd need a technique that could work by day. We definitely wouldn't be able to bring even a small group close enough without being noticed and apprehended."

Shonille's mate drums his fingers on the floor. "Could we create a distraction that would draw some of the guards away and give Lord Sylas an opening?"

Shonille turns to him. "What could we do that would bring enough of them without making even more trouble for Lord Sylas overall?"

He rubs his mouth. "I don't know. Something to think about, at least."

A few more of the pack-kin toss out ideas that one or another points out a problem with. My spirits start to sink. I'd hoped that we'd be able to come up with something concrete so we'd have a plan in place if Sylas needs to rely on us.

I wish *I* could offer more in this discussion, but I still don't know all that much about how the fae world or its magic works—nowhere near as much as the fae around me do, at least.

But Donovan's survival, control over the Seelie realm, the lives of thousands of warriors—and my own safety— could all depend on what happens tomorrow. On whether Sylas can protect his arch-lord ally when it matters. We can't give up.

There are a lot of rules that've come into play in our past conflicts. The vows fae agree to when they're forced to yield, that they then must hold to. Cole breaking out of that obligation by pointing out a crime Sylas had committed against him. The two acceptable ways to displace an arch-lord.

What if what we need isn't magic or trickery but an appeal to some fae policy we can bend in our favor?

"Is there any law that ever allows fae to go into someone else's home without their permission?" I ask the gathering at large. "Or, like… if he had reason to believe something bad would happen if he *didn't* go in, would that be acceptable?"

"He'd have to be able to prove to the guards that there was a major threat first—one they believed they couldn't cope with, or they'd tell him to let them handle it," Charce says.

And Sylas doesn't have clear proof of Ambrose's intentions. So much for that.

But Astrid gestures for attention, her eyes lighting up. "There is one tenet that could force them to give him access. If any of his pack-kin are inside, he has a right to be allowed to go in to speak to them if they won't come out to him."

Brigit knits her brow. "But if they wouldn't let *Sylas* inside, why would they let any of the rest of us in?"

My pulse stutters. I can think of one person here that Ambrose would happily admit into his castle if he thought it meant he'd won: me. Not that he'd trust the situation if I came strolling up to his front door out of nowhere.

But I wouldn't have to, would I? My gaze rises to where Harper is still standing awkwardly at the edge of our group.

Before I've decided what to say and how much I should in front of the full group, footsteps rap against the floor behind us. I glance over my shoulder to see Whitt sauntering into the room.

The spymaster's air is as nonchalant as always, only vague bemusement showing on his face as he takes us in, but his eyes still look a little more sunken than they used to, the corners of his mouth tighter when it pulls into a smile. My throat constricts. It's bad enough we're facing this potential catastrophe at all, let alone while there's so much turmoil between two of the men who watch over this pack.

"Well, well, what's all this commotion about?" Whitt asks lightly. His attention settles on me. "Coming up with more schemes of your own, mite?"

It's a relief to hear him sounding so normal. I suspect he's not going to like my proposal one bit, though.

I push myself to my feet. "Actually, we are. But I think I should probably talk something over with you and August before we get further into it."

August doesn't need any more cue than that to motion to the gathered pack-kin. "Give us some time. Your input has helped us narrow down the possibilities. If we need to put a strategy into action, I'll make sure Lord Sylas knows he can count on you."

As the fae get up and head to the door, disappointment shows on some of their faces, but there's an equal amount of determination. The plan that's forming in my head has no chance of working without at least one of them participating willingly, though.

I raise my voice just enough to carry. "Harper, I need to ask you about something too."

Her gaze jerks to me with obvious surprise. For a second she stays frozen in place. Then she hurries over, a painful mix of hope and apprehension flitting through her expression. "What?" she asks quietly.

I wait until the last of the stragglers have slipped out. My heart is still beating faster with an edge of creeping panic. Do I really want to do this—to walk right into the lion's den?

But I could very well end up there anyway if I *don't* do something like this. I've gotten as far as I have by taking chances, taking my life into my own hands. I can't lie down and give up now.

Whitt and August watch, letting me take the lead. I inhale slowly to settle my nerves.

"It was risky getting those beads to Ambrose's people at the ball," I say to Harper. "Would you be willing to try something even bigger and riskier than that if it would mean protecting the pack—and all the rest of the Seelie—so much more?"

She blinks nervously, but it doesn't take her long to answer. "Yes. I—I want to make up for my mistakes. If it means stopping people who are trying to hurt us, I'll do it."

Then there's no reason this ploy shouldn't work. I turn to the fae men. "Okay. Here's what I'm thinking…"

It's almost dinner time when Sylas finally returns. I'm in the kitchen with August, drizzling icing over the tiny cakes that are our dessert, trying to let the normalcy of working alongside him drown out the jangling of my nerves. It'd be easier if he didn't stop periodically with a wince or a sharp inhale as if he's just remembered what I proposed all over again.

At least he isn't arguing.

Sylas finds us there. He stops in the doorway, running his fingers through his windblown hair, and catches the eyes of the official kitchen assistants. "Thank you for your work today. You can return to your homes—make sure August hands over some of those cakes."

August manages to chuckle as he fills a couple of small baskets, but when the other fae have left, he turns serious. "What happened with Donovan?"

Sylas presses the heel of his hand to his temple. "I managed to speak to him, but he didn't seem to appreciate the gravity of the situation. Or perhaps he can't imagine that Ambrose would truly go that far and believes our information must be faulty. Either way, he insisted on proceeding with the same approach we already agreed on, with me observing through his eyes from a distance. He reassured me very confidently that he'd be all right."

The grim dryness of his tone reveals none of the same confidence on his part. My lungs clench, but I put down the icing tube and ready myself as I swivel on my stool to face him. "We thought that might happen. So we've come up with a plan that should mean you can get into Ambrose's castle if things go wrong and you need to defend Donovan right away."

"Have you now?" Sylas folds his arms over his chest. "Go on."

25

Talia

When I wake up, it's fully dark out. I can tell from the glimmer of stars beyond my window and the mugginess in my head that it's still the middle of the night. I haven't slept nearly enough.

But when I close my eyes, my thoughts weave restlessly through my head, refusing to let my mind settle. After what feels like an eternity of tossing and turning, I get up and limp to the privy in case the walk and emptying my bladder will help me relax.

My nerves haven't calmed at all by the time I make it back to my room. I pause at the door, balking at the thought of lying there sleeplessly for much longer, and a faint creak reaches my ears from somewhere down the hall.

I might not be the only one having trouble drifting off tonight. Is August still up, stewing over tomorrow's plans?

I slip down the hall to where the men's bedrooms are,

but the noise I hear next comes from Sylas's, not August's. There's a rough breath somewhere between a huff and a sigh, and another creak as he turns on the bed.

The fae lord wasn't exactly ecstatic about my idea for getting him into Ambrose's castle should he need to, but he's always so composed, I wouldn't have thought he'd let any worries get that much of a hold on his mind. I hesitate.

So much is on the line tomorrow for both of us. I might not get another chance to show him just how much his trust and affection mean to me. If there's anything I can offer that will set him more at ease, I want to—and I want to soak up any tenderness *he's* prepared to offer while I still can.

As I cross the floor to the bed, Sylas rolls to face me, his eyes open but his eyelids low. His sheet is tangled around his torso, revealing the sculpted planes of his bare chest. I know from experience that he usually sleeps in nothing but his undershorts.

He doesn't look startled—he probably heard me in the hall before I even reached the door. I'm not sure what to say, so I simply hop onto the bed and nestle myself close to him.

Sylas wraps his arm around me automatically, tugging at the sheet so that it covers me too. "Couldn't sleep, little scrap?"

I hum in agreement. "Neither could you?"

He sighs and tucks his chin over my head. "Tomorrow I may have to enter combat with one of the arch-lords I'm supposed to serve. The fact that it'd be in defense of another arch-lord doesn't make the possibility sit that much more comfortably. And all the while you'll be putting yourself under his power..." He trails off with a faint growl.

I slip my arm under his, my hand skimming his muscled back, and hug his brawny frame to me. "If it all works out, then I'll be right back out of his power quickly enough. If it doesn't... I was going to end up there anyway. At least I'll have done everything I could to stop it."

He pulls me closer to him, his heat washing over me. His voice roughens. "I hate the thought of what he wants to do to you, Talia. I look forward to the chance to tear him apart if it means he can never see any of that through. If that makes *me* a traitor to the Heart, so be it."

My throat constricts. "How can it? None of this would be happening if he wasn't scheming against his colleagues in the first place. You—you know I appreciate everything you've already done to protect me, don't you?" I raise my hand to trace my fingers along the side of his face, seeking out his mismatched gaze. "When all you have are awful options, it's not your fault that there's nothing you can do that feels totally right."

He gazes down at me, stroking his own fingers up and down my back through my nightie. "I do feel there was a thing or two I should have done differently the first time my people clashed with Ambrose. I can't see how I could be making a similar misstep now, but I didn't realize it back then either..."

Oh my passionate, honorable lord. My heart swells with so much more than appreciation. "Well, I might not be an expert on any of this, but I can't see any way you could be doing things better right now either. And I promise you that letting me go through with tomorrow's plan isn't a mistake."

"As if you would say anything else." He ducks his head to brush his lips to my forehead. "You know I believe in giving you your freedom, but I do dislike how often these plans of yours involve putting yourself in harm's way."

"I'd rather risk myself than ask anyone else to take the risks for me." I press a kiss to his shoulder in return. The smoky, earthy scent of his skin floods my senses, bringing out a headier heat that courses through me to pool low in my belly. I'm abruptly twice as aware of how little clothing there is between us, only a couple of layers of thin fabric. But I still have to point out, "You're risking more than I am."

"As is my job, as lord over my pack and loyal ally to the arch-lords who *aren't* committing blatant treason." Sylas lets out another sigh. "I suppose it's my fault for naming you our lady. I didn't mean for you to take on quite so many responsibilities to go with the title."

His tone has gone dry enough that a smile twitches at my lips. I scoot higher on the bed, compelled by a dizzying mix of love and desire. "It does seem to come with a lot of benefits too."

He meets me halfway, his mouth claiming mine with a demanding rumble. His tongue sweeps between my lips, hot and fierce, his hands molding me against his muscle-packed body. My skin sears everywhere we touch in the most delicious way.

I kiss him back hard, reveling in the urgency of his

desire. He wants me this much. I *mean* that much to him, at least for now.

I want him too, so badly I'm already aching.

Sylas kisses me again, hunger thrumming through his chest, his fingers tangling in my hair. With a choked sound, he jerks backward. His breath stutters over my lips. Both his pupils have dilated, the dark one and the ghostly one.

"I promised you, when you'd come to me like this— There should be no expectations—" he says raggedly, calling back to the last time things got heated in his bedroom, when my feelings were much more muddled than they are now. But we already have a solution to that problem without any negotiation necessary.

I grip his neck and gaze back at him. My longing turns my voice husky. "Take me to the tryst room."

The words have barely fallen from my lips before he's scooping me up in his arms. He crosses the bedroom and then the hall in a few swift strides to the room he added to Hearthshire's castle like he did to the keep in Oakmeet— the one that's not mine or any of my lovers' but all of ours together, meant for moments like this.

Sylas is already planting a scorching kiss on my neck before we've made it to the bed. I whimper, gripping the thick waves of his hair. Need unfurls from my core all through my body, so intense it's almost painful. "Please," I murmur.

He makes a strangled sound and lifts me onto the bed, his body braced over me. His mouth recaptures mine, devouring me, drinking in every encouraging sound that quivers up my throat. He strokes my breasts, wasting no time in settling his thumbs over my nipples and drawing them to the hardest of points with giddying jolts of pleasure.

"Mine," he growls, nibbling my jaw, nipping my earlobe, as if he can't keep his mouth off of me for more than an instant. "*Mine*."

The word feels less like a declaration of ownership than an adamant warding against the ones who'd take me away from him, like he's daring anyone to even *try* to rip me from this place. It resonates through me. I arch against him, wishing he could claim me so thoroughly that no one beyond this castle could ever even consider doing the same.

"Yours," I answer in a sort of prayer.

Another wild sound spills from his lips. He swipes his tongue across my neck and buries his mouth in the crook. His hand rakes down the front of my body, the tips of barely-emerged claws slashing through my nightgown down the middle.

My pulse hiccups, but only for a second before I'm enveloped in a flood of burning passion again. As fierce as Sylas's desire is, he didn't make one mark on my body, hasn't touched me to bring anything but pleasure.

I know right down to my core that this man would never hurt me.

He palms my breast, stirring another jolt of bliss, and then pulls back, his mouth branding my collarbone, my ribs, my belly in quick succession. Before I've quite caught on to where he's heading, he lowers his head between my legs.

The first urgent stroke of his tongue sets off sparks all

through my sex and shocks a cry from my throat that's a plea for more. I press into his mouth.

Sylas works me over as if his life depends on urging every particle of delight he can from my folds and the sensitive nub above them. I cling to his hair, my hips swaying with each movement of his lips, each flick of his tongue. All I can do is ride the rush of sensation that sends me careening toward my release.

It comes with a burst of pleasure that knocks the air from my lungs. My head tips back into the pillow, a moan tumbling from my mouth. My body quakes as the aftershock tingles through my limbs.

Sylas kisses me once more there, firmly enough to propel the giddy waves even higher, and then prowls up over my body.

Yes. Every nerve inside me sings out in welcome. I grasp his shoulder and splay my legs, reaching to yank at his undershorts. He wrenches them off with the same force he applied to my nightie. His mouth collides with mine, tart with the taste of me combining with his potent flavor.

He slides his arm under my backside, raising me to meet him, and my knees clench around his hips. With a groan, he plunges right into me.

There's none of our first encounter's caution, but I don't need careful. It's thrilling to experience such intense desire from this man who keeps his fiercer emotions so vigilantly in check. To know that he could long to become one with me just as much as I long for him, at least in this way, in this moment.

My hips buck to meld with him of their own accord.

Bliss flares from where he's filled me so perfectly to radiate all through my body. As our rhythm speeds up, our kisses start to fragment, as much panted breath and stuttered gasps as mouths embracing.

Sylas is so big, looming above me and penetrating me to my core. Power radiates off him with every thrust. But I don't feel small beneath him. With each caress, each clutch of his fingers pulling me closer and driving himself deeper, a sense of strength flows through me.

In this moment, I'm his and he's mine. I'm the woman he needs. I'm not a cringing victim or a fumbling human —I'm a fae lord's chosen lover, and I welcome every bit of passion he can pour into me.

The haze of expanding pleasure drowns out any further coherent thought. With a few more strokes, Sylas hits some perfect spot inside me, and my awareness shatters apart. I shudder and clench around him, crying out. He drives into me once more, and his shoulders go rigid as he follows me over that edge.

We rock to a halt at a much more tender pace than the one that brought us to our release. Sylas kisses me softly, drawing it out as I go slack beneath him, and then nuzzles my jaw. His own pose starts to relax, but when he gazes down at me, there's something unexpectedly fraught in the darkness of his unscarred eye.

His voice comes out quiet and a little hoarse. "Are you —all right?" His hand drifts to the shredded edge of my nightgown. "I didn't mean to let out so much of the animal with you. It was just the thought that I might *not* have you—but I should have—"

I interrupt him with a hand against his cheek and a

smile so wide it brings an ache into my cheeks that matches the one around my heart. "I wanted this. I *asked* for this. It was my idea to come in here."

Suddenly I think of Whitt that evening when he first gave in to *his* desire, how he warned me against himself first and only accepted my advances when I told him I wasn't bothered by his supposed faults. I wouldn't have thought Sylas needed any similar assurances, but he is still a man as well as the stalwart lord. I know how deeply his emotions run beneath his controlled exterior.

I lift my head to press a fleeting kiss to his lips. "I'm not afraid of you—I'm *never* afraid of you. I know you'd stop if I asked you to. I wouldn't be yours otherwise."

An echo of a groan escapes him at those last words, and he leans in for a more thorough kiss. As I loop my arm around his neck and kiss him back, I can't help wishing that I could stay his just like this forever, as ridiculous as that hope might be.

At noon the next day, as I walk past the immense black stones that surround Ambrose's palace, the blazing heat of the sun makes me recall the gentler warmth of Sylas's embrace with a pinch of longing.

What I wouldn't give to be spending this day cozying with him in bed rather than marching toward a villain's house. What I wouldn't give to have him—or August or Whitt—walking next to me right now. But it's just Harper, Brigit, and Charce with me, making our way up the slope.

Even Astrid's presence would have been a relief, as much as I've sometimes chafed at her constant presence. We aren't sure that Ambrose's guards will admit us if we have anyone with us who looks like a warrior. Brigit and Charce were among those August has been training who volunteered to come along, chosen partly because of Brigit's past help and partly because Charce had the magic to control the carriage we supposedly stole for this trip.

We need every part of our story to line up for our best chance of seeing this stratagem through.

Another part of that story is making it believable that I'd have come along with Harper despite my previous insistence that I stay in Hearthshire. I let my gaze drift idly over my surroundings for the benefit of any watching sentries, lolling my head to one side and then the other, forcing a giggle at random moments. Drawing on every sensation I can remember from the time Whitt shared his cavaral syrup with me.

As we come up on the towering black form of the palace itself, my heart thumps faster. I will my expression to stay placid.

The luncheon was supposed to start at noon sharp. We're reaching the doors about ten minutes after the visiting arch-lords should have been admitted. We didn't want to leave Donovan unprotected for too long, but we didn't want to risk Ambrose having the chance to interrogate us before his guests arrived either. By now, he should be totally occupied.

Harper strides right up to the guards posted at either side of the main door. "We've come to give ourselves over to Ambrose's care." Hearing the steadiness of her voice brings a glow of pride into my chest. I know how nervous she was about this plan, but she's rising to the occasion.

Her statement isn't a lie—she's just leaving out how short a time we plan to *stay* in Ambrose's care. The guards eye us with obvious uneasiness. The woman on the right focuses on me.

"That's the human—the one with the cure in her blood."

Harper's head bobs. I make a point of humming to myself and tipping my head toward the sky rather than seeming to pay attention.

"I got her drunk on some good wine so she wouldn't argue," my friend says. "I've worked on Arch-Lord Ambrose's behalf before—his pack-kin who visited Hearthshire can tell you. We don't want to be on the wrong side if it comes to war. I thought the cure would make a good peace offering. He wants her, doesn't he?"

The guards clearly know their lord does. They exchange a glance. The man clears his throat. "The arch-lord is busy at the moment. He can't attend to you yet."

Harper shuffles her feet and ducks her head, looking sheepish and not at all threatening. "Could we at least come inside? It'd be easier to make sure the human doesn't wander off. And I'm not sure how long it would take for Lord Sylas to notice a missing carriage."

The woman makes a gruff sound, but after another silent exchange between the guards, she motions for us to follow her. "You can wait in one of the sitting rooms. Just come along quickly."

Harper curls her hand around my elbow. Looking

toward the cavernous doorway, my legs balk. For a second, I'm suffocating.

I think of Sylas's breath grazing my neck as we fell asleep entwined last night. Of August's tight hug before he watched me step onto the carriage. Of Whitt's final murmured reminders of details to keep in mind and the subtle squeeze of my hand as he moved to step away.

I will come back to them. I refuse to accept any other outcome. But to make sure of that, first I have to walk completely away.

My jaw tightening behind my dreamy smile, I propel myself into my greatest enemy's home.

26

Sylas

The warm breeze teases over my fur where I crouch amid the trees at the base of the Heart's hill. Farther up the slope, the stone wall of Ambrose's domain gleams starkly against the grass. Every muscle in my wolfish form is tensed around the urge to bolt across that distance and onward to the palace.

My pack-kin are up there. The woman I love is up there. They got out of their carriage just minutes ago to cross the rest of the distance on foot. Even now, Ambrose's warriors could be—

I clamp down on that line of thought and shove it aside, turning my attention to the more detached impressions trickling into my mind. I know exactly where Ambrose himself is right now. If his guards put out a call for his orders, I'll see it instantly.

When I focus on the faint pressure of the band fixed around my head and specifically of the enchanted gem resting right against my forehead, images and sounds filter into my mind as if I were seeing and hearing them with my own eyes and ears. But it's not my senses taking them in first but Donovan's.

I got into place here an hour ago and activated the gem's magic just before noon. With careful attention, I watched and listened as Ambrose welcomed Donovan and Celia into the palace, charted the route they took through the halls to the smaller, private dining room, and observed their innocuous small talk as the servants laid out the last preparations for the luncheon.

The three arch-lords are still standing next to the table. A woman brings out a carafe of wine, another arriving just behind her with a roast pig on a platter. The meal is about to start.

It's unnerving, experiencing two locations at the same time. Donovan's perspective affects my senses in a subtler, more distant way than the forest around me, but I can still smell the crisp meatiness of the roast, even feel the knot in his stomach as he and his colleagues move toward the table. He spoke about this encounter with confidence, but he *is* nervous.

I'm a little relieved to recognize that. He should be. Ambrose hasn't made any questionable moves yet, but I suspect it's only a matter of time.

My thoughts slip back to the after-image of his tormented face that filtered through my deadened eye all those days ago, the morning after the banquet at Donovan's palace. At the time, I assumed the distress I saw in that impression of him was emotional strain. But the young arch-lord has proven himself adept at conquering the stress of his situation.

Now, I'm more inclined to believe it was the physical agony of a man poisoned.

Was that glimpse a reflection of some future moment when I'll see his face so contorted in actuality? Is it a sign that I won't be able to protect him in time, whether today or on some later date? Do my fleeting visions *have* to show something true, or can what hasn't happened yet still be altered?

Those questions have been gnawing at me since Talia first announced what she overheard from Tristan's pack-kin at the border. The magic that sliced through my flesh and seared my eye right through the socket left lingering traces I still don't fully understand so many years later.

By the Heart, let the risks that my lady, my pack, and I take today be enough to overcome Ambrose's malice.

In the dining room, the servants bow and scamper out at Ambrose's wave. No others have arrived to speak to him about unexpected visitors. The arch-lords move to take their places around the table, and Ambrose pauses, letting out a faint huff of irritation.

"It appears my staff have forgotten my wine glass." He glances around and makes a quick gesture to me—to Donovan, whose eyes I'm seeing him through. "There's one on the sideboard. Would you pass that to me?"

Donovan turns—the sideboard *is* right behind him, with a crystal goblet standing near the edge. It's an innocent enough request, but my skin prickles with more apprehension than I sense from the man I'm linked with.

However Ambrose means to carry out his plot, he

would want every part of it to look innocent to both his victim and outside observers. He wouldn't want Celia raising any concerns about the events that follow.

Donovan hands the goblet to Ambrose. The other arch-lord inclines his head in thanks. "I trust we can all manage to pour our own wine and fill our own plates so that we can talk without disturbances from my faded kin."

"Of course," Celia says, regal and unruffled as ever, and takes the carafe first.

The conversation continues around the table without delving into any subjects I'd think warranted this level of secrecy. How would Donovan feel about my observing if it did? He must have decided his safety outweighs any such concerns.

I can only imagine how much Whitt would have enjoyed getting an exclusive surreptitious peek into the lives of the arch-lords behind closed doors. I thought I noticed a gleam of interest light in his eyes when I explained Donovan's contribution to this plan, although it vanished so quickly behind his new, more reticent manner that I could be wrong. He kept the remarks he made strictly to the practicalities of the business at hand.

Just remembering my last conversation with him— and other conversations before that—sets a prickling sensation unfurling through my chest. My claws dig into the earth beneath me.

I hate the strained wariness between me and my brother. I hate that I don't know how to breach it in a way that satisfies the full measure of my failures and expectations. I closed myself off from Isleen in self-preservation when with more fortitude I would have realized her crime and saved him so much anguish. Something in my behavior led him to believe he couldn't reveal her transgressions to me without my blaming him.

But how long has he held in the resentments he expressed to Talia, that he indicated dogged him long before Isleen's offense? How could he have served me so long behaving as if all was well?

There are no easy answers to those questions either. Right now, they can only distract me. Burying them under my more immediate apprehension, I stretch my legs to keep them limber and resist the urge to pace. Ambrose shouldn't have many if any sentries so far from the center of his domain, but I'd rather not draw the attention of any who might happen to pass by.

Surely Talia and the others have seen through the first stage of her plan at this point? Ambrose's staff had better be treating them kindly. My lips start to curl at the thought of the insults they might aim my lover's way.

Then Celia taps her fork against the side of her plate, drawing my and Donovan's attention.

The eldest arch-lord cocks her head. "This is a very satisfying meal, Ambrose, but I expected to find there was a matter of some urgency you wished to discuss. I can't imagine you called for this very private gathering solely to exchange pleasantries."

"Of course not." Ambrose leans forward with a clank of his plated vest. He takes a swig of wine, opens his mouth as if to launch into a speech—and shudders so hard the liquid sloshes from the goblet he's still holding.

What in the lands?

He tries to speak again but only manages a sputtering

sound. A purplish cast is creeping over his broad face. He pushes to his feet and sways there, looking as though he might collapse at any moment.

His colleagues have leapt up as well. Celia's dark complexion has dulled with shock. "Ambrose, what ails you?"

He coughs and manages to spit out a few words. "I think— The wine—" He staggers toward Donovan and clutches the younger man's wrist. I feel the pressure of his fingers as if around my own foreleg. "I have something— The inner chamber— Help me?" He jerks his other hand toward Celia. "Find—bring my healer."

Celia whips around and darts through the doorway, leaving Ambrose and the man he wishes to kill utterly alone.

My heart lurches, and I'm springing through the trees toward the grassy slope without any further provocation. Whatever he means to do, he's setting it in motion now. I may have mere minutes before it's too late.

I may not get there in time at all.

I hurtle up the hill with every ounce of power I can summon from my straining muscles. Imposed against the grass and stones, another scene unfolds from within my mind.

Donovan glances toward the doorway Celia hurried out through, clearly aware of his vulnerability now that there's no one present to intervene. Ambrose sways again, and the younger arch-lord helps catch his balance. The apparently sickly man gestures toward another door at the back of the dining room.

No. Stay out of there.

But my thoughts can't carry into Donovan's head any more than his are into mine. As I sprint between the standing stones, my haunches and my lungs burning with the frantic pace I'm keeping, Donovan hesitates and says a few words that are drowned out by the pounding of my pulse and my panting breaths.

Ambrose grips his arm tighter and tugs him toward the door with another shudder—and Donovan moves with him.

Dust and doom. I fling myself past the last of the stones and charge the rest of the way to the palace door. The guards jerk to straighter attention, raising their weapons.

Heart bless us and let this gambit work.

I throw myself upright into human form so swiftly my flesh stings with the abrupt transition. My hair falls wild about my face; I can't imagine my expression is anywhere near as composed as I'd prefer it to be. But perhaps that will sell my story.

"I'm Lord Sylas of Hearthshire. Kin of my pack have come here. I must see them at once on a matter of grave importance."

The nearest guard's jaw clenches, but his gaze darts toward the doorway. "They didn't appear to wish to have anything else to do with you."

I glower at him with all the lordly authority I can bring to bear. "Have they sworn vows to another lord yet? I'm assuming not. I have a right to speak with them."

The other guard shuffles on her feet. "I'll ask them to come out." She ducks inside.

They'll refuse, and I'll be granted passage. I only hope the guard doesn't spend too long arguing with them.

In my mind's eye, Ambrose is shoving open the door to the chamber just off the dining room. He stumbles into what looks like a small office containing a rolltop desk, a matching cabinet with two narrow drawers, a few stacks of books on shelves carved into the dark rock of the wall, and a large clay vase in the corner. Donovan hesitates in the doorway, gripping the frame.

Raised voices reach my own ears through the door. The remaining guard shifts his weight, looking twice as tense as before.

Donovan steps into the study—

The first guard shoves the door in front of me wide. "They won't come," she says, frustration sharpening her voice.

I fold my arms over my chest. "Then I must speak with them where they are. *Now*."

Her mouth twitches, but to my relief, she must decide she's better off skipping an argument when she knows fae law is on my side. She makes a brusque beckoning motion. "Come on then."

I follow her into the dark hall, only a sliver of the tension clutching my chest releasing at this minor victory. I'm inside—

Donovan is standing over Ambrose in the cramped room. The older arch-lord points to something on one of the shelves. I catch a glint of a metal blade—

There's no time left. I must act now.

"I've arrived," I call out, just loud enough to be sure

the words will reach my pack-kin, and then I leap forward, releasing my wolf.

The guard who was escorting me gives a shout. I've already dashed as far as the bend in the hall where I watched Donovan take a right turn. A thump and a snarl behind me tell me that my pack-kin have sprung into action. Brigit and Charce will be holding back any guards who made to charge after me as well as they can, with Harper protecting Talia. If need be, my fierce little human will toss salt into the mix.

A pang of worry rings through me, picturing Talia so close to the fight, but she put herself in this position so I could keep going. If I can end this quickly, she won't be in danger for long.

I race around another corner, spotting the door to the dining room up ahead.

Donovan wraps his fingers around the wooden handle of the dagger Ambrose indicated. His confusion echoes into me with the hesitation in his movements, a twinge in his chest. He would have expected his colleague to aim a blade at him, not to offer one.

As he lifts the dagger, Ambrose snatches at his wrist. The older arch-lord yanks Donovan's hand forward with so much strength that Donovan's shoulder jars in its socket.

The dagger slams into Ambrose's chest, just beneath his armpit. Not a fatal strike by any means, but solid enough that Ambrose flinches at the pain, even though he must have been braced for it.

Donovan heaves backward, startled panic speeding his pulse. He flings the dagger to the side. It skitters across the floor to the vase. As I wheel toward the dining room door, he stares at Ambrose. "What game are you playing? Will you say I stabbed you—and perhaps poisoned you too with that cup? Do you think I won't speak up and tell whoever's judging us the truth?"

I barge through the dining room doorway, and Ambrose's lips stretch with a thin smile turned taut by pain. "You won't if you're dead."

My own blare of panic sends an extra burst of adrenaline to my feet. I burst past the study door just as Ambrose whips a needle-like blade from his sleeve and stabs it at Donovan.

I crash into Ambrose, slamming his arm to the side— not quite soon enough to totally deflect the blow. The narrow blade slices across Donovan's chest rather than piercing straight into it. A searing pain echoes from him into my own flesh.

I chomp my jaws around Ambrose's hand hard enough that his fingers spasm and drop the weapon. But as I kick it away, he shifts, wrenching his hand-turned-paw from my grasp. I manage to send the needle-blade spinning away into the dining room, but the door swings shut in my wake. I have to slam against it to avoid Ambrose's lunge.

Bracing myself against the frame, I rein in my wolf and stand tall while I draw my sword. When I brandish it in warning, the arch-lord backs up, muscles coiled through his shoulders and haunches. I don't want to skirmish with Ambrose any more than I have to. And Donovan—

The younger arch-lord has teetered and toppled onto his ass. Blood wells all along the thin line carved through his tunic into his flesh. Dizzyingly, I see both him and myself through his eyes. His vision doubles, turning my form into hazy twins. And his face—

His face is the image that swam before me those weeks ago in his office, contorted and shining with sweat. Ambrose might not have gotten the poison in as deeply as he meant to, but it's acting on the other man all the same.

It's acting quickly. A rattle has crept into Donovan's breath even as he murmurs the words of a spell that must be meant to protect him. I feel his lungs straining. As a green tint spreads over his face, his body slumps farther, his eyelids drooping, his voice failing. The hazy impressions cut off completely as he loses consciousness.

He's still alive. He didn't get the full dose of poison, and he had the chance to ward off at least a little of its effects. Healing has never been a particular skill of mine, but I can slow the flow of his blood, calm his nerves so the poison doesn't spread as quickly. Buy time for Celia to bring the healer.

If Ambrose will allow it.

I step toward Donovan, and Ambrose's dark wolf shoves me aside. As I raise my sword threateningly again, he rises back up as a man, gripping the hilt of the sword at his waist. Blocking my way to his dying colleague.

"So," he taunts with a sneer, "the great Lord Sylas shows his traitorous inclinations after all. Do you mean to run me through with that sword?" He pulls out his own.

The jab lands hard enough that I wince inwardly, but the sight of Donovan's sprawled body gives me all the resolve I need to hold my ground. *I* am not the traitor here.

I grit my teeth. "I don't want to. But I'd be betraying

the arch-lord you've attempted to murder if I don't do all I can to help him survive."

Ambrose gives his sword a casual swing. "Is that what you're telling yourself?"

"It's what *everyone* will see. Fighting off someone who's attacked an arch-lord, even if he's an arch-lord himself, can never be treason."

"Hmm. That assumes that either of you will be around to tell your version of the story. Let me rectify that impression. Neither of you will leave this room alive, and I'll be sure your name and your pack go down in blazing infamy."

My gut twists with nausea, but an eerie calm settles over the rest of me. The memory of Talia's arms around me floats up through my mind alongside her soft voice, telling me with such certainty how much she trusts me.

I know she's right. I know *I'm* right. If killing an arch-lord is what it takes to defend the one who needs it, then as much as I abhor the idea, I'll do it. Not out of greed like Isleen and her kin. I don't care who becomes arch-lord when Ambrose is gone as long as he can't continue to risk all Seelie kind with his own lust for power.

And clearly that's what it's come down to: my life and Donovan's or his.

"Move out of the way, Ambrose," I say in one final warning.

He simply readies his sword. So be it.

I feint in one direction and lunge in the other. Ambrose parries, our blades clanging together. He pushes forward with a stab, a feint, and a swing, taking up every bit of the tight space in his attempt to press the advantage.

I dodge to the side, and he rams me into the shelves, books thumping onto the floor. Pain that's all mine splinters through my side. With a knee to the gut, I send Ambrose reeling backward, but only a couple of steps.

At my next strike, he smacks his blade against mine so hard the clash reverberates through my arms. As I swivel, he snaps out a word that turns my blood cold. "*Fee-doom-ace-own.*"

From Talia's lips, that true name can bend spoons, warp knives, and lift thin chains. She wouldn't be able to damage this sword in any significant way with its built-in enchantments specifically to prevent any ill effects in battle. But Ambrose is an arch-lord with all the power that runs in his family and that's built up in him with his proximity to the Heart. My blade sags from its hilt as if it's turned to melted wax.

I bash it at him from the side, but the lopsided mass throws off my balance. He dodges too easily. There's no chance my magic is enough to conquer whatever protections he's added to his own blade over however many months or years, especially when I've only been back from the fringes for a short while.

Sucking a breath through my clenched teeth, I make the best gamble I can.

I toss my ruined sword away. As the movement draws Ambrose's attention for the briefest of instants, I slam my hands at his sword-arm's wrist with a swift twist. The flat of his blade smacks my temple, but an instant later, bones crack.

I wrench the weapon from his fingers. It clatters to the

floor. At a swipe of my heel, it skids across the floor behind me.

Ambrose doesn't waste any time bemoaning his broken wrist. He hunches into wolf form, already lashing out with his curved fangs. Thankfully I expected him to make the shift. As I spring backward, I unleash my own wolf.

I hurl myself at him, and he meets my charge. Our bodies collide, rolling over one another, claws scrabbling and teeth biting at every bit of flesh they can reach.

My tail brushes against Donovan's sprawled form, and my heart lurches. How much more time does he have?

I need some way to get the upper hand. As Ambrose attempts to pin me down and we grapple against one another, my gaze flicks around the room. My sword is useless. I'd wager his is charmed to burn any hand other than his that attempts to grasp its hilt. The poisoned knife he cut Donovan with is out in the dining room.

But there was another blade he doesn't even know I'm aware of. I wasn't in the room when he forced Donovan to stab him with that dagger, not in any way Ambrose could observe.

Where did Donovan fling it to? It knocked against the base of the vase…

I manage to heave Ambrose off me far enough for me to hurtle toward the vase. My furred shoulder smashes through the pottery. Ambrose throws himself onto me, making the broken shards beneath me dig into my muscles, but I've caught the gleam of bronze.

There's no chance of demanding a yield. This isn't a fight for dominance but a desperate bid for survival.

I shift faster than I've ever changed before, snatch up the dagger, and ram it right between the arch-lord's eyes.

The blade slams home all the way to the hilt, shattering skull and slicing straight into Ambrose's brain. A groan and a spray of spittle bursts from his gnashing mouth. His wolfish limbs spasm and slacken.

The massive beast tumbles off of me, returning to the form of a man as he hits the floor on his back. Ambrose stares blankly at the ceiling, his body limp, blood dribbling from around the blade still lodged in his forehead.

My throat is throbbing where he dealt a shallow but broad gash, my torso aching with at least one cracked rib, but I don't pause to tend to myself or him. I spin toward Donovan. The younger arch-lord's chest is still hitching with erratic breaths, his eyelids quivering.

I press my hands over the wound on his chest, muttering the true names for blood and muscle with all the power I can pour into them.

Slow the poison. Save his life. *Please*.

I'm not sure how many times I've spat out the syllables in the fading rush of adrenaline when a voice carries from the room beyond. "Ambrose? Donovan?"

It's Celia. "In here!" I shout hoarsely.

She flings the door open, urging a man who must be Ambrose's healer ahead of her. "I came as quickly as I could. I—"

They both stall in their tracks at the sight of the arch-lord's corpse.

I heave myself to my feet. "You can't do anything for Ambrose. He poisoned Donovan with a blade. Donovan's still alive, but he won't be much longer if he doesn't get proper help."

Faced with the death of his master, the healer wavers for only a second before dropping to his knees at Donovan's side. From his urgent incantations and his fumbling with his pouches of supplies, I don't think he has any interest in carrying out Ambrose's intentions now that the man is gone, if he ever would have.

Celia stays by the door, staring at the scene. As I take in her horrified expression, my heart sinks.

Ambrose may have his revenge yet. She has only my word that he was the one who attacked Donovan rather than me. She might very well accuse me of attempting to slay them both. I did burst in here uninvited under technically false pretenses; I had every reason to wish Ambrose dead for my own gain. Even if Donovan recovers enough to speak to his own injuries, she might claim the poison has addled his mind or see it as some conspiracy of our own.

She lifts her gaze to meet mine, taking in me as I was observing her. Her attention appears to settle on the band with its gem still pressed against my forehead. One corner of her lips slants upward.

"My young colleague was most thoroughly prepared," she says, and tips up the simple crown she's wearing to show a gem that matches mine fixed underneath.

Donovan gave her the means to see what happened too. Based on the fact that she's making no move to arrest me, I'm going to suppose that she heard Ambrose declare his intentions before the poison took hold. Thank all that is merciful.

I bow my head to her, the surge of relief mingling with the aches of my body. If I didn't have every muscle in my legs tensed, I'd sway on my feet. "Thank the Heart for that."

"It did no harm to accept his request, but I thought him rather paranoid." Celia considers the figures slumped on the floor again. "Clearly I was mistaken."

As if in response to those words, Donovan jerks to the side, folding over at the waist. With a quake of his abdomen, he spews yellow-green bile from his mouth onto the floor. The healer eases to the side, watching.

The young arch-lord coughs and gags again, but the sickly color is already fading from his face. He blinks, looking up at us with a dazed expression, and swipes at his mouth.

After a moment, a weak smile crosses his face. "Well," he says hoarsely, "this is not at all a respectable position for an arch-lord to find himself in, now is it?"

Celia snorts. "From the looks of things, you're lucky to be in the position of keeping your life. Worry about respect once we're sure you're doing that."

I sink down next to Donovan, ready to steady him if he wishes to sit up. He extends his hand, but when I grasp it, he doesn't make any attempt to pull himself upright just yet.

"I think you can count on this being the last time I don't fully heed your advice, Lord Sylas," he says. "Your conduct today should earn you rewards far better than becoming a colleague of mine, but I'm afraid that's the highest honor I'm capable of presenting. Perhaps I should be kinder and send you on a century-long vacation instead."

I offer a small smile in return. "I served as I've sworn to, and as I'll continue to in whatever way you will it, my lord."

A thin hum emanates from his throat. "In that case… You'd better get your affairs in order, soon-to-be-Arch-Lord Sylas."

27

Talia

The Bastion casts a golden light over everyone within its walls, pulsing gently with the flow of energy from the Heart just beyond the building. Brilliant sunlight streams through the high windows into the huge central room with its vaulted ceiling. The gold ore laced through the warm stone gleams.

The expansive glow matches the crown Celia and Donovan are setting on Sylas's head together in the final stage of his initiation as arch-lord. The light wraps around him as if the Heart of the Mists itself is embracing him in his new role.

Which in some way it is. Even with my human senses, I felt the thrum of energy rising with the current arch-lords' words as they carried out the ceremony and asked for the Heart's blessing.

Whitt and August stand a few steps behind their lord, August beaming, Whitt sporting a crooked smile that's maybe not quite as enthusiastic but pleased nonetheless. I'm back by the edge of the circular room, where the spectators from the arch-lords' packs, Hearthshire's, and many other lords and their cadre-chosen have come to witness Sylas's ascension. The size of the crowd and the intensity of the moment make my nerves jitter, but Astrid's no-nonsense presence besides me keeps my anxieties in check.

"Welcome to the trio of the Bastion, Arch-Lord Sylas," Celia and Donovan say in unison. The crown on Sylas's head sparks with a brighter light. The arch-lords each take one of his hands, raise them in the air, and turn with him as if displaying their new unity to the entire crowd around them.

Sylas is smiling too—typically reserved, but there's no mistaking the awed pride in his expression. Just weeks ago, he wasn't even respected as a lord. Now he's one of the three most esteemed figures in the entire summer realm.

As I watch, so much affection wells up inside me that my chest aches with it.

When the arch-lords finish their rotation and lower Sylas's hands, a cheer rises up from the crowd. A smattering of applause grows to a deluge. I add my hands to the clamor, suddenly grinning uncontrollably.

The assembled fae stream outside to the grassy field that lies directly before in the vast, pulsing glow of the Heart, its light flowing over us and out into the hazy border that stretches into the distance on either side. Food and drinks have already been laid out on tables along the fringes of the field; several musicians strike up a rollicking tune.

The serious parts of the ceremony are over. It's time to revel.

Sylas makes his way through the crowd, shaking offered hands, acknowledging bows, responding to eager compliments. He stops when he reaches me.

"Congratulations, Arch-Lord Sylas," I say, aiming my grin at him.

He gives a low chuckle. "Maybe in a few decades that'll start to sound normal." He reaches to grip my shoulder, his dark eye speaking of all the things he'd like to say if we didn't have so much of an audience, but he's already said plenty over the past two weeks. "I won't forget how I got here and who I have to thank for that."

"I know." I rest my hand over his for a brief moment, and then the other fae draw him away into their midst again.

Several of the attendees begin to dance in the center of the field. August catches my arm and tugs me to join them. Gazing up into his joyful face, I tune out the stares I know are aimed our way.

Even a lord's cadre-chosen giving a human this much attention was unusual. An arch-lord's? It must be nearly unthinkable.

For a few songs, swaying and turning in his arms, it doesn't matter. But then pain creeps up my ankle from my warped foot even with my braced boot, and I can't ignore *that* discomfort any longer. August leads me back to Astrid before I'm outright hobbling, and in a few minutes he's been swept back into the festivities again.

I sit down on a cushion to watch. The flow of conversation and music carries on around me. The fae move from one partner to another, but none of my three lovers is ever without one—the women with their unearthly beauty, their feral grace, and jewels sparkling along the curve of their pointed ears. And when they pause to grab a drink or a bite to eat from the tables, they're surrounded by men as well, all seeking favor with the new power by the Heart.

Why wouldn't it be like that? It's all just a sign of how much favor my pack has gained since I joined them. Everyone is recognizing what a devoted and honorable leader Sylas is. I can't let myself see that as anything other than a good thing.

After I've rested my foot for a while, I venture to one of the tables with Astrid trailing behind me. My men are off among the dancers again; none of the fae around me pays me any mind. As I lean over to pluck a skewer of roasted fruit chunks from one of the platters, the voices of a nearby cluster of Seelie in low but audible conversation reach my ears.

"He'll be wanting an heir, though. He'll need a true-blooded mate for much chance at that."

"Oh, I've already seen a few widows positioning themselves. I'm sure he'll have plenty of choice even so."

"Too bad for you two, huh?"

A tinkle of a laugh. "Well, there's always his half-brothers. They're quite impressive too, and that heir will need a cadre, after all."

My gut clenches. My fingers tighten around the skewer, my gaze fixed on the fruit I'm no longer sure I can force down.

I carry it back to my cushion anyway and pick at the

smoky, juicy bits for several minutes, doing my best to convince myself that I don't care at all about anything I overheard. That I already knew everything they said perfectly well.

It's just a little different hearing confirmation from outside my own head.

The music lilts on, winding through the chatter and laughter, but I can't will my spirits to lift again. I set down the half-eaten skewer and get to my feet, needing space from the bustle of the celebration. My gaze falls on the Bastion, the gold seams running through the rock glinting warmly.

"Can I go back inside?" I ask Astrid, tipping my head to it.

She shrugs. "I don't see why not. I'd imagine anything the arch-lords don't want messed with is locked away."

I wander across the grass and through one of the side doors. My uneven footsteps echo through the wide hall. Avoiding the huge central room where the ceremony took place, I veer toward a flight of stairs and limp up it to the second floor of one of the smaller towers.

In the landing at the top of the stairs, the small arched window gives a view over Sylas's new domain. He hasn't touched Ambrose's obsidian castle or wall yet, waiting until his appointment was official, but over the past week he and the pack-kin who are skilled with the right sorts of magic have been working on a new home to suit their tastes. Several immense trees already stretch toward the sky, not yet melded together or shaped into rooms, but giving a clear impression of how they'll make a castle like the one in Hearthshire.

Sylas told us he's changing the name of the domain too, to fully claim it and match our pack. Instead of Dusk-by-the-Heart, it'll be Hearth-by-the-Heart.

My fingers curl against the window ledge as I gaze out at it. That'll be my home too for as long as we stay here, which will hopefully be the rest of my life. I helped Sylas earn it. It can be a happy home, free from any fear of cages or other sorts of imprisonment.

And if it becomes too lonely once—once things play out as everyone expects, then I'm sure Sylas would allow me to make my way back to the human world if I asked to. He could send Astrid or someone to collect the blood they need every full moon until they find another cure, and otherwise I could let this all fade into a dream.

But I don't want to.

I close my eyes against the sudden burn of tears. I have to pull myself together. Soon I'll need to go back to the revel, and I have to look as happy as everyone else. I can't distract my lovers from the greatest triumph of their lives.

Apparently it's too late to avoid that, though. Footsteps rasp on the stairs below, and Astrid stirs where she's been leaning against the wall nearby. Her voice comes out wry. "It appears I'm no longer needed."

I turn to see her already slipping away down the spiral stairs—and Sylas, August, and Whitt emerging from the shadows.

I blink hard, but I'm too startled to hide my emotions that quickly. August's eyes have already widened with worry at the sight of me. So I start talking before they can. "What are you doing up here? You're supposed to be celebrating."

Sylas walks right up to me, the thin crown gleaming against his dark hair, and brushes his fingers over my cheek. "So are you, Talia. Whitt noticed you leaving and was concerned, and it appears he was right to be. What happened? Was someone unkind to you?"

A growl is creeping into his voice just at the thought. An arch-lord for only a few hours, and he's already preparing to use that authority to defend me. My gaze slips past him to Whitt—of course it'd be the spymaster who observed me slipping away—taking in the tensing of his shoulders and the dark flash in his eyes, equally protective. August comes up beside Sylas and grasps my hand, stroking his thumb gently over my knuckles.

"No," I say, willing my voice to stay steady. "Nothing like that. I just got a little overwhelmed by the crowd. I'm all right."

Whitt makes a soft sound, stepping closer while noticeably careful not to infringe on Sylas's personal space. "I may not have the occasion to hear many lies from my brethren, but I know one when I hear it. What's the matter, mighty one?"

"Whatever it is, we'll deal with it," August assures me, so firmly that tears prick at the back of my eyes again.

How can I explain that it isn't something they *can* deal with? That it's just my selfishness and nothing anyone's done wrong?

I resist the urge to hug myself. "I'm just being silly. Really, it's fine. You should go back to the party. People will wonder where you've gone."

A rumble reverberates from Sylas's chest. He wraps his arm right around my shoulders, tugging me to him. "If you're so concerned about me keeping up appearances, the fastest way to ensure I go is to tell me what's upset you."

I lean my head against his solid chest, clenching my jaw and clamping my eyes shut. But the familiar, delicious smell of him fills my nose, and the thought that I don't know how many more times I'll get to be held by him like this chases after it. Before I can catch it, a sob hitches out of me.

All three men have circled in on me in an instant, August squeezing my hand, Whitt resting his hand on my back. The spymaster's voice turns fierce. "If someone said one nasty comment to you, I'll—"

"No." I pull back from Sylas, holding myself rigid as if that will seal in any other reactions I'd rather tamp down on. I guess there's no getting out of this. Embarrassed heat tickles over my cheeks. "I—I know this is stupid, and I don't expect anything else. I shouldn't be letting it bother me when there's so much to be happy for. I just—"

I can't look them in the eyes while I say it. I lower my head, my voice dropping with it. "The pack isn't outcast anymore. You've received the highest honor there is. So of course—of course you'll want to take proper mates now that you can. Maybe not right away, but— And that's *okay*. That's what you should do. You need heirs and all that. I promise you I'm not—"

"Talia," Sylas interrupts, his voice rough. He lifts my chin with his fingers, and then he's kissing me, so deeply and urgently I'm barely aware of anything other than the hot press of his mouth and his strong fingers sliding along my jaw.

August lets out a ragged sound and nuzzles my hair;

Whitt plants a kiss on the shell of my ear. I'm completely encompassed by them, and in that moment I don't care what kind of future there is, I only want to lose myself in this feeling of shared devotion.

Sylas draws back, leaving me aching for more, but he stays close enough that his breath grazes my face. "I am *not* tossing you aside, no matter how many offers I get from the fae down there. *You* are the one I want, and I intend to spend every moment I can with you by my side. I have centuries to worry about heirs. I don't even need one of my blood if I choose to carry on my line by decree instead. There is nothing in this world or theirs I would give you up for." He pauses, and his voice thrums with emotion. "I love you, Talia. I should have said that the first moment I understood it."

I stare up at him, my pulse fluttering against my ribs like the wings of a frantic bird. I never expected to hear those words from August, let alone the fae lord. But the force of his declaration leaves no doubt that he means it. Still, I can't help saying, "You do?"

He kisses my forehead. "You own my heart. You've become my guiding light through so much turmoil, and as far as I'm concerned, there isn't a single woman in the fae realms who could hold a candle to you. And I don't think I'm alone in feeling that way."

He glances toward his cadre. August guides my face to him and steals a kiss for himself, all tenderness. "If I'd had any idea you were thinking that way," he says raggedly, and shakes his head. "You're everything I could possibly want or need, Sweetness. I can't imagine being happier than you make me. I'd sooner never set foot in a kitchen again then spend a day when I could have you without you."

My lips twitch with a smile at that last declaration, and then Whitt is turning me toward him. His mouth collides with mine, as fierce as his voice was a minute ago and searing with a passion much headier than just hunger. He lets the kiss linger on before releasing me, his fingers still teasing over my hair, and then tucks me against his chest like Sylas did before.

He hesitates, eyeing Sylas as if he's not totally sure whether his lord will object to his participation in this moment after all. The other man simply offers a slight smile and a dip of his head like a benediction.

Whitt hugs me tighter. "I may be a man of many words, but I'm not much of one for grand declarations. Let it just be said that I'm certainly not about to let these two lunks hoard you all to themselves. I expect we have many more adventures ahead of us, mite, and I wouldn't miss sharing them with you for anything."

Tears are filling my eyes again, but they're giddy rather than painful now. I hug him back and then turn in his arms to look at Sylas. "So what does that mean? We'll keep on the way we have been, with everyone thinking I'm only with August?"

"No," the fae lord says. "If you are ours and we are yours, it's only fair that we make that claim for all to see. You deserve that recognition." He frowns. "It's rare but not unheard of for fae to commit to a mate bond with a human. I'm not sure I've heard of any joint mate bondings where those sharing a lover made it quite so official all around. Perhaps our strategist can investigate an appropriate approach?"

Whitt grins, looking totally at ease with his lord for the first time I've seen in weeks. "It would be my pleasure."

"A mate bond," I repeat. The giddiness is spreading through my whole body. Can this really be happening? Can they really want—but how can I doubt it after everything they've said? I'm not totally sure what that means, though. The only thing I'm really sure of is— "It isn't like the soul-twined bond."

Sylas nods. "It's the formal exchanging of vows and entwining of magic that all those who aren't soul-twined mates can use to bind themselves to their chosen mate in love and loyalty. There would be none of the intense effects, but there's something to be said for a choice freely made."

Yes, there is. I remember the way he described the forming of a soul-twined bond. *It hits you like a lightning bolt straight down the center of you, like being suddenly burned through.* What I feel for these three men is plenty powerful enough without that, thank you.

Only one worry remains. "Wouldn't the other fae think it's strange?"

Sylas lets out a challenging guffaw. "They'll be welcome to tell me so to my face and discover the consequences. Let them gossip however they wish elsewhere. If my rule as arch-lord doesn't command enough respect to quell any disparagement, then I'm not doing my job well enough."

Whitt gives a lock of my hair a playful tug. "We'll

remind them that you do have some small trace of fae blood in there somewhere, and you take to true-blooded coloring so well you might as well be one. Auggie can keep you in hair dye, hmm?"

August laughs. "I'll mash up a whole vat if it'll—"

"My lord!" Astrid's voice carries up the stairs with the thumping of hurried feet. She sounds rattled, so unlike her usual unflappable self that my body has already tensed before she hurtles into view.

She dips into a swift bow at the top of the stairs and straightens up, her jaw tight. "You're needed below, Arch-Lord Sylas. They—the arch-lords of the Unseelie have come across the border to parley."

Sylas can't rein in his shock. "They're here—*now?*"

Astrid motions for him to follow, and we all rush down the steps together.

My heart hitches behind my ribs. What could the Unseelie want? Astrid didn't say they'd attacked us—no, they can't. For any fae to cross the border near the Heart, they have to take a vow that they won't harm anyone on the other side.

The real question is, what could possibly have prompted the rulers of the winter realm to take that risk at this exact moment?

"They say they have magic on them that would retaliate if any of us attempt to hurt them," Astrid says breathlessly, filling Sylas in on the way down. "No one's dared to test it."

When we emerge from the Bastion, the musicians have stopped playing. The dancers have fallen back to the fringes of the field. Only seven figures remain in the clear span just in front of the Heart, outlined in its glow.

Donovan and Celia stand their ground before five fae in finery of pale gray, blue, and ivory—like the colors of ice. Silvery crowns gleam on all of the strangers' heads, and true name marks unfurl along their brows and jaws. Their expressions are coolly haughty. Broad wings rippling with black feathers stretch from their backs.

Apparently the Unseelie can use their wings in human form just like the Seelie can bring out their fangs and claws. And they have five arch-lords rather than three. I didn't know. I wonder if Sylas even did.

He strides through the crowd to join his new colleagues, his shoulders squaring. Whitt and August follow to the front of the throng, ready to leap in if called on.

Astrid tugs me to the side. We circle the clearing until we find a spot where the spectators are less densely packed and ease forward there to get a better view. She keeps one hand clamped around my forearm, the other on the hilt of her dagger.

When Sylas joins the other arch-lords, Celia is the one who speaks. I guess her age gives her the most seniority to speak for all of them.

"The three of us are before you now. What is the meaning of this visit?"

The Unseelie fae in the middle of their group is a woman so brawny even her tattooed neck bulges with muscle. She swipes her turquoise hair back from her face. "We heard there's been a changing of the guard in the lands of summer. Is it so strange that we'd want to see the new line of authority on the other side of the Heart?" Her chilly gaze skims over Sylas.

"Here I am," he says amicably enough, but his dark eye is wary.

I study each of the other Unseelie, searching for any clue of their true motives. There are three women and two men in total. I have trouble judging the age of fae, but they appear to range from a man with curly blue-black hair and bronze skin who looks to be as young as August to a slight, spindly woman I suspect is much older even than Celia.

They all stand straight and regal, their eyes fixed on the Seelie arch-lords, totally motionless—except for the young man, whose wings give a restless twitch behind him.

As I focus more intently on him, his attention slips away from the rulers in front of him to consider the crowd. He glances across the assembled fae so swiftly I don't have time to jerk my eyes away before our gazes collide.

And it truly is a collision.

The second his dark eyes catch mine, a wave of energy sears through me. As I hold in a gasp, it crackles into every nerve all the way to the roots of my teeth and the tips of my toes. It wrenches down the middle of my chest as if I'm being carved apart by a blade of fire.

As if I've been hit by a lightning bolt, straight down the center of me.

The bottom of my stomach drops out. My mouth falls open, but no sound comes out.

The Unseelie arch-lord stares at me as I must be staring at him, his own jaw going slack—and then a roar of sensation floods into the burned-out space where the energy blazed through me. The pinch of a belt buckled too tightly. The pang of a stomach too tensed to risk filling.

The image of a pale girl with vivid pink hair gaping at me—at *him*—from amid the crowd.

No. It's impossible. It *can't*—

I stumble backward in Astrid's hold, slamming my eyes closed, but there's no escaping the words that rise up in an unfamiliar voice that's somehow resonating from deep inside me.

How can— It's you. My soul-twined mate.

Royal Mate (Bound to the Fae #4)

Love bound us together... but fate has other plans.

Just when a happily ever after with my Seelie men was within reach, the Heart of the Mists tied me to one of the foreboding winter arch-lords. I can't escape the connection between us. The enemy can speak from right within my soul.

I'm not willing to give up on my happiness that easily, but I can't let the realms descend into all-out war. I'll brave the uncertainties of the winter lands if that's what it takes to protect the men I love.

My chilly Unseelie arch-lord isn't quite what I expected, though. As the lines between ally and enemy start to blur, can I stop the clash of winter and summer before even more blood is shed?

ABOUT THE AUTHOR

Eva Chase lives in Canada with her family. She loves stories both swoony and supernatural, and strong women and the men who appreciate them. Along with the Bound to the Fae series, she is the author of the Flirting with Monsters series, the Cursed Studies trilogy, the Royals of Villain Academy series, the Moriarty's Men series, the Looking Glass Curse trilogy, the Their Dark Valkyrie series, the Witch's Consorts series, the Dragon Shifter's Mates series, the Demons of Fame Romance series, the Legends Reborn trilogy, and the Alpha Project Psychic Romance series.

Connect with Eva online:
www.evachase.com
eva@evachase.com

CPSIA information can be obtained
at www.ICGtesting.com
Printed in the USA
FSHW010711210321
79706FS